FEAR CITY

AXEL BLAZE THRILLER
(BOOK SEVEN)

BILL RUNNER

RUNNER HOUSE BOOKS, LONDON
www.bill-runner.com

This is a work of fiction. Names, characters, places, and incidents either are the product of the author's imagination or are used fictitiously. Any resemblance to actual persons, living or dead, events, or locales is entirely coincidental.

First eBook edition May 2024

978-1-7393196-6-3

www.bill-runner.com

From Soldier to Vigilante: Blaze's Path

Dear Readers,

First off, thank you for joining Axel Blaze on his journey. Whether you've been with him since *Blaze Returns* or are just diving in now, I'm thrilled to have you along for the ride.

When I first created Axel Blaze, I envisioned a man who couldn't stand by when innocent lives were at stake—a man who acts decisively, even when it means crossing dangerous lines. In his first adventure in *Blaze Returns*, he was still tethered to a semi-official role, stepping in to help his old boss at the U.S. Marshals track down a missing Deputy.

But as the series unfolded, Blaze began carving his own path, driven by his unwavering sense of justice and a deep disdain for the wrongs he saw around him. In the first seven books—*Blaze Returns*, *Lethal Force*, *Hard Target*, *Mean Streets*, *Unchained Fury*, *No Escape*, and *Fear City*—all set across different American cities, Blaze operates as a lone ranger. He steps into situations where innocent lives hang in the balance, doing what others can't—or won't.

Starting with *Dead Calm* (Book 8), the series takes a deeper dive into Blaze's past. In *Dead Calm*, we see him as a Captain in the U.S. Army Rangers, followed by his Delta Force missions in *No Mercy*, and the upcoming *Warpath* (April 2025) and *Crossfire* (July 2025). These stories explore the intense operations and personal losses that forged Blaze into the man he is today.

The upcoming Book 12, *Nemesis* (November 2025), will be the final book exploring Blaze's military career. It's a deeply personal story where Blaze seeks justice for his brother Ryan—a U.S. Marine. This pivotal story will mark the turning point in Blaze's life, as he ultimately decides to leave the army. Disillusioned by the failures of the system, he becomes a man willing to cross lines to ensure justice prevails. Beginning in 2026, Blaze will be stepping fully into a world where the lines between right and wrong blur, and he's left to rely on his own moral compass to guide him.

In his words: You have to pay your dues. Period.

Your feedback and support have been instrumental in shaping this series. Blaze's journey has been as much yours as it has been mine, and I can't thank you enough for coming along for the ride.

Thank you for being part of Blaze's story.

Sincerely,

Bill Runner

CHAPTER 1

It was supposed to be a clean, professional hit. The idea was to keep it simple, making it easy for the cops to close the case, no big deal. Something that would look like random street chaos, maybe a mugging gone wrong. Nothing that would get cops overly interested. No breadcrumbs leading back to the men who ordered it. The other choice, staging it as a suicide, needed way more time than the guys had been given for the job.

I knew the hitmen wouldn't make a move out in the open. Pros don't leave witnesses. Not that hits can't go down in open spots with folks around. And I'm not talking about long-range sniper shots. You could be elbow-to-elbow with the mark at a packed intersection, and nobody would catch a whiff. All it takes is a second to discreetly whip out a knife or a suppressed gun and—boom, it's done. You're a ghost before the guy hits the ground. Big city folks are too caught up to pay attention. And Boston was one hell of a big city.

The man walking along the sidewalk didn't seem to have a clue that the hitmen were watching his every move. Lost in his phone but glancing up occasionally, he made his way through the stream of pedestrians. Even though it was close to 11 a.m. and rush hour was over, the pedestrian route linking Exchange Place with State Station in downtown Boston remained bustling with activity. That was mainly because apart from being in the heart of the financial district, the location was also adjacent to several tourist hotspots.

The day was as close to perfect as it gets. The sky dazzled in a brilliant shade of blue. Fall had begun its slow approach. Leaves were changing hues from green to an array of gold, amber, and fiery red, creating a picturesque backdrop against the cityscape. A gentle chill in the air felt crisp and invigorating. Not the kind of day you'd expect danger lurking around street corners. But you didn't need to be a genius to figure out that neither the two guys closing in on the man, nor the occupants of the suspicious black van edging nearer, were planning to have friendly chats with him. They were there to take the man out. Plain and simple.

The man was dressed in sharp but kind of crumpled clothes—pants, a jacket that fit just right, and boat shoes that gave off a semi-casual vibe. He was of medium height, around five foot nine. But even though his movements suggested he was recovering from an injury, he looked like he had been in the habit of hitting the gym on most days. His hair was a bit all over the place, like he had just rolled out of bed. The specks of gray in his stubble suggested he was probably in his mid-40s. He had a crossbody satchel slung across his torso, like he was ready to bust out some papers or maybe a laptop. To any casual observer, a likely guess would be that the man was a journalist out chasing a story.

As for me, I didn't really need to guess. I knew the man was a seasoned reporter at the Boston Globe. His name was Josh Dillon. I also knew it hadn't even been five weeks since he barely survived being shot by gunmen in the middle of a forest in Wyoming. Josh had been lucky to make it out of that place alive.

It was sheer coincidence that I happened to be around in Wyoming at that time, helping an old friend—Marine Staff Sergeant Logan Davis. Logan wasn't just a friend; he was more like a brother. He got set up by a nasty crew he got mixed up with in Wyoming. It was David Wolfe's crew. Wolfe was a cult leader with ties to a rogue pharmaceutical company. He was exploiting troubled veterans battling with PTSD, using them as guinea pigs while also creating a small army of highly trained hitmen.

Logan and I went way back, over a decade, from back in the day when I was an Army Ranger. When he called for help, I left everything and rushed over. Josh had got into trouble investigating the same guys who had framed Logan.

It hadn't been easy tracking Josh in Wyoming and ensuring he made it out alive after taking three bullets. So, I was more than a little surprised when I realized that a little over a month later, he wasn't just back on his feet, but also digging deep into powerful, shadowy people who didn't take kindly to anyone looking at them too closely. Josh clearly wasn't the kind of guy who got scared easily and backed down.

That morning, he was on his way to the FBI's Boston Division office in Chelsea to give evidence. A distance of not even five miles. Barely a 15-minute drive even in downtown Boston traffic. But a lot can happen in 15 minutes. I had received reliable intel yesterday that a contract had been floated on Josh. The men tailing him were there to make sure he wouldn't make it to the FBI office. But I wasn't about to let that happen.

Before Josh exited the Globe's office in the Exchange Place building at 53 State Street, I was already positioned at a bus stop next to it. I was certain the building was being watched. I was there to assess the threat level. I had been on countless recon missions in the army and as a U.S. Marshal—handling countersurveillance was second nature to me.

I was in full-on tourist mode, sporting a Patriots navy blue jersey and backpack, and a Red Sox baseball cap. Bright colors. Not even remotely trying to be inconspicuous. It's what we call blending in by sticking out. Look like a tourist and act like one. I was near the Freedom Trail, Boston's top tourist magnet, with the Old State House and Faneuil Hall less than half a block on either side. Leaning casually against a wall, I stood clutching a tourist map, seemingly trying to make sense of it, playing the part of a confused sightseer.

Within moments, I had spotted two suspicious-looking vehicles—a Ford pickup truck fitted with a giant rammer at the front, and a black van—parked in an alley across the street. The van had direct lines of sight to the exit of the Globe office as well as its underground parking garage, which was on Congress Street at one corner of the building, about fifty yards away from the front entrance. Two men were stationed next to the parking lot exit, scanning every vehicle that left the building.

These guys clearly meant business. They were waiting for Josh to exit the building in a car. I was sure they must have figured out a couple of ambush spots on the route to the FBI office in

Chelsea. It wasn't like there were multiple options for getting there. The only choice was in the initial part—depending on the flow of traffic, you could drive either north or south on Congress Street after exiting the parking lot. But both routes would eventually mean getting on to U.S. Route 1 to cross Mystic river and drive into Chelsea. With those guys on the lookout, there was no way of making that journey safely without at least one escort vehicle. There could be any number of points along the way where a single vehicle could get boxed in and forced into a corner.

That's the way ambushes are set up. Decide on a kill zone, where you either force or lure the target to isolate and trap him. Once a target is stuck there, his chances of escaping are very low. Once they grabbed Josh, it wouldn't take much for them to stage a "clean" hit.

The immediate safe option was for Josh to not get out of his office at all. But that would simply delay the attack. Those men weren't just going to give up and walk away. They would pick another time and place. And next time, I might not be around to see it coming. The best option was to tackle the threat head on. Deal with it once and for all.

Ambushes work only when the target remains clueless about what's going to happen. The best way to mess it up for the attackers is to avoid getting stuck in the kill zone. Screw up their carefully laid-out plans, and force them to improvise. If the ambushers lose the element of surprise, the target can move the battleground—take it to a place where the attackers won't have an inherent advantage. That's exactly what I was planning to do.

When I spotted Josh at the building entrance waiting for his ride, I rang him to tell him to ditch the car. We had never met before. Josh only knew me as a voice on the phone. He was unconscious when they airlifted him from the forest. Once Logan was cleared of any wrongdoing and released, I had headed back to my ranch in Colorado. Josh and I had chatted on the phone a few days later. I had also called him the previous day, warning him about the hit and asking him to watch his back. But he had no clue I was in Boston.

A couple of conversations are usually enough to size up a man. When I called Josh that morning, I knew he wasn't the type for pointless questions. The only thing that could screw up my plan was him second-guessing every move. If he aimed to make it out alive, he needed to stick religiously to the plan and follow my lead, even if it didn't add up at the time. I gave him precise instructions. He followed them to a T. That's what kept him breathing that day.

"Hello?" Josh answered cautiously, his tone guarded, as he picked up my call.

He didn't recognize the number. I was using a burner phone. There was a good chance Josh's phone was tapped. I didn't want to get on these guys' radar as well. It was best to stay low until I had a handle on what was up.

"It's the cowboy from Colorado. No names. Stay put. Don't leave the building. Call me back immediately from a burner," I instructed.

"Oh. Yeah, sure," he replied, picking up on the urgency in my tone.

Josh called back within thirty seconds.

"Are you in Boston?" he asked incredulously before I could utter a word.

"Yeah. That's not important. Those guys I warned you about, they're here to take you out," I declared, getting straight to the point.

That got his full attention. The seriousness of the situation hit him like a ton of bricks.

An uneasy "Oh!" was all he managed to utter in response.

"Don't make it obvious, but there's a black van at your 11 o'clock across the street, and a mean-looking truck behind it."

"I see them," Josh confirmed. "Um, where are you?"

"Your three o'clock. I'm the guy rocking the Patriots jersey."

"Got you," he exclaimed, a touch of relief in his voice. "So, this is how this goes down, huh? These killers will make a move in broad daylight? Right in the heart of downtown?" Josh asked, still a little incredulous, but the reality of his situation was finally sinking in.

Even though I had warned him about the threat to his life, and Josh trusted me enough to know I wasn't one to exaggerate things, especially in matters of life and death, there's a human instinct to downplay impending dangers. It's like you're trying to wish away the threat. The seriousness of such situations often doesn't hit home until you're staring directly into the killer's eyes.

"They won't make a move here, not with so many witnesses. That's why I told you to stay put. But these guys are going to be relentless. They'll keep tailing you and strike when they've got you cornered in a spot of their choosing."

"Shall I call the cops?" Josh asked, sounding a little nervous.

"Cops can't do much. These guys haven't broken any laws. At most, cops can ask them to get moving, but it'll only tip them off that you're onto them. They'll be more cautious and strike when you least expect it."

"Oh, man, you sure know how to lift a guy's spirits. Remind me not to come to you for a pep talk next time I need some cheering up."

"Just serving up some reality bites, pal," I replied, chuckling. "But I've got your back. No need to fret. How's that for a ray of sunshine?"

"Much better. So... what's the plan?"

"For starters, grab a notepad or papers from your bag. Pretend like you've got to check your notes. Don't look like you're waiting for a ride."

"Got it," Josh replied, grabbing a stack of papers from his bag. "What next? Should I stay put or head back inside? I'll have to get out eventually. You know I can't miss this appointment," he added, sounding more like he was trying to convince himself about it.

"Yeah, I know. You know what, pal, let's wrap this thing up while we still have eyes on these suckers. We don't want them circling back to take a shot at you later. At least not the same guys. I've got you covered, but you'll have to stick your neck out. You cool with that?"

"If you've got my back, I don't mind strolling over and banging on that van's windscreen."

"That might be pushing it a bit on the badass scale," I replied, chuckling.

"Well, then, tell me what to do."

"Ditch the plan of going by car. Have the taxi wait and take off. You're leaving on foot."

"Uh, sure, but it's not a taxi. Kelly and Jason are giving me a ride. I tried talking them out of it, but I guess you've known Kelly long enough—she can be stubborn."

"I know," I replied, my mind wandering back to the stunning Kelly Walsh who could be drop-dead gorgeous and a real pain all at once.

Kelly and her sidekick, Jason Kim, had come looking for Josh in Wyoming and got entangled in the chaos. I had barely managed to snatch them from the jaws of certain death at the hands of those psychos.

A fleeting thought crossed my mind—did Josh have any inkling about me and Kelly? We had a thing back in Wyoming. Some tender moments delicately balanced with the unspoken understanding that it was fleeting. It wasn't just the physical distance; our lives and commitments pulled us in different directions.

"Where are they now?" I asked Josh, snapping myself back to the present.

"They'll be driving out of the parking lot any second now."

"What car is it? We need to stop her."

"Red Malibu. Should I call her?"

"She might argue with you and drag this out. We don't have time for that. Let me handle it. I'll call her and get back to you in a minute. Hold your position."

I hung up and rang Kelly. It was crucial to keep her and Jason under the radar. I avoided telling Josh that anyone spotted with him would become a target for those guys. I couldn't possibly keep all of them safe simultaneously.

"Hello?" Kelly answered a little impatiently, not recognizing the number.

Her voice stirred some memories, moments shared together, not too long in the past. She wasn't a woman easily forgotten. But I had pressing business requiring my immediate attention. I spotted a red Chevy Malibu exiting the parking garage as her voice came through. It was still too far off to make out who was inside it.

"Kelly, it's Axel. Listen carefully. It's urgent."

"Axel? What the... What's happening?" Kelly responded, sounding a bit thrown off.

"Are you driving the red Malibu that just came out of the parking garage?"

"Yeah. But how... Where are you? Are you in Boston? What's going on?"

"I'll explain later. Just keep moving. Don't stop for Josh. Don't even look at him. You guys will walk into an ambush if you drive him. I'll take him through a different route. Can you trust me and just roll with it?"

"Uh, yeah, sure. What do I do? Where should I go?"

Kelly had known me long enough to not take my warnings lightly. When I say there's a threat, I don't mess around, and she had learned to trust my instinct on these things.

"Just circle the block a couple of times and head back. I'll call you again."

"You're going to owe me one hell of an explanation, cowboy," she said.

"Yeah, I know," I said before disconnecting the call.

I called Josh again to give him exact directions.

"Jump on the T. Head toward State Station. Use the Old State House entrance," I instructed him, asking him to make his way to the subway, known as the T in Boston—short for MBTA (Massachusetts Bay Transportation Authority).

"Not the entrance next to me?" he inquired.

He was talking about the 53 State Street entrance, practically within spitting distance. The one I directed him to—the Old State House entrance—was a good three hundred yards away.

"No. I want to draw these guys out. See if they tail you. Keep it casual. Let them see you strolling, no rush, no scanning the area. Play it cool. You're just a guy who's figured it's a fine day to ditch the car, take a leisurely walk, and hop onto the T."

"Got it."

Josh exited the building onto Congress Street, took a right turn, and headed toward the traffic intersection at the State Street junction. Along the way, he brushed past a tourist sporting a Patriots jersey and a Red Sox cap, leaning against a wall, and deeply engrossed in a map. Josh barely spared me a fleeting glance, keeping his pace steady, eyes glued to his phone, never missing a step. We both had Bluetooth earphones on, keeping us connected in real-time without tipping off any onlookers.

The moment Josh stepped out of the building and started heading my way, the two men stationed near the parking lot exit clocked him and immediately shifted gears. They were roughly halfway down the block from where I stood. Swiftly, they began striding in my direction, displaying an air of restraint, holding back from breaking into a full sprint while Josh continued walking away from them.

Just a few seconds before Josh reached the intersection, the pedestrian lights switched to green, and the walking figure lit up. Without delay, pedestrians began crossing the street.

"Miss the signal. Cross at the next one," I directed Josh.

"Copy that," he responded, promptly dropping a piece of paper at the same moment, then pausing, turning around, and bending to retrieve it.

When he straightened up, the pedestrian signal had turned red, and traffic started flowing once more.

"I'll be behind you. Don't look back. Make sure you flash your CharlieCard. Make it obvious you're heading for the T," I instructed Josh, asking him to conspicuously display the smart card required for traveling on the subway.

"Sure thing," he responded, digging into his pocket and retrieving his CharlieCard.

At that moment, Kelly's car passed by me. She was scanning the sidewalk as she drove. Her eyes locked with mine. She looked even more gorgeous than I remembered, if that was even possible. A couple of seconds later, she was gone beyond the intersection.

By then, the two men were just a few yards away from me. That was my cue to start walking toward Josh, clutching the map, like I had finally figured out which way to go. I wanted to remain between the men and Josh. Both were wearing light jackets that could easily conceal a weapon, even though neither was openly carrying one. But for a guy trained in the game, it only takes a moment to draw a blade and strike the target.

Meanwhile, the van exited the alley and merged with the slow-moving traffic heading toward the intersection. The pickup truck stayed put, seemingly waiting for a signal from the men in the van.

At the intersection, a small group had gathered again, waiting for the pedestrian lights to turn green. I positioned myself behind Josh. The two men seamlessly blended into the crowd. When the lights switched to green, we began crossing. I matched steps with Josh, but the two men picked up speed and overtook us. It dawned on me that more players might be entering the fray, approaching us from behind. My suspicion was confirmed when I glanced back at the van, caught in traffic and inching ahead slowly. I spotted four men exiting from its side and onto the sidewalk.

Two guys sported overcoats, a bit of an overkill considering the temperature was around 70. Definitely concealing weapons. The other men had light jackets on, but the way they adjusted their pants upon exiting the van hinted at a gun tucked at the back.

Despite their potential danger, the men were on the far side of the bustling street. The two guys in overcoats started walking briskly toward the intersection we had just passed, but it would still take them a couple of minutes to cross over to where we were.

But I was a little puzzled when the other two men who had exited the van began walking in the opposite direction. Then it hit me—the CharlieCard had done its trick. The message must have been passed that Josh was planning to take the subway. This was their contingency plan, in case he managed to somehow make it into the station. Those guys would enter the station from the 53 State Street entrance and trap Josh from both sides. It made me realize this was a well-organized, professional crew—not a bunch of gun-toting wannabes looking for an easy buck.

By then, we had made it across the street. The Old State House stood in front of us. The two men ahead of us had moved toward the Freedom Trail. The Trail runs alongside Old State House in front of the entrance to State Station, which is located at the side of the building. The entrance leads to the basement and onward to the platforms. The men had moved ahead to set up a trap.

"Pause at the Massacre marker, fiddle with your phone, keep an eye out for two guys in overcoats behind you. They're still on the other side of the intersection. Let me know as soon as they've crossed," I instructed Josh while I kept walking toward the station entrance.

"Copy that," Josh acknowledged, halting near the circle of granite pavers marking the historical site of the Boston Massacre from 1770. The medallion-shaped marker rests under the balcony of the Old State House.

I stepped inside the station entrance and saw a short passage leading to steps that went down to the basement level. When I descended the steps, I noticed a corridor leading to the subway platforms, culminating in the fare gates. But my focus was more on a nook adjacent to the steps, where the restrooms were located a little out of sight.

Even though marked by signage, the restrooms were a bit tucked away around a corner, not immediately obvious. However, front and center were the two men I had my eyes on. Both guys matched my size—standing at six foot two, each carrying a little over two hundred pounds.

One man, leaning against the wall, had his thumbs hooked in his belt, shooting the kind of menacing glares that could make a guy decide to hold it in and skip the bathroom break rather than mess with him. The other guy lurked a bit behind him. No weapons drawn yet—there wasn't any need for them to draw unnecessary attention until their mark showed up.

This was their kill zone. No eyes from security cams. And with rush hour being long over, barely anyone was coming down the steps making a beeline for the platforms. State wasn't a busy station outside of rush hour. It was a perfect place to stage a deadly mugging. With these two in the basement and the other two tailing Josh, there was nowhere for him to go.

But there was a major flaw in their plan—they hadn't prepared for contingencies. They didn't have a clue I was part of the equation. I was the unpredictable wildcard they had overlooked.

CHAPTER 2

I figured I had a thirty-second window to take out the men and sprint back to Josh. It would take the guys up on the street level at least that long to cross the intersection.

I hadn't stopped for a second while I was assessing the scenario and deciding on a plan of action. It was quite simple, really—knocking the living daylights out of the men in front of me. Use surprise and speed to neutralize that first threat with overwhelming force before dealing with the others. Speed and overwhelming force were the operative terms. I didn't have time to mess about with prolonged fights.

I glanced at the restroom sign above the man in the front, the one pulling an intimidating look. He seemed a little surprised when I walked straight toward him, my walk signaling a desperate need for a leak. He was just about beginning to open his mouth to tell me to beat it, but I never gave him the chance.

I slammed the heel of my palm right under his chin. The impact jolted his head backward violently, a move that alone could have knocked the guy out by rattling his brain against the walls of his skull. The fact that there was a solid wall conveniently placed about half a foot behind his head ensured he went to deep sleep instantly. The resounding thud of his skull banging against the wall echoed in the confined space. That surely was overwhelming force if anything ever was.

I didn't wait to confirm if my blow knocked him out. It was a done deal that man had checked out of the conscious world. I had already moved toward the other guy, who was stunned and rendered motionless by what happened. It took him a full second to start reaching for the gun tucked into the back of his pants.

In close-quarters combat, a second's hesitation often seals the deal. And after that delay, opting to shift your arm to your back instead of blocking your opponent's charge is practically asking for a knockout. That tucked gun won't be of any use unless you create some space between yourself and the adversary. The guy's costly blunder ensured he didn't stay conscious for another full second.

I nailed him with a clothesline move—holding my arm nearly straight and swinging it in an arc, smashing my forearm into the side of his neck while the heel of my palm slammed into the back of his head. The force of the blow sent such chaotic signals to his brain that it opted for a temporary shutdown. Either of those hits alone would have knocked him out, but the combination meant he was in for a prolonged nap.

Two strikes, three seconds. Speed and overwhelming force used to near perfection.

Both men were down with plenty of precious seconds to spare. I utilized some of that extra time to ensure they wouldn't be a threat when they regained consciousness. These guys were killers—until I had figured out what the hell was going on, I wasn't going to leave any of them in a condition for another assault. I lifted the right arm of one man and drove my knee into the back of his elbow, breaking bones and contorting the arm at a bizarre angle. I replicated the move with the other guy before frisking them.

Both men were packing unmarked guns and knives. They wouldn't have hesitated for a second in using them on Josh. I also found brass knuckles stashed in the back pocket of one of them, and slid them into my own pocket. I had no idea how many more men I would have to deal with. It's always a good idea to go easy on your knuckles when you've got no idea how many jaw-breakers you'll need to dole out.

After dumping the men in the restrooms, I was about to sprint back up the steps when I caught a crackling sound coming from the earpieces of one of the men. I grabbed the earphones and put them on.

"Where you at? You in position?" a voice inquired.

"Yeah," I grunted into the mic on the man's jacket, muting my own phone.

"You gonna haul him into the restrooms?"

"Yeah."

"Alright. We got the back covered. He's dead meat."

I didn't have time to hear more. As I sprinted up the steps, unmuting my phone, Josh's voice came through my earphones.

"Overcoat guys have crossed the intersection," he informed me.

"Copy that. Enter the station and take the steps down to the basement. Don't move toward the platforms yet. Get into the restrooms. OK?"

"Yeah, got it."

"Ignore the couple of knocked out guys lying there. Just get inside a cubicle and wait for me."

I finished my directions just about the time I made it to the street level and saw Josh walking toward me. He gave me a slightly weird look when he heard my last statement, but simply nodded as he passed me and moved down the steps.

Getting Josh trapped inside a cubicle didn't sound like the ideal option, but it was the best alternative under the circumstances. I didn't want him to be caught out between two groups of men converging from opposite sides. They ideally wouldn't want to take him out in public view but, if they got desperate, they would take the chance. It was a safer option for me to take them out in pairs rather than having to deal with four armed men simultaneously.

I took out my map from my back pocket and hung around a few seconds, waiting for the two men to follow Josh. My plan was to tackle them on the stairs—trip them and let gravity do half the work.

But it wasn't meant to be. A young couple who had been hanging around decided at that very moment to get on the subway. They began moving toward me, with the two hitmen following a few feet behind. I realized I would have to take out the two men a little more discreetly. Gravity wouldn't be doing me any favors—I would have to do it the hard way.

I folded my map and turned around to go back down the steps. The two men didn't want to get stuck behind the couple. They took a few quick steps to cut ahead of them. But I was too close to the entrance for them to get in front of me. I began going down, taking my time, with those two on my heels. I could sense their frustration, and how they were itching to push me out of the way. But they faced the same problem as me—they needed to be discreet to avoid attracting attention.

As I went down the steps, I took off my cap and put it on with the back facing front. When the time came, I would need to take down the men as quickly and noiselessly as possible. And it would be close quarters combat once more. I didn't want to rule out a headbutt just because the hat's bill was in the way.

Once I got down to the basement level, I acted like I was about to move down the corridor leading to the platforms but suddenly noticed the restroom signs and decided to head that way. I knew that so long as the young couple was behind the men, they couldn't risk attracting attention by trying to physically stop me from going there. The thing was, so long as the couple was around, I too could not knock the guys out. I too couldn't attract attention until I was sure all threats were down.

I stopped just before turning the corner, took off my backpack, and began rummaging through it. There wasn't much inside, except for an extra cap, jersey, and a couple of T-shirts. I grabbed a pen, put on the backpack, and began making notes on the map.

The men looked at each other, unable to figure out how to deal with the situation. So far as they were concerned, their partners were inside the restroom, standing over a badly beaten, and possibly dead, Josh. They stepped aside to let the couple pass. And then they just stood facing me. About ten seconds passed with none of us changing position.

I could almost hear a clock ticking inside my head. I knew the men's partners would have already entered the station through the 53 State Street entrance. It wouldn't take too long for those guys to rendezvous with their partners. Every fiber in my being was itching to launch myself at those two. But none of that was visible on my face as I scribbled the words on my map: Surprise, Speed, Controlled Violent Action. Kind of reminding myself of the essence of close-quarters combat drilled into our minds back in Ranger School at Fort Bening.

I could sense by the subtle change in the men's body language that the couple was out of range, and they were ready to send me packing from there. One man stepped forward and ordered me in a low growl that was borderline menacing: "You gotta clear out."

"Excuse me?" I responded.

The man shifted his overcoat a little to show me a glimpse of a gun in a shoulder holster, moved a step closer, and really got in my face. He was itching to get his face smashed. It was a good thing I had my cap on backwards. When he spoke again, the menace in his tone wasn't borderline anymore.

"You heard me. Fuck o..."

He never got a chance to finish his sentence. The man was about my height, but I had been lightly leaning against a wall when he moved toward me. And when he began his routine to scare me, he never noticed me slip down another couple of inches. So, when I propelled myself forward and slightly upward, the hard part of my skull, just around the hairline, smashed into his nose, rupturing his nasal septum, and turning it into a bloody pulp.

A headbutt is one of the most devastating blows you can inflict on an opponent. A vicious but effective way to blow out a person's fuse. The man's head jerked back, his legs began giving out under him, but before he collapsed unconscious on the floor, I pushed him onto his partner standing less than a couple of feet behind him.

That guy was too busy multitasking—reaching for the gun in his shoulder strap while trying to get out of the way of his falling partner. It didn't even occur to him to try blocking my next move. That's what packing a gun does to most people—they get too focused on trying to pull the gun even in extremely close quarters situations, where unless you have your hand on the trigger, a gun isn't much use as the opponent can easily grab it.

I took a quick step forward and jabbed the guy in the neck. The blow took his breath away. He tried taking a step back, but I had planted my right hand behind his neck by then, forcing his face down as I launched my right knee upwards and smashed it into his face. I could feel his upper jaw crack and cave in, taking most of his front teeth with it, while his nose went flat against his face. The man's lights blew out as he collapsed.

Three strikes, four seconds. Surprise, Speed, Controlled Violent Action. The enemy was down.

I took a quick peek toward the platforms. There wasn't any sign yet of the two guys I had seen heading for the 53 State Street entrance.

"All clear. Time to get moving," I spoke into my phone.

I knew Broken Jaw Man wouldn't be biting anyone's head off for a while. Headbutt Guy would have a killer headache lasting a few days, but he could still pack heat. I stomped down hard on his gun hand, making sure one less trigger-happy dude was in the mix if this spilled into tomorrow. By the time Josh emerged, I had dragged the pair around the corner—out of sight of passersby, unless someone decided to take a leak. The look on Josh's face told me he had a load of questions, but he understood that wasn't the time for them.

"What's the play now?" was all he asked.

"We've got no idea about what's going on up on the street. We can't risk getting caught off guard. The best bet is to jump on the T and figure out our next move. Two more guys took the 53 State entrance. Let's try to avoid them if we can."

We moved briskly toward the platforms. Josh tapped his CharlieCard on the card reader, and the gates swung open for him. Every second counted. Though I hate fare dodging, that day, I couldn't spare the time to get a ticket. I just tailgated him to breeze through.

We crossed the gate to move toward a pedestrian tunnel leading to the platforms. A man's loud shout, "Someone call 911", from near the restrooms told me the knocked-out guys had been discovered. That saved me the trouble of calling the cops. With the unmarked guns with their prints on them, cops would keep those men busy once they opened their eyes.

I kept some distance from Josh, maintaining the illusion that he was flying solo. I was still trying to use the element of surprise, though its edge was dwindling, as I had no idea where the other two men might spring from.

My plan was to board the first departing subway train and put some distance between us and the guys on the street. The next train, an Orange Line heading north to Oak Grove, was due in a minute. The destination didn't matter; we just needed to get the hell away from there.

But sixty seconds felt like an eternity, especially in a near-empty platform. There wasn't any crowd for Josh to blend into and disappear. His best bet was standing by one of the thick pillars scattered across the platform. I took position by the next pillar, roughly fifteen yards from where he stood.

My sigh of relief at the sound of the approaching train was cut short when the two men charged onto the platform from the far end. They had realized what happened to their partners lying broken in the restrooms. I knew they would be re-evaluating Josh's combat capabilities, as they likely still assumed he was alone. However, this presented a challenge; they wouldn't consider it a straightforward task anymore. They were likely to approach with extreme caution, guns at the ready, posing a more significant threat.

"Stay behind the pillar. Don't move," I ordered Josh.

The two men were still a hundred yards away as the train rolled in. Josh remained concealed from their line of sight. As the few passengers started boarding, one of the men stayed at the other end, while his partner began walking briskly toward our position. His pace escalated with each passing second as he walked our way, glancing inside the windows of each car. They were trying to ensure

Josh wouldn't attempt to board the train from some hidden corner just before the doors closed.

I realized I could no longer remain in the shadows. Nearly fifteen seconds had passed since the doors opened. I was getting worried about missing the train. If that happened, we would be left facing two gunmen on an empty platform.

"Be ready. Wait for my command, and then dash into the car," I instructed Josh.

I was positioned between him and the two men. I decided to take out the man approaching us and deal with the other guy later. As he sprinted toward us, I swung my arm and clotheslined him, the radius bone of my forearm striking his neck. His own momentum amplified the impact. His feet flew out from under him as he fell hard on his back, his head crashing on the floor, knocking him out.

"Now. Run for it," I yelled to Josh before the man's head hit the floor, while sprinting toward the doors at the same time.

A second after we entered, the doors began to close. But it was enough time for the other guy to get in. With about five cars between him and us, I had some time to devise a plan before he charged into our car. This time, the stakes were higher. I was no longer Josh's concealed asset. The man knew he was dealing with two individuals. The only potential advantage we still had was that he had been too far away to have seen my face. All he had observed of the man who knocked out his partner was someone of my height and build wearing a Patriots jersey.

"Take off your jacket, throw on my jersey over your shirt, and stand by the connecting door to the next car. The moment you see the gunman cracking open the door on the other side, swing it wide and step into the next car. I'll handle the rest," I directed Josh, yanking off my jersey and revealing my bare chest while he removed his jacket.

There were three other passengers in the car—a well-dressed kid, likely an intern from the financial district, and two casually-dressed middle-aged guys. All three sat scattered. The middle-aged guys watched me with curious expressions while the kid looked distinctly nervous. Josh handed me his jacket while he put on the jersey. I struggled to squeeze my arms into it; there was no chance of buttoning it up. Standing shirtless in a jacket two sizes too small wasn't a fashion statement I would typically make, but desperate times called for desperate measures. We had a mad-as-hell gunman rushing in our direction with the intention of pumping bullets into us.

Ditching the jersey significantly reduced the chances of the gunman recognizing me. That jersey was a dead giveaway. That's why I positioned Josh at the far end. I wanted to provide a target for the gunman's eyes to fixate on.

As I approached the door where the assailant would enter, I spotted one of the middle-aged passengers sporting a bucket hat.

"I'm undercover, part of an ongoing operation. I need to borrow your hat, pal. Is that cool?" I asked, though it was more a declaration of intention than a question.

"Uh, OK, just make sure I get it back," he replied.

"Thanks, you'll get it back for sure."

I put on the hat and took the last seat right by the connecting door where the gunman was about to burst through. The seat had a big window beside it, giving me a clear view into the next car. I would be able to clock the exact moment that guy would storm in, but he too would catch sight of me before making his move. Still, I was sure the hat and the jacket combo would throw off anyone casting a quick glance at me, making him think twice about linking me to the dude rocking the Patriots jersey.

I had made doubly sure by painting a bull's eye on Josh's back. It was a strategy of misdirection, presenting something very similar to what the assailant anticipated and watching it play out. In a tense situation, falling for such tactics was nearly unavoidable.

I considered using my boot knife. Sheathed in my cowboy boot, the hand-crafted knife with a double-edged razor-sharp carbon steel blade was a formidable weapon. I knew the man would rush through the door with his finger on the trigger. Disarming him wouldn't be easy. There was a chance he could let off wild shots. I needed to incapacitate him within seconds. I had enough experience with blades—I could do that without giving him a chance to squeeze the trigger. A deep slice on the inside of his elbow, below the bicep, would sever ligaments and nerves, paralyzing his arm.

The downside was blood, lots of it, in a public place. Dismissing the idea, I retrieved the brass knuckles I had stashed in my pocket earlier—they would serve the purpose.

As soon as the gunman entered the adjoining car at the far end, I put my head down. He only got a view of a man's head wearing a bucket hat. Then I began counting the seconds. As the door swung open and the man burst inside, he was positioned above me, and all he observed was a guy in a bucket hat and a snug jacket. The fact that I was shirtless and the jacket was too small went unnoticed from his vantage point. My ploy had worked—his attention was solely on Josh, the man in the Patriots jersey, who was opening the door at the opposite end to slip into the next car.

Before the man could aim his gun, I grabbed his wrist with my left hand and forcefully yanked it skyward. At the same time, my right fist slammed into his chin. Fueled by the lift of my body, my fist packed some serious punch, especially with the brass knuckles on. The man's jaw snapped. The cracking sound reverberated through the whole car. He went limp, out cold in an instant. I managed to secure his gun before it could slip from his grasp and hit the floor.

"Clear!" I hollered to Josh.

Addressing the other three passengers, I reassured them, "Guys, the threat's over. Nothing to worry about."

The train had begun slowing down while I was incapacitating the gunman, and it came to a halt at Haymarket by the time I settled the unconscious man into a corner seat. The young passenger promptly exited as soon as the doors opened. The other two guys remained seated. Leaving the train at Haymarket wasn't a good option. It was too close to State, not even a five-minute walk. I decided North Station, the next stop and a busy terminal, would be a safer bet.

As the doors closed and the train resumed its journey, Josh joined me. I handed him back his jacket.

"Put it on over the jersey," I instructed him in a hushed tone.

Without hesitation, he followed my guidance. I retrieved an extra jersey from my backpack for myself. I no longer needed the borrowed bucket hat.

"Thanks, pal," I said, handing the hat back to its owner.

"It gives you superpowers, don't it?" he quipped, offering a toothy grin.

"It sure does. Whenever you're ready, dial 911. But I'd suggest waiting until your stop. Once the cops roll in, this train won't be moving for a bit. And as for him," I nodded toward the knocked-out guy, "he won't be waking up for a while."

We stepped out at North Station. It was a bustling hub, being the commuter rail and Amtrak terminal as well. I slapped on my Red Sox hat, pulling the bill low. Josh did the same with the hat I tossed him. I asked him to ditch the jacket, which I stuffed into my backpack. As we strolled away, we looked like regular tourists, decked out in some gift shop gear.

The imminent danger had passed. It was time to figure out the next move.

CHAPTER 3

It had all begun last morning when I got a call from an unfamiliar number.

I was a long way off from Boston—at my ranch in Colorado. Savoring my second cup of coffee after a hearty breakfast, I was gazing vacantly at the autumn-kissed landscape of the Colorado Rockies, watching the aspen leaves shimmer like liquid gold in the crisp September breeze. It was a serene, contemplative interlude before embarking on the day's endeavors.

The ranch was the home I left more than sixteen years ago to follow in the footsteps of my brother, Ryan, who enlisted with the Marines after 9/11. I joined the army a few months later, serving for a decade, primarily with the 75th Ranger Regiment. I left the army to be with mom during her final year battling cancer. Before that, we had already lost Ryan. After mom's passing, the ranch didn't feel like home anymore.

After a period of feeling adrift, I found a new purpose when I joined the U.S. Marshals, sticking with them for five years. When I finally returned home after leaving the Marshals, the family I once had was no more. But I had confronted many of my past demons and gained new brothers along the way. The ranch felt like home once again. It didn't take me long to reacquaint myself with the familiar rhythms of ranch living.

After savoring the last drop, I departed the coziness of the kitchen, and headed to the barn, my thoughts shifting to the day's chores—checking on the cattle, mending fences, gearing up for the shifting seasons… the usual cowboy stuff. However, a call from an unknown number interrupted my thoughts. The area code was 307. Wyoming. It turned out to be a collect call from the Wyoming correctional facility in Torrington.

I was more intrigued than surprised. I had been a Marshal for too long—I was accustomed to receiving such collect calls. To stay ahead of the game, you had to keep your ear to the ground. Often, it meant connecting with those on the other side of the law. Guys behind bars often had the inside scoop on what was brewing beyond prison walls. But ever since I left the Marshals, these kind of calls had stopped.

"Blaze, it's Samy," a voice with a distinctly French accent resonated from the other end of the line when I accepted the call.

Samy had once been a Legionnaire. The Algerian who had once served honorably with the French Foreign Legion had ended up with the wrong crowd in Wyoming—David Wolfe and his mercenaries who had framed Logan. Samy wasn't as rotten as the rest of the crew, even though I realized that only after I had pumped four bullets into him. I didn't have a choice—it was a hostage situation, the kind of scenario where you shoot first and ask questions later.

Anyway, he gave me timely intel, something that helped me save the day. And his testimony helped in clearing Logan. In return, I ensured he received a lenient sentence. My being an ex-Marshal helped. So did the recommendation of

Cheyenne's police chief, who kind of owed me one. Samy hadn't forgotten what I did for him.

"Samy? Don't tell me they've decided to let you walk," I replied.

"I wish," he chuckled, before turning serious. "I heard something. Thought you'd want to know."

"Go on," I said, getting more curious by the second.

"It's about this guy, a mutual friend. But names don't matter. You know how it is in here—the walls have ears."

I instantly caught his drift. Every call from the prison gets scrutinized. And not just by the authorities but also by anyone in the queue waiting for Samy to wrap it up. Those prison walls are notorious for eavesdropping—they do have ears. Whatever Samy was hinting at, he couldn't afford the guards or fellow inmates catching a whiff. Being labeled a snitch would be a death sentence. He was taking a serious gamble by trying to convey a message.

"Yeah, got it. Names don't matter," I affirmed.

"Right. Well, this guy, he's the one who digs deep, gets ink on his hands, the truth seeker in that forest of darkness where you bumped into me... you follow?"

It wasn't rocket science to figure out who he meant. Samy and I didn't share a long list of acquaintances. His subtle hints pointed unmistakably toward an investigative reporter. My bet was on Josh. Yet, there was a slimmer chance it could be Kelly. She, too, was big-time into reporting. And she, too, had come wandering in the Wyoming wilderness.

"You mean the guy who went swimming in the river and went off the radar?" I probed, seeking confirmation.

Josh had been shot by Wolfe's men and managed to escape only because he fell into a river and got swept away by the current. Samy was well aware of that.

"Yes," he affirmed, sounding satisfied that his message had landed.

"So, what's the deal with him?"

"Word is, the pen's scribbling a big story, some real big deal. That's ruffling feathers. It's got some big birds feeling really nervous. You catch my drift?" Samy inquired, maintaining a deliberate level of ambiguity.

Up to this point, all I could decipher was that Josh was tangled up in a story as perilous as the one in Wyoming, which had stirred up some serious trouble and nearly cost him his life.

"Go on."

"Those birds, they're scribbling too, making lists, writing contracts..." Samy continued with his mysterious words.

That didn't sound good. Samy's words strongly hinted that a contract had been floated on Josh's life.

"And this guy's on the list?" I sought confirmation.

"Yes. It's a serious list. Word has it they're playing for keeps. There's some heavy chatter about someone wanting those stories buried, for good."

That sealed it. Samy was undoubtedly referring to Josh being targeted on a hit list.

"Any teams already in the field?"

"I can't say for sure, but the action will kick off soon."

Samy couldn't have been clearer—the threat was imminent. Still, I couldn't wrap my head around how Josh had jumped from one life-threatening situation to another in the matter of a month. I needed to confirm it wasn't connected to the events in Wyoming.

"You know that medicine man in the forest... wasn't that the end of that story?" I asked, maintaining the same ambiguous thread of our conversation.

I knew Samy would easily connect the dots, understanding that the medicine man I referred to was Wolfe—the soulless devil who had been preying on vulnerable veterans battling with PTSD. He had been amassing a cult following until I put an end to his set up. The last I heard was that the shady pharmaceutical startup he had colluded with had gone bust, and the CEO took a swan dive from his penthouse perch. A messy end for a guy messing with the lives of good men.

"I don't think so. That was just one chapter, it seems. The real narrative is still unfolding."

Samy's words implied there were some heavy hitters pulling the strings behind Wolfe and the Wyoming saga. That came as a shock. Wolfe and his men were a vicious crew. It had taken me a whole lot of effort to put them down. Hell, I even got stabbed in the process. Realizing that the main guys behind that bunch were alive and kicking made my blood boil.

"That guy who took the leap, I think that was just someone tying up loose ends," Samy added. "Those birds whose feathers this guy has ruffled, they soar way up there, hidden behind clouds, almost like ghosts."

"No intel on them?"

"No. That's the way they play this game, you know? Names don't get tossed around."

What he said made sense. In these deals, everything happens in the shadows, and staying anonymous is the name of the game.

"I get it. Where's the story being written?" I asked Samy.

I knew Josh operated out of Boston, but his recent escapade had him chasing shadows in Wyoming. I had to make sure of his current whereabouts before plotting my next move.

"The city where they print the book. The hometown of Barbie and cowboy Ken."

That confirmed the location: Boston. Josh worked at the Boston Globe, the so-called book in Samy's cryptic talk. As for Barbie and cowboy Ken, that was Samy's way of referring to Kelly and her intern sidekick, Jason, who had ventured from Boston to Wyoming in search of the missing Josh.

While the stunning Kelly was a gutsy reporter relentless in pursuit of the truth, she tended to stick out in her chic city attire amidst the small-town vibe of Wyoming's Bison Creek, where flannel shirts, well-worn jeans, and worn-in cowboy boots ruled the fashion scene. On the other hand, Jason, the nerdy Boston kid of Korean descent, tried too hard to blend in, offering up awkward "Howdys" while wearing a pair of new cowboy boots that were always killing his feet. His efforts to assimilate into the cowboy culture were about as successful as a polar bear navigating a desert. Though no one said it to their face, they earned the nickname "Barbie and cowboy Ken" behind their backs.

"Got it. Is it solid intel?" I asked for confirmation.

"I wouldn't be playing Russian Roulette if it wasn't."

"I know. Appreciate the heads up. I owe you one."

"No, we're square. I wanted out of that crew. You threw me a lifeline. I'll be out in a couple of years with good behavior. That's all the break I needed."

When I wrapped up that call, I knew Samy was giving it to me straight. There was a real threat on Josh's life. From what I knew of Josh, he had a habit of playing fast and loose. Not cocky, just damn impulsive. Taking a bullet out in Wyoming didn't seem to have put a dent in his behavior. I respected his grit, but I sure as hell didn't want him ending up as another statistic in this twisted conspiracy that ran deeper than I figured. I couldn't kick back until I had peeled back the layers on this thing. Too many stand-up guys had met their end in Wyoming while these scumbags roamed free. I wasn't about to let them stroll away without answering for it.

My top priority was to reach out to Josh to get the lowdown on his situation. If these shadowy figures pulling the strings were half as powerful as Samy made them out to be, they probably had eyes on Josh and were tapping his phone. I couldn't risk tipping them off by calling him from my own phone and laying it out for him. I had to play it smart and stay in the shadows myself. Using a burner was a must to make that call, and I had to make sure my name didn't get tossed into the mix. To any nosy eavesdropper, I had to be nothing more than a mysterious voice on the line. Luckily, Josh was a smart guy. I was confident he could handle it.

I strolled back to the ranch house and made my way into the study. In the bottom drawer of the desk, I found a stash of burner phones. As it turned out, I needed those more often than I anticipated when I left the Marshals. Even though ranch life seemed laidback on the surface, my reality wasn't exactly a snooze-fest.

Luck played a part, sure—being in the wrong place at the wrong time. But that wasn't the whole story. This world's messed up, full of scumbags lurking in the shadows, hell-bent on making everyone's life miserable. Somebody's gotta clean house.

That's why I enlisted—to go out there and ensure 9/11 never went down again. It's also what drew me to being a Marshal—hunting down fugitives who had no business mingling with decent folk. More often than not, the justice system does a good enough job of that. But I soon realized that when it comes to combating evil, "good enough" just doesn't cut it.

Law-abiding citizens put their trust in the state's criminal justice system to maintain order and dispense justice. That's an implicit social and political contract. But in a system that's merely scraping by with "good enough", there are bound to be instances where the state drops the ball on punishment and protection. I started feeling disillusioned as a Marshal when I witnessed some scumbags walking free in exchange for snitching.

It's easy for folks to kick back in their recliners and brush it off as minor sacrifices for the greater good. But moments like those made it crystal clear to me: when the system falters, someone's gotta step up. Looking the other way wasn't an option. In my book, you have to pay your dues. Period.

I started meting out my own version of justice when the system fell short. It all kicked off with a scumbag pimp dealing drugs, specifically getting minors hooked on heroin, then pimping them out on the streets. The system cut him a deal—witness protection in exchange for ratting out a big shot in the drug game. They were planning to set him loose with a new identity, ready to blend into some unsuspecting community. But I knew damn well he'd be right back to his old tricks the minute he touched down.

So, I played along, set him up with his new identity. Then, a few days later, I tracked him down in the shadows. Ensured he would never walk straight again.

It happened again with another witness. And then another. That started to weigh on me. I had sworn an oath to uphold my duties faithfully. Playing the vigilante on the side didn't align with that. I didn't want my actions tarnishing the fine reputation of the Marshals. So, I handed in my resignation. But that urge to intervene and make things right never really left me. I guess it's just part of who I am. I can't turn a blind eye when bad stuff is going down.

All these thoughts were racing through my head as I tore off the plastic and pulled out the burner phone. Josh and I never really had a face-to-face, man-to-man kind of thing. I only saw him knocked out cold when they choppered him out of the forest. But I had respect for the guy. He had gone out there in the Wyoming wilderness by himself, putting everything on the line to uncover the dirt on those scumbags and their shady dealings. That kind of gutsiness doesn't go unnoticed. Josh gave me a ring later, thanked me, and spilled the beans on the aftermath. But that was a solid two weeks ago. A hell of a lot seemed to have gone down since then.

It was time to call Josh and find out what was up. I scrolled through my contacts, found his number, and punched it into the burner.

CHAPTER 4

"Hello?" Josh answered, his tone more of a question than a greeting, as he picked the call from an unknown number.

"Josh, pay close attention. It's the cowboy from Colorado. Don't mention any names. Got it?" I asked.

"Yeah, got it. Keep talking," he replied, picking up on the urgency in my tone.

"Grab a burner and ring me back on this number."

"Sure thing," he said and hung up.

A couple of minutes later, my phone buzzed. It was an unknown number.

It was my turn to say "Hello?" in a questioning tone.

"It's Josh. How's it hanging, cowboy? Everything good?" Josh's voice resonated on the phone.

"Josh, pal, what have you got yourself into this time? Word on the street is that some heavy hitters are sore at you."

"If I had a dollar for every heavy hitter who's got a grudge against me... But seriously, dude, what's up? I know this isn't a casual catch-up call."

"You're right it isn't. But before we dive in, you're calling from a burner, right?"

"Yup, just ripped off the shrink wrap. I've mostly been using burners for over a week, changing numbers every day. My own phone's still on, but it's mostly been gathering dust. I'll bring you up to speed. But what's with all the cloak-and-dagger stuff?"

"What I've heard is that what went down with Wolfe in Wyoming and the CEO killing himself, that didn't wrap up that story. Is that right?"

"How the hell did you catch wind of that? You've got no idea how much legwork it took me trying to get to the bottom of it," Josh replied, sounding genuinely surprised.

"Ears to the ground, pal."

"Yeah, I know. Wish I was hooked into that network of yours. But you're spot on. There's this group of private investors. Loaded guys, old money types, and they're knee-deep into some seriously shady stuff. They're running the show through this investment outfit called Phantom Ventures. Wolfe and Raven Pharma were just the tip of the iceberg."

Raven Pharma was the Boston-based startup that was betting big on a groundbreaking drug focused on treating PTSD. It was in a fierce race against two rival startups, Apex and Intech, each vying to be the first to hit the market with their version of the drug. All three were gunning for the FDA's approval, and whoever hit the bullseye stood to strike gold—not just making a killing on the stock market but also by locking in hefty military contracts. However, Raven's competitors had a lead on it in the drug testing department.

Raven played dirty, using Wolfe and his crew of mercenaries to target scientists and sabotage manufacturing facilities belonging to Intech and Apex. Wolfe also helped Raven by using his followers as guinea pigs for trials of the company's experimental drugs. The whole game changed when I took out Wolfe. Raven got caught in the crosshairs of the authorities. The suicide of its founder and CEO, Frank Grant, seemed to have wrapped up the whole mess. Or so I thought, until Samy's call flipped the script.

"I don't get it," I asked, somewhat puzzled. "So... are you saying the Raven CEO was just a fall guy, and the real culprits were these Phantom Ventures guys?"

"Frank Grant, the CEO, wasn't exactly a saint. He was neck deep in it, but he wasn't flying solo. These guys at Phantom run a slick operation, and they skillfully distanced themselves from the fallout. They spun it like Grant was the mastermind and they were just innocent investors, played for fools with no clue about what went down."

"What made you think they were in on it?"

"It started as a gut feeling. Well, more than just a gut feeling, really. The thing is, I was completely out of commission for about ten days after coming back from Wyoming. Drugged up, mostly in dreamland. When I finally started getting back on my feet, I discovered everything neatly wrapped up. Grant was dead. His company folded up. It just seemed too damn straightforward. Kelly and Jason were keeping close tabs on the whole saga. What they dug up was that Apex, Raven's competition, was riding high. Sounds logical, right? Three companies in a dogfight, one drops out, so one of the remaining two takes the lead."

"Yeah, it does sound logical. What set off your alarm bells?" I asked.

"The reasons behind Apex's sudden rise. It was swimming in cash all of a sudden. Scooped up most of Raven's researchers and even poached some from Intech. It's crystal clear to everyone that Apex is on the verge of hitting the jackpot. But here's the kicker: all that cash was flowing in from two offshore funds, one holed up in the Cayman Islands, the other in Switzerland. Both notorious offshore havens used to funnel funds into the U.S., skating around direct U.S. jurisdiction."

"Hmm... so they channeled all this money into Apex. Any particular reason they went after Apex? Why not Intech?"

"Apex was the only one with intact manufacturing units, even though it had lost key scientists. With Phantom's backing, Apex went in for a recruitment blitz and is now well in the lead."

"But still, it could all be a regular part of business. Doesn't necessarily mean that Phantom is crooked. I'm sure there must be many such setups, using these offshore money channels, operating near the boundaries of the law without stepping on the other side."

"That's a good point," Josh conceded. "It's not been easy getting a fix on these guys. They are really good at this game, manipulating investments and the stock market. They've got stakes in several hedge funds and private investment outfits. Crafted a sophisticated setup, hiding behind a tangled web of interconnected companies with no clear ownership, remaining practically invisible. When I couldn't crack it by myself, I brought in a financial whiz to dive deep into it. Eventually, he traced it all back to Phantom."

"You found a clear connection with Apex?"

"Yeah. So, while Raven was biting the dust and the case files were getting shelved, the Phantom crew had already covered their tracks. The law agencies don't have a clue, while Phantom continues to pull the strings from the shadows. And all they're concerned with is getting the product out in the market. This drug Apex has been working on, it has the same problems Raven had with its version—memory lapses, entire chunks of memory wiped out. It has to do with how these drugs work, apart from acting as mood elevators, these drugs induce memory suppression, which helps PTSD sufferers tackle their trauma head-on. You must've heard about that problem with Raven's drug."

"Yeah, I remember. This memory suppression has to be temporary and reversible, but it wasn't. And until that was resolved, the FDA won't touch it."

"Exactly. It would have taken Apex a lot more research to overcome the memory issues. But Phantom is calling the shots now, and they plan to fast-track FDA approval and get on the market next year. Phantom has the connections and the money to get FDA to close its eyes to those issues."

"That's not good at all."

"I know. And it's not just about Apex, these guys are funding a lot of dubious setups, across a range of industries."

"Like what?" I asked.

"They've cast their net wide. IT startups, specialist IT hardware companies, especially ones focused on microchips and GPS modules, social media startups, think tanks..."

"That sounds a little random. Is there a connection between them?"

"Yup. The Russians."

“Russians? You’ve got to be kidding me.”

“I was waiting for that reaction,” Josh chuckled. “Here’s where the waters really get murky. Those funds coming in through the Caymans and Switzerland, that’s Russian dirty money making its way onto our shores. The IT hardware is to get their hands on the best technology that goes into drones. You must’ve heard about the drones Iran has been supplying Russia. Not just Russia, but many terrorist outfits in the Middle East. Well, most of the navigational components in them come from western companies. They’re trying to go one better by getting their hands on the source of the technology. As for IT and social media, that makes it easy for the Russians to interfere in our elections and generally create disharmony. And that’s why they’re funding think tanks as well. That’s how you get credibility for your disinformation campaigns. Financial resources are channeled into lobbying, covert political contributions, and spreading disinformation.”

“Election interference? What have you got yourself into, pal? You sure you don’t have Putin gunning for you?”

“I doubt that,” Josh replied, laughing. “But Phantom surely isn’t in love with me.”

“You can say that again. But, tell me one thing—what about the CEO’s suicide? You think that was for real?”

“There’s no way to prove it, but I think it was murder. Grant’s death was too damn convenient. Everything got tied up too neatly. I’d been tracking him for a while, even met him a few times. Grant was a slick guy, hard to corner. Not the kind of guy who runs out of options and throws in the towel. I know he was planning to skip town, had a private jet ready to fly him south of the border. But instead, he decides to go home, get wasted, and take a nosedive from his penthouse. I don't buy it at all. But the way his body was all smashed up, no coroner can say for sure if he was pushed. Like I said, it can't be proved... unless there's a witness."

"Are you saying there's one?"

"I'm not sure. There's this guy, Frankie... his brother saw something. The brother worked as a parking attendant in the high-rise where Grant had his penthouse. I don't know what he saw, but whatever it was, it got him killed. What I've heard is that he got greedy and tried blackmailing someone. His body was found floating in Charles River next day. Frankie's sitting on something that proves Grant's death wasn't a suicide, but he's scared shitless and has gone into hiding."

"It sounds like this thing runs deeper than I thought. But so does the risk to your life. You think these Phantom guys are on to you?"

"I don't know. I guess they must know I've been digging into them. They are connected guys. I've tried to be discreet, but you can only stay under the radar for so long."

"I know. Word has gotten out. Whatever dirt you've dug up must be heavy because you've stirred up quite the hornet's nest. That's why I rang you up today. I've got solid intel these guys have got a hit out on you. You've got to watch your back, pal."

"Oh," was pretty much all the reaction he gave me.

The man was cool-headed, no doubt about that. And he was dead set on uncovering the truth. But there's a fine line between bravery and downright recklessness, and it doesn't take much to cross it.

"This is something you need to take very seriously," I emphasized.

"Yeah, I know. Seriously, I'm not looking to be a hero. I haven't fully bounced back from taking bullets last month. That's an experience I definitely don't want to repeat. I do know there's a risk, but I've been playing it safe, staying under the radar. That's why I've been relying on burners. But I have to see this thing to the end. I can't let these guys get away with murder."

"I hear you. But did something happen today that pushed them to make a move? I'm trying to figure out what might've triggered this. Have you kept your inner circle tight?"

"Yeah, I think so. Only Kelly and Jason are in the loop, and you know them—no worries there. Also, my editor. He's my boss, so he's aware of what I'm working on. But he's solid."

"Anyone else in the loop? What about that financial whiz who helped you connect the dots?"

"Well, he's one of my regular guys. But he only knows bits and pieces, not the whole story. I don't think I'd be worried about him."

"What about cops? You shared this with anyone?"

"Well, yes, the FBI. They've got a couple of guys in DC digging into Phantom. They've got an active file on them. I've been sharing info with them. In fact, I'm headed to the FBI office tomorrow."

"What? Are you going to DC?"

"Not me. There's a Special Agent in Charge flying in from DC to record my testimony," Josh clarified.

Special Agents in Charge, or SACs, as they're commonly known, are pretty high up in the FBI chain of command. A SAC flying in for that meeting meant that stakes were seriously high.

"There's a SAC flying in especially for your testimony? What's it about?" I asked, genuinely surprised.

"I'll be sharing all my findings linking the money trail from Apex and some of those other startups back to Phantom and the Russian money."

"Is this SAC in charge of financial crimes?"

"Yeah. He's the head of the FCS."

The SAC was the real deal when it came to financial crimes. As the top dog of the FBI's Criminal Investigative Division's Financial Crimes Section (FCS), he was responsible for investigations covering fraud, corruption, money laundering, and all white-collar crimes.

"I think that's why there's this rush. They don't want you spilling the beans in that testimony," I observed, as the pieces fell into place.

"I guess you're right."

"You've got to lie low for a while. Don't brush this off just because you're on your home turf. The streets of Boston can be as dangerous as those deserted jungle paths in Wyoming. You get what I'm saying?"

"Yeah, I get it. I certainly don't have a death wish. I promise I won't take this lightly. Thanks for the heads up."

"When's your testimony?" I asked him.

"I've got to be there by 12 noon."

"Can you move this to another day and time?"

"I don't think so. I don't want you to think I'm being full of myself and not taking your warning seriously. It's just that the Feds are pushing hard for this even though they've been facing a ton of pressure to bury it. They've put in serious work to set up this testimony. The SAC flying in tomorrow—he's the one who'll give it the final push. I can't bail on him at the last minute."

"Even if your life's on the line?"

"I know it sounds corny, but I guess so. I can't let these guys off the hook. It's not just about a lousy byline on a story. It's personal. You know how it is."

I knew the feeling too well. There are times when things hit close to home. For Josh, it was as personal as it gets. These guys had tried to take him out. He couldn't let them walk away.

"Yeah, pal. I get it. Don't you worry about me. But you've got to watch your six, head on a swivel. And if you need me for anything, just say the word."

"I sure will. And I'll be super careful. Thanks for the heads up."

After I hung up, I stood there in silence, staring out the window without really taking in the view. The landscape outside was bathed in the warm tones of red, orange, and gold as the aspen trees embraced their seasonal change. The rugged peaks of the San Juan Mountains in the backdrop wore a dusting of the season's first snow.

Yet, despite the peaceful scene, my mind was anything but calm. The truth was, this tangled affair with Phantom wasn't only personal for Josh. It carried just as much weight for me.

I got involved in Wyoming because Logan, who I considered a brother, reached out for help. When my older brother Ryan, a Captain in the U.S.

Marines, met a treacherous end at the hands of scumbags within his own platoon, it took me a long time to unearth the truth and get to the killers. Throughout that ordeal, Logan, who had served as a Staff Sergeant in Ryan's Company, was the one guy who had my back no matter what. He risked his own career to help me track down Ryan's killers. There was nothing I wouldn't do for that guy.

I tore apart Wolfe's operation in Wyoming to prove Logan's innocence. Wolfe framed Logan because Logan was on the verge of exposing him for what he truly was—a predator preying on vulnerable veterans. Even though Logan, grappling with PTSD himself, initially fell into Wolfe's trap, he quickly came to his senses. Once he did, he resolved not to let Wolfe exploit others.

With the destruction of Wolfe's set up, I felt a sense of closure, thinking all that devilry had come to an end. However, it dawned on me that it was only half the battle until Phantom faced its downfall. Merely warning Josh didn't sit right; it wasn't sufficient to ensure his safety. I couldn't simply brush it off and go back to business as usual. Once a professional crew took up the hit, it was almost certain the target would go down. The threat to Josh's life would never go away. Unless someone stepped in and eliminated that threat.

Without really thinking about it, I began packing. Less than five minutes later, I had thrown my rucksack and a small suitcase into the back of the Silverado parked outside the ranch house. Inside the suitcase, I stashed a Glock, a couple of spare magazines, and my boot knives. After a brief chat with Rob, the foreman, letting him know I'd be gone for a day or two, I hit the road bound for Denver.

Once I hit the highway, I dialed Logan's number. This was as much Logan's battle as it was mine, and I knew he wouldn't forgive me if I kept him in the dark.

"Hey, Rockstar," a gravelly voice answered from the other end.

Logan was the only person in the world who called me by that nickname. It originated from my big brother Ryan, who bestowed it upon me during the Guns N' Roses era when Axl Rose was huge, and I was just another teenager rocking rebellious long hair tamed by a badass bandana. Ryan and his crew affectionately dubbed me "Rockstar". Most of them are now gone, casualties of war. Those who remained, like Logan, held an even more special place in my heart.

"Logan, pal, the wickedness Wolfe was tangled up in isn't finished."

I briefed him on the conversations I had with Samy and Josh. Though he mostly remained silent and simply listened, I could sense his tension when I detailed the involvement of Phantom and how Apex was now pushing the same drug as Raven.

"I'm on my way to Denver, catching the evening flight to Boston," I concluded. "I'll keep you posted once I assess the situation there."

"Which flight?" Logan asked, brushing off the last part of my statement.

"There's one at 1555 hours. That's the earliest I can make it. I'll hit the airport around 1445 hours."

"I'll start packing. Meet you at Departures. 1445 hours."

"Are you sure?"

"You're kidding me, right?" he retorted.

That shut me up.

"I'll see you at 1445 hours," I confirmed.

"Copy that."

About an hour before I reached the airport, Josh's text landed on my phone: *"Thanks again for the heads up. I'm being extra cautious. Staying away from my apartment. Crashing on the office couch. The place is guarded. All good."*

It eased my mind a bit. By the time Josh left the office next morning, I would be waiting outside. The time was 1440 hours when I parked the truck and entered the departures area at Denver International Airport. Logan was already there, packed almost identically to me, a rucksack on his shoulders and a small suitcase in his hand. I spotted him almost immediately.

Logan stood leaning lightly against a railing, a commanding presence in the bustling departures lounge. A man of roughly forty years, Logan possessed the unmistakable air of a seasoned soldier. Standing just over six feet tall, he carried his frame with the solid bulk of around two hundred pounds of pure muscle. Veins prominently traced their paths across his powerful forearms, visible under the rolled-up sleeves of a cotton shirt tucked into well-worn jeans. A scattering of gray peppered his trimmed beard.

Logan's demeanor exuded a quiet confidence, seemingly relaxed yet keenly attuned to his surroundings, his eyes ever vigilant, betraying years of military training. There was an aura about him, a subtle intensity that hinted at the readiness to swiftly transition from calm repose to decisive action.

He spotted me about a second after I saw him. The grin on his face mirrored mine as we hugged big time. The flight and check in at an airport hotel were rather uneventful, almost leaving us itching for the imminent action that awaited us the next day.

After breakfast and coffee at a diner, we parted ways. Logan dropped me at an intersection in downtown Boston in the rental truck we picked at the airport. He headed to the FBI office in Chelsea to do a recon of the area. I made my way on foot to the Boston Globe office in the Exchange Place building at 53 State Street, grabbing a couple of Patriots jerseys and Red Sox hats on the way there.

I conducted a quick recon of the area, inspecting every subway entrance, before positioning myself outside the 40-story building. It wasn't hard to spot two suspicious-looking vehicles—a Ford pickup truck fitted with a hefty rammer at the front, and a black van—parked in an alley across the street.

These guys meant business. So did I. A little before 1100 hours, Josh made an appearance at the imposing entrance of the building. That's when all the madness began.

CHAPTER 5

We stepped off the train at North Station, blending in like a couple of tourists in our Patriots jerseys and Red Sox hats pulled low. Moving swiftly, we navigated through the busy station, staying inconspicuous within the crowd. I had taken out six men, but I knew the danger wasn't over yet. Those guys would keep coming for Josh. It made more sense for me to fall back a little, so I could spot anyone showing undue interest in him.

"Keep walking toward the exit. I'll fall back a few steps, keep an eye out for any other hostiles. Don't look back. Call me if you need to talk. Once you're out, locate any coffee or breakfast joint and get inside. We'll take a breather there and figure out the next move," I instructed Josh as we passed through the fare gates.

"Got it," Josh replied as he picked up speed while I slowed my pace slightly.

As we emerged from the station, TD Garden loomed in front of us. However, the home arena for the Boston Bruins and the Celtics barely registered on my consciousness. My attention was elsewhere—I was too focused on keeping Josh in my sights while also scanning the area for any more suspicious vehicles or pedestrians passing by us.

Josh glanced sideways a couple of times, as if checking out his reflection in the glass fronts of the shops he passed. He ran his fingers through his hair, acting all cool, but I could tell he was checking the area behind him to make sure I was tailing him. I got it—that impulse to be doubly sure. The dude had been through the wringer lately, recovering from a bunch of gunshot wounds. Then, in the last half-hour, hitmen had been on his tail. No telling how many more could pop up from any direction. Any regular Joe who hasn't seen action would be a jittery mess by now.

I rang him up.

"Yeah?" he answered.

"I'm about ten yards behind you. It's all looking good."

"Great," he replied, sounding relieved. "There's a Starbucks up front. I'm heading in there. Cool?"

"Cool."

"Need a caffeine fix. You think we've got time? Want one?"

"Sure. We've got a few minutes. Get me an Americano. I'll grab a table. Join me there. No need to keep up the pretense in there."

"Got it."

"Oh, and one more thing, get the code if they have one of those keypad locks for the restrooms," I added as an afterthought. We were going to be in a confined space. It's always smart to have a backup plan in case things went south.

Josh quickened his pace, urgency in every step, as he made his way to Starbucks, pulled open the doors, and stepped inside. I could almost feel his sigh of relief as the glass door closed behind him. It might not stop any killers or bullets, but there was a psychological comfort in that door closing.

The aroma of freshly brewed coffee wafted through the air as I entered the place after Josh. Ignoring the cushy armchairs and the bar-style seating along the windows, I headed straight for a corner table. I opted for the seat against the wall, providing a clear view of the entire area. Instinctively assessing positions of dominance had become second nature, even in everyday scenarios. But inside that coffee place that day, I needed to be hyper-alert.

I did a quick check on the restroom layout before taking a seat. It was slyly stashed away, keeping it off the customers' radar. You had to slide through what looked like some concealed alcove, beyond which was a short passage leading to the solo restroom. Just as I suspected, the door was sealed up tight, locked down with a keypad. You had to punch in the digits to get inside.

I had barely settled into the chair when my phone buzzed. It was Kelly.

"Hey there, gorgeous," I answered.

"Easy there, charmer. We've been driving around the block, waiting for your call? What the hell's going on?" she asked, sounding impatient.

"Sorry. Haven't had a chance to catch my breath. Those guys after Josh just wouldn't stop coming."

"What do you mean 'they wouldn't stop coming'? You mean they were out to get Josh?"

"They weren't exactly handing out friendship bracelets."

"Oh boy, that's not good. So, you handled it, the usual way?"

"Not sure what you mean by the usual, but yeah, I took care of those immediate threats to Josh."

"That's what I meant—going all Army Ranger on them. But right in the heart of downtown? Seriously?"

"Yeah, dead serious. But what's the deal with you Boston reporters attracting hitmen? Can't you stick to cute little stories, like a puppy parade or a bake-off?"

"Sure thing, cowboy, I'll add it to my to-do list. But why aren't you guys in Chelsea? What are you doing down at North station?"

It was my turn to be surprised.

"What? How do you know that?"

"How's that for being a crack investigative reporter?" she declared triumphantly.

"You got me. Wait, did Josh share his location with you on the phone?"

"Bingo. You're not the only one with tracking skills. But where are you?"

Her answer left me a little worried. If those men were tracking Josh's phone, anyone with access to the phone's location would also get on their radar. Despite my spending the past half-hour drilling into Josh the gravity of the threat to his life, Kelly was still in the dark about the situation. I wasn't certain if she and Jason were in the sights of those men, but hanging around near him could easily make them targets.

The morning's events had made it clear to me that I couldn't leave Josh's side until this whole mess was wrapped up. I had no idea how it would end, especially since I didn't even know who these Phantom bad guys were. My immediate objective was to escort Josh to the FBI office, where he could provide his testimony and share any intel on those guys. It didn't mean the threat would vanish instantly, but at least it would take some heat off, and he could lay low in a secure location.

As for Kelly and Jason, the best move was to ask them to come to us, brief them on the situation, and then split up. Even if those guys were tracking Josh's phone, they would only have a vague location, in the general vicinity of Starbucks. Just like Kelly did. It would take them a while to reach North station and narrow down his exact location. By the time they caught on, I needed to ensure we were long gone from that spot.

"We're inside Starbucks. How long will it take you guys to get here?" I asked Kelly.

"Five minutes tops. Just need to park and walk over."

"Make it four. We've got to keep it moving. Can't linger in one spot for too long."

"Got it."

Meanwhile, Josh walked over to the table with the coffees.

"Thanks," I said, grabbing mine. "Kelly's en route, by the way."

"Got it. Thanks for having my back today. I've been left feeling like a kid who can't cross the street without a babysitter. And it's not like I didn't take your warning seriously."

"No sweat. Look, without some real battlefield action under your belt, it's damn hard to gauge how serious a threat like that can be. Normally, it's logical to figure you're not going to get jumped cruising through downtown Boston. It's just that this situation isn't normal at all. Good thing you bunked down overnight at the office. That was a smart move—probably kept you alive till morning."

"Ah, there you go with your pep talk again," Josh shot back with a wry smile. "But seriously, I never thought they'd set up an ambush in this neck of the woods. I mean, we're not exactly out in the boonies."

"That just screams desperation on their part. You'll have to be extra cautious now, watch every move."

"Trust me, I'm fully on board now. But..."

"What?"

"What's the deal with those guys you left in pieces back there? Are they all, you know, still breathing?"

"Yeah, they're breathing, but they're out of commission for a while. No sense leaving them in good enough shape to come after you again," I explained.

"I get it. And trust me, when I ask, I'm not passing judgment. I've done lots of shit as a crime reporter that's been just about borderline legal. But won't this land you in hot water with the law?"

"I doubt it. Those guys were packing unmarked guns. Cops will figure they're not exactly choirboys. They won't lose much sleep over finding out what exactly happened to them. They'll be more interested in uncovering what the hell were those guys up to. But that won't happen because those guys will get lawyered up. I've seen this scenario played out hundreds of times. And anyway, the legality of it all was the least of my worries. Keeping you alive was all that mattered. Not that the threat's over yet."

"I know. I owe you big time. You've saved my life twice already."

"Forget it. Just stay focused on dealing with Phantom. That's all that matters."

"Yeah, I know. You think you can get me to the FBI office by noon?"

"Yeah, absolutely. You don't need to ask. It's the only play we've got at losing the bull's-eye Phantom's painted on your back."

"Great. That's all I needed to hear. Whatever plan you have in mind, count me in."

"I'm still working on it. The main thing is to keep these guys guessing about your location. First step, get rid of your phone. I'm pretty sure they're using it to trace your movements. There's no point using a burner if you keep your main phone with you."

"Yeah, true. I'm carrying it mainly because there are some contacts who only have this number," Josh clarified.

"Those contacts can wait. The only ones you should worry about are the ones at the FBI, and Kelly and Jason. Everyone else takes a backseat until we've taken care of this. Deal?"

"Yeah, sure. But I'm kind of stuck with it. Can't just leave it here. And if I turn it off and carry it, they can still track it, right?"

"Exactly. We'll have to drain the battery. That'll make it untraceable. What's the charge on it?"

"38 percent," Josh glanced at the screen before answering.

"Turn the screen brightness to maximum, then play any video and leave it on. It'll be out in about half an hour. Forty five minutes tops. I've got something in mind once Kelly gets here. She'll have to ditch her phone as well. Your phone sharing its location with hers might've put her phone on the radar too. They'll go after her if they can't get to you. You're only going to be using burners until this thing's over."

"Sure. Whatever you say."

"What about Jason? Did you share your location with him?"

"No."

"He should be fine then. Starting now, we're going off the grid. That means no digital traces. No Uber or any other app-based services. We're sticking to rentals or old-school taxis—the kind you call up and they come get you. You got anyone at the office who can handle that? Someone sharp, gets the job done without needing to be micromanaged."

"That's Maggie. You need something done, she's the go-to. Total efficiency queen. You're stuck someplace on a tight deadline, need to get to a breaking story across town. Maggie will have a car ready for you. I once spilled coffee all over myself right before a big interview. I panicked, but Maggie didn't even break a sweat. Next thing I knew, I had a change of clothes, and right on time."

"Just what we need. We need to hop into a ride the moment we're out of here. Sticking around in the open is a risk. That street outside is too exposed. I suggest grabbing a taxi at the other entrance."

"That would be Nashua Street. Sounds like a plan. Less chance of running into anyone there. Do you want a car with a driver? Or we could have someone hand us the keys, catch the T back to the office. Gives us more flexibility. Your call."

"It's like you read my mind. Think your girl Maggie can handle that? We don't have a lot of time."

"We pull this off regularly, and Maggie's a logistics pro. You have to be when you're running operations for the entire Globe team. When do you need the car?"

"Ten minutes. It's 1130 hours. We'll hit the road at 1140. It's no more than a 15-minute drive, right?"

"Yeah, 15-minute tops."

"Perfect. Give her a ring. Regular car, nothing flashy. An old, beat-up one would've been ideal, but those are hard to come by unless you're at a used car lot."

"I'm sure she can arrange something. Anything else?"

"See if you can manage a couple of hoodies and sunglasses. I've got a basic change of clothes for the two of us, but always good to have a backup."

"On it," Josh replied and got busy on the phone.

I got a call on my phone a few seconds later. It was Logan. I signaled to Josh before taking the call.

"Any interesting intel?" I inquired as soon as I got on the line.

"You bet. Looks like we've got Russian mercenaries in the mix," Logan reported.

"Sure about that?" I questioned, surprised by the revelation.

My question was largely rhetorical. Logan, a former Scout Sniper in the Marines, was the go-to guy for reconnaissance, surveillance, and long-range precision firepower. To earn the title of Marine Corps Scout Sniper, you had to be not only an exceptional marksman but also an elite recon operator. If Logan identified them as Russian mercenaries, there was no room for doubt. They couldn't be anything else.

"Affirmative," Logan replied. "We've got two crews holed up in two SUVs. These aren't your run-of-the-mill rides. They look like mean, reinforced beasts, ready to roll through anything. I'll send you photos I've clicked."

"Think they're ready for an ambush?"

"You bet. They're strategically positioned on both flanks of Everett Avenue, approximately a couple of hundred yards out from the FBI office. Everett's the main route running in front of the office, the route you'd take to approach the building. My assessment is they're posted up there, ready for your arrival. It's the prime spot to set up an ambush and box in a vehicle. I kept my distance from the trucks but managed to catch snippets of their chatter. Recognized enough Russian to confirm their language. The parabolic mic proved its worth."

I had used parabolic mics plenty back in my days as a Marshal. They're remarkable for picking up distant sounds. Look like radar dishes with a microphone. Point them in a direction, and you can pick up sounds from sources well over 200 yards away.

"Smart move having one in your kit."

"Yeah. The moment you mentioned Russian money was involved, I knew we were dealing with some serious high-stakes action. But Russian mercs? That caught me off guard. And here's the kicker... at least one of them looked like he could be ex-Spetsnaz. I've been keeping my distance and using the binoculars, but I'm pretty sure he had that batman tattoo on his forearm."

This latest intel raised some serious red flags. Spetsnaz are no joke—they're Russian special forces. The batman tattoo is the symbol of Spetsnaz GRU, elite units of Russia's top military intelligence agency. It's a bat spreading its wings over a globe. Take away the globe, and it's practically the Batman logo.

"Spetsnaz, huh? Sounds like these guys are the backup plan if the target manages to make it that far," I replied, deliberately sidestepping any mention of Josh's name.

Josh was sitting across from me. Even though he was busy with his own call, hearing me speak out his name might draw his attention to the conversation I was having. I didn't want to spook him any further.

"That's the game plan. It implies there's gonna be a play on your turf."

"You got that right," I affirmed, giving him a quick recap of recent events.

"That's six less tangos on the board. You figure that's the end of it for now, or are there more where they came from?" Logan asked.

"There's more, but we've shaken them off for the time being. We'll be heading your way soon. Any specific spots at your end that are prime for a hit?"

"The FBI building is in an open area, with plenty of space all around. The prime spot for an ambush is on Everett Avenue, which is what you'll normally take, unless you make your way through side streets and alleys. Once you exit the Avenue and turn toward the building, there's a fortified barrier with a guard's cabin behind it. That's the most exposed spot for a sniper shot. Now that we know Spetsnaz is in the mix, I'd bet my bottom dollar there's a sniper ready to take a shot as a last resort."

"How many potential locations for a sniper are we looking at?"

"There are four structures tall enough for a sniper to set up shop on the top floor or the roof. I've ruled out the nearest and simplest one, a hotel to the north. Trees are obstructing the view, no clear shot to the barrier. Apart from that, there are a couple of offices west of Everett Avenue, and the fourth is MGH Chelsea hospital to the south. All within the 200 to 250-yard range. There's a bit of wind, but it's a clear shot. Not an issue even for a reasonably skilled sniper."

"Any signs of activity at these three locations?"

"Can't confirm. The only vantage point high enough for me to scope out all three roofs is the FBI building. No time to conduct physical recon at each site. The area is too extensive for thorough ground surveillance. Attempting such a maneuver could potentially tip off hostiles. The safest play is to prevent Josh from exiting the vehicle at the barrier. Sniper can't engage if he's not exposed. The snag is, all incoming vehicles are directed to the open parking lot beside the building. Occupants have to hoof it from the vehicle to the building across wide-open ground. But I'm sure there must be some underground parking facilities."

"Copy that. I'll figure it out. Hold tight. I'll reach out once we're mobile."

Josh had finished his call by that time and was waiting for me to get off mine.

"All done. There'll be a car waiting for us. I'll get the license plate number in a couple of minutes," he informed me.

"Perfect," I replied.

I was trying to figure out how much to tell him about the Russians. I didn't want to spook him. Even though he was holding up well under the circumstances, I knew he would be a little high-strung after the multiple attackers we had encountered in the last hour. The added information of Russian mercs getting in the mix wouldn't really help.

A message from Logan dropped on my phone. It had photos of the SUVs as attachments. He was right—the vehicles weren't run-of-the-mill rides. The mercs looked like they were armored up and ready to roll through anything.

My thoughts were interrupted by the melodious chime of the opening door. In the doorway stood the type of woman who can make men gawk and unwittingly stumble into walls. She was about five foot four, wearing a dark blue cotton jacket over a white T-shirt and snug-fitting jeans, which traced the curves of her finely sculpted body. Her dazzling white Converse sneakers further enhanced her sporty look. Her Red Sox hat struggled to tame the cascade of chestnut waves that spilled out from under it. Her hazel eyes scanned the café until they locked onto me.

Kelly tried to put on a stern expression but couldn't hide the radiant smile that emerged when her eyes met mine. Unconsciously, I found myself rising from my seat, a reflex ingrained by the timeless code of the old cowboy residing deep within my psyche—one doesn't stay seated when a woman enters the room. Briefly, Kelly diverted her eyes as she approached us, her gaze shifting to Josh.

That break in eye contact got my focus on a black van pulling up along the bustling Causeway Street outside. It bore an uncanny resemblance to the one stationed outside the Globe office building. Four men disembarked and fanned out. Two men took opposite trajectories, canvassing the shopfronts along the street, while the other duo made a beeline for the station. Their moves shouted loud and clear—they were on the hunt. That clinched it for me—Josh's phone was under surveillance.

I was debating the next move when the two men moving toward the station made a sudden detour and headed straight for Starbucks. They were still a good forty yards out, giving us about a forty-second window before they busted in. There was no way we could slip out without these guys clocking Josh.

CHAPTER 6

The two men needed to be neutralized. Swiftly and discreetly. It wasn't a simple task, especially when the options were between dealing with them on the bustling sidewalk or inside Starbucks. I opted to do it inside. There was a slim chance of some privacy inside.

Kelly had joined us by then. She greeted me with a quick, friendly hug, giving no hint that we were anything more than pals. That pretty much clarified my doubt about whether Josh was aware of our past encounter in Wyoming. Turned out, he wasn't. I took the cue, returning the hug somewhat absentmindedly, my focus still on the approaching men.

"Easy there, cowboy. Don't go spoiling me with all this attention," she quipped, her tone tinged with sarcasm, before catching on that something was amiss.

Kelly and Josh followed my gaze, sensing the urgency in the air. We didn't have the luxury of time, but I had a plan in mind. Grabbing the backpack I had carelessly tossed onto a chair, I took out two plain T-shirts—one green and the other brown.

"Those guys are coming for you. They must have tracked your phone," I informed Josh, handing him the green T-shirt. "You need to remain invisible, or bullets might start flying in here. Hit the restroom, change into this, and lay low until you hear from me. Kelly, grab a seat."

Josh wasted no time, darting into the corridor leading to the restroom. I trailed behind him, shedding my Patriots jersey and slipping on the other T-shirt. Our entrance had been far too conspicuous in those jerseys. The plain T-shirts would help us make a lowkey exit.

"Where did you park the car?" I asked Kelly as I swiftly changed.

"Over there," she replied, pointing north. "North Station garage, directly below TD Garden. Barely a minute's walk from here."

"Perfect. Watch out for those guys. They'll hit the entrance in thirty seconds. You're my lookout," I instructed Kelly.

I walked back to the table and took a seat on a different chair, turning my back to the entrance. It felt unfamiliar, almost alien, given my usual vigilance and ingrained sense of situational awareness. But desperate times call for desperate measures.

I was fairly confident that five of the six guys I had taken down at State Station were probably still out cold or, if awake, in no shape to alert their crew. However, the sixth one, whom I had clotheslined on the platform, when I was in too much of a rush to put him to sleep properly, could have regained consciousness. There was a chance he had relayed the message that Josh had someone assisting him. But all they would have to go on was a vague description of a guy my size sporting a Patriots jersey. Someone walking in and seeing me in a nondescript T-shirt, with my back turned, wouldn't give me a second glance, especially with a woman at my side.

"Can't we just call the cops?" Kelly asked.

"And tell them what? Cops can't do shit until a crime has been committed. And technically, they haven't committed one yet."

"Well, what do you know, huh? So, this is for real?" she asked, her tone tinged with disbelief.

"Yup. Like I said, maybe consider covering bake-offs from now on. It'll be a lot less drama."

"Ha ha. You're a real funny guy. So, what do I do now?" she asked, a hint of nervousness in her voice.

"Just sit around looking pretty. It might distract those guys a bit. They might leave without checking the restroom. And if not, I'll step in," I explained, gesturing toward the passage to the restroom. "We'll get out of here as soon as I take out the second guy."

"And how many have you taken out already?" she asked, emphasizing the last three words.

"Six."

"Oh boy, you live in some parallel universe I had no clue about until I met you."

"I don't know, Kelly, I'd much rather be a plain old cowhand on my ranch. Twenty seconds to go," I said, looking at my phone screen, which I had switched to selfie mode to keep an eye on the entrance behind me.

"Right. I've got them in my sights."

"Good. Check your phone screen and tell me what's your battery charge."

"56 percent," she replied, giving me a weird look.

"We've got to drain the battery. Crank up the screen brightness to the max, play a video, and let it run. You'll be sticking to burners until this blows over. Your phone might be on their radar."

She appeared on the verge of protesting, but my final statement made her think twice.

"Oh, OK," was all she said, before complying.

"Where's our urban cowboy, by the way?" I inquired about Jason, aiming to distract her a little and lighten the mood.

Back in Wyoming, Jason got some ribbing from me for strutting around in cowboy boots in which he looked about as comfortable as a squirrel tap dancing on ice. My comment achieved the desired effect.

"He's on his way. Should be here any second," Kelly replied, a smile breaking through her slightly tense demeanor. "Forgot his phone and had to run back for it."

"Let's hope he doesn't accidentally bump into those guys."

"Knowing Jason, I wouldn't be surprised if he does. But, you haven't told me yet, what are you doing in Boston?"

"Long story. The short version is, I got word that there's a hit out on Josh. I couldn't just hang around at home and let this shit go down. You get that, right?"

"Not many guys I know would step up like that, but you're a different breed somehow. So, yeah, I think I get why you're doing it. And guess what, it's showtime—those men are at the door. And, oh boy, Jason's there too. He's actually holding the door open for those guys."

I glanced at my phone screen and spotted Jason by the entrance. He was a slim, fresh-faced young guy in his early twenties, just dipping his toes into the world of journalism as an intern under Kelly's wing. Jason courteously held the door, allowing the men to enter first. However, only one of them eventually walked in, while the other loitered by the entrance. Jason expressed his frustration with a subtle shake of his head as the man strolled in, without so much as a nod, let alone a "Thanks". While Jason made his way to our table, the other man hung around the entrance, scrutinizing every face.

"Hey, Axel, how you doin..." Jason began calling out as he approached our table, but his sentence got cut off midway by a stern expression and subtle headshake from Kelly.

"How you doing, cowboy," I greeted Jason without looking back, only holding up my hand. "Take a seat and act normal."

Jason gave me a weak high-five and sat down, trying to wear as normal an expression as he could.

"Fiddle with your phone, check messages, do stuff that you'd normally do," I instructed Jason.

"He's moving toward the restroom," Kelly's sharp whisper cut through.

"Right. Party time. You two, keep chatting, act normal, and keep your eye on the other guy," I said, rising, stretching, and heading toward the restroom passage.

I stopped as the man almost bumped into me. I took a step back and let him pass. He didn't give me a second glance. He was too focused on his next task—checking out the restroom.

As he entered the confined passage, he cast a brief glance back at me. Holding my phone in my left hand, my eyes focused on the screen, and my thumb scrolling through content, I played the part of a guy absorbed more in the virtual world rather than the reality around him. The man mentally clocked me as a non-threat, pivoted, and proceeded into the passage.

That was what I was waiting for. I took a couple of quick steps, pushing the phone into my pocket while I moved, and entered the passage, completely hidden from the view inside the café. Just before the man reached the restroom door and altered his course, I lunged forward and delivered a powerful punch to the back of his neck. My knuckles struck the fleshy area just below the base of his skull, a highly vulnerable spot where the brain stem meets the spinal cord. I deliberately avoided using the knuckledusters. That could have killed the man. All I wanted was to knock him out. My knuckles were more than enough for that. The man's lights blew out instantly. The only sound was the impact of his body against the washroom door, muffled by the ambient music outside.

"Josh, it's me. Open up," I said, rapping on the restroom door.

When Josh opened the door, his reaction was less surprised than it might have been on any ordinary day. He had grown somewhat accustomed to the idea of knocked out guys lying scattered around restrooms.

"He's not going to wake up," I assured him as I dumped the unconscious man inside. "Shut the door again and stay put. Just one more guy to deal with, then we're out of here."

"Got it, boss, whatever you say," he replied, locking himself back in the restroom.

I called Kelly.

"Where's the other guy?" I asked.

"He's getting antsy, peering in to locate his partner."

"That's fine. His partner's in the restroom with Josh. I'll wait for that guy to come in. You and Jason can chill, act casual, just like you normally would."

I walked over to the entrance of the passage and stood there, my back against the wall, visible to Kelly and everyone else. I kept my eyes glued to my phone—just a guy waiting for whoever was inside the restroom to finish up and get out. A few seconds later, the door chimed, and the second man walked in, heading straight toward me. My eyes stayed fixed on the phone, my hat still concealing most of my face.

"It's occupied, pal. Waiting for the other dude to get out," I informed the man, still engrossed in my phone.

"I'll get him out," he grunted, striding past me into the passage.

I immediately followed him, but he was wary. He half turned, signaling me to back off. I missed the chance to take him down like his partner. However, retreating wasn't an option. His next move would likely involve banging on the door. And if he didn't get a response, I would lose any element of surprise I still had.

Without a moment's hesitation, I took a quick step and drove the heel of my boot into the side of his knee, which was half turned and at a vulnerable angle. Ligaments inside his knee snapped as his knee buckled unnaturally. The man dropped slightly, struggling to maintain his balance. I delivered a couple of forceful jabs to the side of his neck, then grabbed his hair and slammed his head into the wall. That did the trick—the man was out cold.

"Josh, open up. Time to go," I said, rapping on the restroom door.

As Josh emerged, I dragged the unconscious man inside and shut the door.

"I'll scout ahead and watch for the other guys. When I signal, grab Kelly and Jason, and follow me quickly," I directed Josh, striding swiftly toward the entrance.

Seeing no trace of the other two men, I signaled Josh to join me. I knew they were bursting with questions, but that wasn't the time. I maintained a brisk pace, making them struggle a bit to keep up, forcing them to almost run. As we moved, I continued speaking, finding it easier to control the conversation while they were busy keeping up.

"We've got to move fast. The clock's ticking. Josh has to reach the FBI office in 20 minutes. The car will be here any moment. I don't have time to explain everything now. All questions and concerns will have to wait. Agreed?" I addressed them all, glancing back as they struggled to keep pace.

"Yeah, sure," Kelly replied.

"Where did you park your car?" I asked her.

"On the lower level. Elevator's over there. Or we can take the stairs."

"Alright. Josh, what's the status of your battery?"

"Almost gone. It'll switch off any minute," he replied.

"Good. Kelly, yours?"

"25 percent."

"Leave the video on. It'll shut down in a few minutes once the battery runs out. You guys need to ditch your phones. As in now. Toss them in the trunk of the car."

"But..." Kelly began, but I cut her off.

"No buts. This is about life and death. Josh's got hitmen looking to take him out. If they can't get to him, they'll come after you two. You've got to be untraceable. Got it?" I asked, leading them down the stairs to the parking garage.

"Yeah, got it. So, what's the plan, Captain America?" Kelly grumbled, annoyed but falling in line.

"You're all using burners until this blows over," I stated, trying to hold back a smirk. "Where's the car?"

"That way," she answered, taking the lead, and stopping next to her red Malibu.

"Toss your and Josh's phone into the trunk. Quick. We're heading back now. Gotta keep moving," I urged, keeping up the pressure.

As soon as Kelly stashed the phones in the trunk, we made our way up the stairs to the ground level.

"The guys tracking the phones will assume you're still hanging around here. Buys us some time. And soon, the phones will go dead, throwing them off," I explained, as we rushed up the steps.

"Uh-huh," was all Josh could muster in response.

"What about me?" Jason asked.

"I'm coming to you, pal. You and Kelly are catching the T back to your office."

"Nuh-uh, not happening. I need to stick with you guys. Josh will need backup info for the testimony. He needs me around. Right, Josh?"

Kelly interjected, and before he could reply, she declared, "There, all settled."

"Nice try," I quipped. "But let's be real, Kelly. There's another crew lurking near the FBI office to stop Josh. I need to keep him safe, stay laser-focused. You and Jason jumping on this one will only give them more targets. Trust me, we'll circle back to the office as soon as we're done. And keep you in the loop the entire time. Deal?"

"Yeah, fine," she grumbled, not exactly jumping for joy. "Are you absolutely sure there are more men lurking out there? You think you can handle that solo? I mean, I get it, you're a total badass and all, but still..."

"I don't know about being a badass, but do you remember Logan?" I asked.

"Your Marine buddy?"

"Yeah, him. Remember what I told you guys about him?"

"I remember," Jason, the odd mix of a philosophy geek and martial arts junkie, chimed in with excitement. "You mentioned he was part of an elite Marines unit. A real lethal fighter. Took down two armed guys using just a knife."

"Exactly. Well, Logan's waiting for us in Chelsea. He headed there this morning to scope out the area."

"Oh, boy, what else have you not told us yet?" Kelly asked.

"For now, all you need to know is that with Logan as my wingman, I've got Josh covered. I'll keep you updated. Text me the number once you're back at your office and get your hands on a new burner."

"Just one little problem, genius," Kelly interrupted.

"Yes?" I asked, suppressing a chuckle at her sarcasm.

"Your number's chilling in the phone I just tossed in my trunk. This is 2024—people aren't exactly toting around little black books with phone numbers scribbled inside."

"Fair point," I conceded, a grin spreading across my face. "Any of you fine reporters happen to have a pen handy?"

All eyes turned expectantly toward Josh, who promptly fished one out from his satchel bag.

"Extend your wrist, please," I directed at Kelly.

She complied, looking puzzled. I hastily jotted down my number on her wrist.

"There. Written the old-fashioned way. Now hop on the T before those other guys come looking," I said, walking with them until the fare gates.

"I recall saying this back in Wyoming too," I whispered to Kelly as Josh and Jason led the way.

"What?"

"You want my number, just ask. I won't say no."

"Yeah, right, smartass," she retorted, rolling her eyes.

Once Kelly and Jason passed through the fare gates, Josh and I moved toward the Nashua Street entrance, where our car awaited us. It turned out to be a Honda Civic, a plain gray color, looking like it hadn't seen a wash in days. There was nothing about it that screamed, "Look at me". The driver got out as we approached, handing Josh the keys.

"Hoodies, track pants, and shades are in the back seat," he informed Josh.

"How did you pull off that dusty look?" Josh inquired.

"Emptied the vacuum cleaner on top of it, then used a blower to blow it off, leaving that nice film of dust," he grinned, before walking off toward the subway.

Josh tossed me the keys as he hopped into the passenger seat. Maggie had nailed every detail I had asked for. Josh wore a satisfied "I told you so" expression.

A sense of relief flooded over me as I pulled away. For once, there were no pursuers visible in the rear-view mirror. I knew it was only a temporary respite. Those guys wouldn't stop coming until they were all stopped for good.

CHAPTER 7

It didn't take us long to navigate through the bustling streets of downtown Boston, weaving our way through the skyscrapers looming overhead. We were soon driving toward the entrance ramp for Tobin Bridge, a towering structure that spans Mystic River. Satisfied that we had put ample distance between ourselves and any potential threats, I pulled out my phone, accessed the Contacts list, and passed it to Josh.

"Mind sending a message to Logan? Just a short one—'Rendezvous 1155 hours'."

"Yeah, sure. Uh, that thing you mentioned to Kelly about another crew waiting in Chelsea, is that for real?" Josh inquired as he keyed in the message.

"You think I was just trying to scare Kelly off?" I chuckled. "I did want her out of the mix, but the threat's for real. There's a bunch of guys hanging around the FBI building. And not just any guys, it's a crew of Russians, likely ex-military."

"Russian mercenaries? Are you serious?" he asked incredulously, handing back my phone.

"Dead serious. I wouldn't be playing all these covert games otherwise. The men staking out your office were likely a local crew who picked up the hit. They were good at their game, the way they had planned the ambush, but they weren't as dangerous as the Russian mercs. These guys look like the backup plan in case the first crew failed."

"Oh," was all Josh could muster in response, suddenly at a loss for words.

"Honestly, I would've been more surprised when Logan told me, but you'd already filled me in on the Russian cash mixed up in Phantom's scam. It adds up. If Phantom's involved in funneling Russian money, it's a safe bet they've got access to Russian muscle as well."

Even if Josh didn't display it, I could feel the tension in him at the thought of Russian mercenaries awaiting us. Just then, Logan's reply landed on my phone: "Copy that."

"Logan's got it under control. We should be fine," I reassured Josh, attempting to ease his tension.

As we merged onto U.S. Route 1, the urban sprawl of Boston gradually transitioned into a blend of commercial and residential areas. Skyscrapers receded into the background, replaced by a more suburban ambiance as we made our way through Charlestown toward Mystic River. However, my focus wasn't on the changing scenery. I had more pressing matters on my mind, like preparing Josh for the possibility of a sniper targeting him. There was no gentle way to deliver that news.

"There's another thing you should be aware of," I started. "You'll need to coordinate with your FBI contact. We'll need someone to meet us at the entrance barrier outside the building."

"Why? I mean, they'll want to know why."

"I know. The way it's set up there, we'll have to park in the external parking lot and approach the building on foot. That's too risky—there's a real risk of a sniper taking a shot at you."

"Sniper at the FBI building?" Josh asked, disbelief evident in his tone. "But... that's the FBI field office for all of New England. Isn't that like the safest place there could be?"

"When a sniper's locked onto you with a high-powered rifle, there's nothing like a safe place out in the open. That's what we're trying to avoid. The only way we ensure you make it into the building is if we roll straight into the underground garage. We can't pull that off unless your contact comes down to the gate and escorts us in."

"Oh," he replied, taking a brief pause before continuing. "I'll call Special Agent Vasquez. It's just that it feels kind of strange to tell someone I suspect there's a sniper gunning for me."

"Trust me, a Special Agent handling such a high-profile case won't find it weird. These guys deal with these kinds of threats regularly. Just let him know you've already had a bunch of guys come after you this morning. This is serious stuff."

Josh didn't need more convincing. He dialed Vasquez's number, but it just kept ringing before going to voicemail.

"It went to voicemail," Josh informed me with a hint of concern in his voice.

His apprehension eased when a text message popped up on his phone moments later.

"It's from Vasquez," Josh relayed. "Says he's in a meeting and will call back soon."

"Well, we've still got some time. Give him another call if he doesn't respond within five minutes."

"Yeah, I'll do that. These guys are usually on top of things. There's probably a last-minute sit-down for the Special Agent in Charge coming in."

"Got it. What's the SAC's name?"

"Dan Carter. I've never met him. Word from Vasquez and Jess is he's had Phantom in his sights for a long time."

"Jess?"

"That's Special Agent Jessica Hayes."

"Got it. But why are these Phantom guys so dead set on blocking your testimony? Financial crimes are usually a tough nut to crack. I can't wrap my head around how a single testimony can shut them down."

"It's not an instant shutdown, you're right. These things take time—building cases, pulling people in. But what I've uncovered is the mastermind behind Phantom, the one orchestrating it all, pulling the strings on these shady deals. Phantom is a mixed bag of financial investors; not all of them are dirty. Some are just investors, throwing in money based on the Templeton family's reputation. The Templetons were like Boston's royalty, old money with deep roots here since the days of Boston's role in the War of Independence. They made their fortune through shipping and maritime trade."

"You're talking in past tense. Are you saying they're not high and mighty anymore?"

"Well, yeah, their glory days are gone," Josh replied.

"So, what happened?"

"What happened is this one guy—Nick Templeton. His old man, Edward, was the last in line. But old man Edward and his wife were childless. They were looking at adoption, and that's how little orphan Nikolai from St Petersburg came into the picture. He landed in Boston and became

Nick. The old man never made any secret of the adoption, and he also didn't want Nikolai to cut ties with his roots completely. So, officially, Nick remained Nikolai, but he hated it. Spent his whole life trying to erase his past and then, ironically, ended up getting in bed with the Russians."

"What happened to old man Edward?"

"He's gone. Car crash. The old man had a thing for sports cars. Had a sweet collection of classic cars."

"Who wouldn't with that kind of cash?"

"Yeah, that's true. It was a 1965 Shelby Cobra 427. I laid eyes on it once, when they showcased Templeton's cars alongside other classics. A badass roadster in Guardsman blue, rocking those signature white racing stripes. Worth at least a cool two million. Anyway, he took it for a spin along the Maine coast. They found the car at the bottom of a cliff near Penobscot Bay."

"Just a freak accident? Nothing suspicious about it?"

"It's never just an accident, is it? Especially when there's big money in play. And when a snake like Nick is in the mix. Rumors have always been circulating. Nothing concrete surfaced, but once the old man was out of the picture, the Templeton empire took a turn into uncharted territory. Nick's mom went off the grid. She used to be a staple at fundraisers, but that all came to a screeching halt. Nobody's laid eyes on her in ages."

"So, Nick's the one you're dragging out of the shadows?"

"Yeah. Back in Wyoming, I was clueless about this whole mess. Nick had everything twisted up real tight. All I knew then was Raven Pharma was screwing around with the cash, and the company's CEO, Frank Grant, was pulling the strings. Nick had a sweet setup, but he screwed it up when he staged Grant's suicide. That's something I never bought. I wouldn't have started digging further otherwise."

"I asked this yesterday on the phone, but after what you've experienced this morning, and knowing there are Russian mercs waiting for you in Chelsea, I ask again—are you still committed to seeing this through to the end?"

"Yes," Josh affirmed, trying to inject as much resolve into his voice as possible. "I'm not pretending I'm not scared. But I can't let them intimidate me and bury the truth."

"I get it. I just needed to hear you say it loud once more. And you know what, scared is OK. Panicking is the problem. Panic leads to irrational actions and can get you killed. But being scared keeps you hyper-aware. It'll keep you alive."

"But what about you? You don't have to put your life on the line. I'm not saying I've got a problem with that. I can't get to thank you enough. I mean, I wouldn't even be alive today..."

"Josh, pal. Let's make a deal. I'm in this with you till the end. But you don't have to thank me every now and then. I respect what you're doing to uncover the truth. It takes balls of steel. Both of us are doing a good job of what we do. We're in this together. We'll see it through together. End of the story. Deal?"

"Yeah, sure. You won't hear me say it again."

"Good. As for putting my life on the line, dealing with those dumbasses back there didn't exactly qualify as that. You need a different breed for that."

"Like ex-army Russians?"

"Yeah, possibly. But my motivations are aligned with yours. I thought I'd put an end to it in Wyoming. Turns out, I was wrong. Can't leave it unfinished if I have a shot at bringing these guys to justice."

"And what about Logan? Why's he risking it?"

"He came simply because he knew I was headed to Boston. It's a soldier's code. If a brother's in peril, you charge through hell to have his back. But for Logan, it's even more personal. They tried to exploit him when he was at his lowest, dealing with demons and battling PTSD. They even took out veterans to protect their secrets. That's a line you don't cross. Because if you do, and I catch wind of it, I'll be coming for you. That's why I took out Wolfe and his crew back in Wyoming. That's why we're not resting until Nick Templeton and whoever else is involved pay for it."

"I get it," Josh replied, nodding gravely.

"But it doesn't seem like your testimony alone will put an end to this guy. He'll remain a threat as long as he's out there. What's the deal with the witness you mentioned. Some guy named Frankie, right?"

"Yeah, I'm not entirely sure what he's holding, but whatever it is, his brother got killed over it. It's supposed to debunk the idea that Grant's death was a suicide. If that comes out, it could expose Nick's connection as well."

"Maybe. It all hinges on what Frankie's got. And you have no idea how to track him down?"

"Haven't had the time. Got this lead yesterday morning. Word is, he's just a kid, not even twenty, and scared out of his wits. If he hasn't skipped town, chances are he's holed up in Dorchester. But that place is like a whole city. It's gonna take some serious asking around. But your call came in, and well, I haven't really had the chance to move much since."

"Well, we'll need to figure out how to track him down. In the meantime, you better give Vasquez another ring. We'll be hitting Chelsea in less than five."

"I'll give Jess a try this time."

"Sure. Whatever works for you."

While Josh made his call, we cruised over Tobin Bridge to cross the river. As we left Boston in our wake, the rear-view mirror treated me to panoramic views of the Boston skyline and the vast harbor. Downtown Boston's soaring skyscrapers stood proudly against the canvas of the clear blue sky, their reflective glass exteriors catching the sunlight. The skyline formed a dynamic fusion of glass and steel, dominated by iconic structures like the Hancock Tower, the tallest building in all of New England. Meanwhile, the sparkling waters of Boston Harbor sprawled under the cityscape, adorned with sailboats, ferries, and cargo ships gracefully navigating the shimmering expanse. The sunlight danced on the water, amplifying the harbor's scenic allure.

"She was in the middle of a meeting, whispering into the phone. But she's promised to call back within two minutes. I don't understand what's going on," Josh updated me, beginning to look a little frustrated.

"We still have a few minutes. And we're fine so long as we don't stick our necks out in that wide-open FBI parking lot."

Once we crossed Mystic River and entered Chelsea, the look and feel of the area underwent a noticeable transformation. Leaving behind the financial district's skyscrapers and the historic charm of Charlestown, we had landed in the industrially flavored streets of Chelsea. The streets become narrower, and the buildings took on a more industrial appearance, with warehouses and factories lining the roadside. The neighborhood had a gritty, urban feel, with graffiti-covered walls.

Taking the Fourth Street exit from the bridge, I deviated from the direct path to the FBI building through Everett Avenue, where Logan had spotted the Russians waiting in two vehicles. Instead, I headed in the opposite direction. My plan was to continue toward Sixth Street, approaching the building from the rear. But before that, it was time for a change in our appearance. We were less than a mile away from the building.

"Time to slip into the hoodies," I announced, pulling over to the curb.

Josh reached for a bag in the back. Inside it were two dark, oversized hoodies with a graffiti-style print, a perfect fit for the neighborhood we were traversing. Once we put them on, we exuded a streetwise vibe, a far cry from the appearances either of us had earlier in the day when Josh left his office. With the sunglasses on, we would be virtually unrecognizable.

"Your Maggie must have some telepathic powers. Pull the hood down low and you'll blend right into these streets. I doubt those mercs will give you a second glance," I remarked.

"I told you so," Josh replied smugly. "We don't need these, right?" he asked, holding up the matching track pants.

"I'm sure we can survive without them."

Josh's phone buzzed at that moment.

"It's Jess," Josh informed me, sounding relieved.

I received a call on my phone at the same time. It was Logan. I stepped out to take the call. There isn't enough room inside a vehicle for two guys on different calls—causes too much disruption.

"What's the sitrep? Any movement at your end?" I asked Logan as I got on the call.

"Yeah, that's why I called. These guys are getting antsy. One SUV is on the move. It crawled toward the FBI building at the junction of Everett Avenue and Maple Street. It turned into Maple Street and is moving slowly, not stopping, not speeding up. Looks like they're splitting up to cover both ingress routes to the building."

"Copy that. What's the status of the other SUV?"

"That's stationary. What's your location?"

"Approximately three minutes out. Holding position until we receive confirmation from the Feds that they'll come down and escort our vehicle into the underground parking."

"Smart move. That eliminates the sniper risk," Logan commented.

"That's what I figured."

"But there's still the risk of an assault by the tangos in one of the vehicles. Should I shift my position and move closer to you?"

"Where are you?" I asked.

"Near the junction of Maple and Everett."

"Hold your position. We need eyes on that second vehicle. Can't risk being caught with that one behind us. I'll call back as soon as we receive confirmation from the Feds."

"Roger that."

I was glancing at Josh while talking to Logan. His expressions and body language gave me the vibe that his call wasn't unfolding the way he had imagined. Something big was amiss. Josh soon wrapped up the call, frustration etched all over his face.

"I don't believe this," he grumbled in an exasperated voice, popping the door open to get out.

"Woah, hang on, tiger. Stay inside. What's going on?" I asked, jumping back into the driver's seat.

"The testimony's been pushed to tomorrow."

"What?"

"Carter couldn't fly in today. Meanwhile, we're out here risking our necks like a couple of fools."

"And no one bothered to give you the heads up?"

"Jess mentioned another agent, Miller, said he'd inform me."

"Did he tell them he'd informed you?" I asked, alarm bells going off inside my head about the possibility of a mole inside the FBI.

"She's looking into it, going to find out what happened and get back."

"What did you tell her about where you are?"

"That I'm nearby. I wasn't sure if there's any sense in going inside now."

"No, I guess not. It's not worth the risk. Did you tell her about the men coming after you?"

"No, I was getting too worked up. Didn't want to lose it on her. She sounded more rattled and pissed off than even me at the fuck up. So, I just ended the call saying I'd talk later."

Something felt seriously off. I couldn't believe that Federal agents could be so oblivious to the threat looming over Josh.

"Did any of those agents advise you about the risk to your own safety?"

"Yes. They even offered to pick me up. I just didn't want to be a hassle. But that was before your call yesterday; otherwise, I might have taken them up on it. After the call, I did play it safe by bunking out in the office, but didn't really fancy going back and saying, 'Hey guys, on second thoughts...'"

That settled my doubts about the agents' competency. But there was something else bothering me. Why were the Russians lurking near the FBI building? There wasn't any doubt they had been sent by Nick Templeton and his Russian backers. That implied they knew about the testimony and its scheduled time. That could only happen if they had inside information. There had to be a mole within the FBI.

What troubled me further was that the presence of the Russians indicated one of two scenarios, neither of which was favorable for Josh. One possibility was that the Russians were as clueless about the meeting being rescheduled as we were. They were under the impression the meeting was still taking place and were there to make sure Josh didn't get into the building.

The second scenario was even more troubling—that the Russians were informed about the cancellation of the meeting but also knew Josh would show up, aware that he hadn't been informed. The FBI mole, whoever he was, was luring Josh from the safety of his office to the killers waiting for him outside.

But there was no time to dwell on that thought because another, more urgent concern flashed in my mind, compelling me to take immediate action. Why was the other van slowly making its way down Maple Street, seemingly obstructing the path I intended to take? One logical explanation could be that the men planned to block both routes of approach. However, why execute it at the last minute when they had been parked on Everett Avenue all this while?

I was getting a strong feeling that the van was actively on the hunt for us. This could only be the case if those guys were somehow tracking us. There was a strong possibility that they were homing in on Josh's burner phone. If there was a mole inside the FBI, he would also likely have access to the details of the phone Josh was using.

Getting rid of the burner was a simple solution. However, the situation became more complicated when another possibility occurred to me—someone might have discreetly placed a tracking device on Josh. Now that I had realized the kind of influence the men who were after Josh wielded, it wasn't too farfetched an idea. Locating and removing a tracker would require a few minutes. But the luxury of time was one thing we didn't seem to have.

The clock was ticking. There was a sword hanging over our heads. I had no illusions about the danger posed by the crew moving toward us. These guys wouldn't be a walk in the park like the ones I took out at the subway station. They'd be armed to the teeth and prepared to unleash firepower. Confronting such a group without matching firepower, even with the element of surprise, was out of the question.

I needed to get rid of any tracking devices and extricate Josh before we found ourselves cornered.

CHAPTER 8

"They're tracking your burner. You need to lose it. Remove its battery and SIM card," I directed Josh, simultaneously zooming in to Google Maps on my phone screen.

I was searching for a safe place where I could stop briefly to inspect Josh's stuff and sweep the car for tracking devices without those men breathing down our necks. I zeroed in on a Salvation Army community center nearby. That looked like a place that would have a bustling parking lot. It had the added advantage of having exits onto two different streets. We would have a backup escape route if we got blocked by a vehicle on one exit.

The urgency in my voice prompted Josh to act swiftly, without wasting time asking questions. Burners are essentially the basic cellphones from the pre-connected devices era, limited to voice calls and messaging. As they don't have internet connectivity, they become untraceable once their battery and SIM card are removed.

"Done," Josh informed me. "But are you sure?"

"Can't be entirely sure about these things, but those guys are moving toward us in an SUV. They know our location. I can't see any logical explanation for that," I replied, pulling away from the curb and heading toward the community center on Chestnut Street.

"Oh," was all Josh could muster in response.

"What're you carrying in your satchel bag?"

“Just my laptop, tablet, and some odds and ends... papers, pens...”

“Empty the bag on the back seat. We need to make sure there isn’t a tracking device planted in your stuff,” I instructed him as I pulled into the parking lot and stopped between a pickup truck and a van.

“Tracking devices? Man, this shit’s gone way over my head,” Josh replied while dutifully emptying the contents onto the back seat.

I grabbed the laptop, flipped it over, and inspected the screws securing the back panel. They were all intact and showed no signs of tampering. Satisfied that the laptop didn’t have a hidden tracker, I moved on to the satchel. Besides the laptop, there was nothing sizeable that could contain a concealed tracker.

I grabbed the empty satchel, and systematically ran my fingers along every seam, pocket, and crevice. The soft leather yielded slightly to my touch as I searched for any irregularities. As my fingers traced the interior of an internal pocket, I detected something hard and unyielding. It was a square-shaped tracking device, about an inch in length and width and half an inch deep, cunningly concealed within the pocket with a thin tape securing it against the pocket wall. The tape was the same color and texture as the satchel’s leather—I would have missed it with just a cursory visual inspection.

“You’ve got a mole in your office. This tracker was discreetly placed inside your bag. Done with finesse to evade easy detection. Whoever did it probably had guidance from a professional. This isn't a cheap device you can pick up online. Here, take a look," I handed the tracker to Josh.

"Oh, man, I don't know what to say," he said, looking at the tracker in bewilderment.

"Check your wallet, clothes... anything else that you didn't have on you at all times since yesterday. The size of what you're searching for is similar to this. We're on a tight schedule. I'll quickly check under the car for any additional devices."

I checked the tire wells and found nothing. As I got down on the ground to examine the undercarriage, I called Logan.

"It's past 1200 hours, brother. What's the sitrep?" Logan asked.

"It's FUBAR out here. The meeting was cancelled. No one informed Josh. I'm pretty damn sure we've got a mole inside FBI and another one inside the Globe. Someone planted a tracker in Josh's bag. I'm sweeping the vehicle for additional trackers."

"Holy crap. What's the play?"

"Still working on it. What's the status on the SUV? Still have eyes on it?"

"Affirmative, it's holding position," Logan confirmed.

"I'm sure it'll move soon. Tail it. I've got a plan to draw out the other one and shadow it."

"Copy that. We maintain observation, no engagement?"

"Affirmative. No engagement until we're ready to take them down."

The car was clean, no tracking devices attached. After inspecting the undercarriage, I straightened up to find Josh decked out in some hardcore street gear—rocking the graffiti-covered hoodie and track pants, all in sync. The pants he had been wearing were in his hands, as he meticulously checked them for bugs.

"I've seen this in movies—tracking devices in the seams of pants and the belt. It's all clean, I think. But you better double-check," Josh said with a hint of nervousness.

"I will, but there's something I need to do first," I replied, eyeing a pickup truck parked a few vehicles away.

Two men had loaded some stuff into the back of the truck and were getting ready to get inside the cabin to drive off. Walking toward the truck, I timed my approach just as it began to move, swiftly planting the magnetic tracker inside the open rear end. As the truck slowly advanced toward the exit, heading for the street, I returned to the car, running my fingers over the seams of Josh's pants for a final check. They were clear.

"Get in the back and stay low," I instructed Josh as I jumped into the driver's seat, with Josh obediently taking cover in the rear.

"Slide into the space between the back and front seats. Just a precaution until we get away," I added, tailing the truck.

I maintained my position until the truck was about a hundred yards away. When it slowed down to make a turn onto Fifth Street, I rolled out of the parking lot right on its tail, keeping a consistent gap. The truck was taking its sweet time, just a couple of workers not in any rush to reach wherever they were headed. After a couple of turns, the truck merged onto the busier Washington Avenue.

"Stay low. It should happen any second now," I informed Josh.

"What's about to happen?" he asked.

"Me giving you the signal to relax and sit up straight."

Moments later, the thing I had been anticipating unfolded. Rolling in from a side street, a hulking, black SUV with tinted windows smoothly merged onto Washington Avenue, about fifty yards ahead of us. The license plate matched the intel Logan had shot my way a few moments back. That was the ride carrying the Russian crew, closing the gap on the truck, patiently waiting for the opportune moment to intercept it and bring it to a stop.

"You're good to sit up now, but stick to the back seat. If my estimate is right, you'll soon have to hit the deck again."

"Got it," Josh replied, getting up and settling into the back seat.

"Keep the hood up and put on the shades. If someone takes a peek inside, they won't connect you to the sharply-dressed reporter who walked out of the Globe office this morning."

"There you go. What's going on?" he asked, yanking up the hood of his hoodie and sliding on sunglasses.

"See that black SUV? Beyond the couple of cars ahead of us."

"Yeah. That's one mean-looking vehicle," Josh replied, leaning forward. "What's going on? I'm still trying to wrap my head around the tracker in my bag. Still can't believe it. Who's in the SUV?"

"The Russian crew looking for you. We're supposed to be the hunted, and now we're tailing the hunters. How's that for irony, huh?" I said, trying to get him to relax a little.

"Well, the irony is right up there but... doesn't common sense dictate that we try and avoid them?"

"You're right. But they don't have a clue we're shadowing them. They're too busy tailing the pickup in front of them. You can't see it from here, but it is there."

"Is that the same truck that pulled out from the parking lot? I knew you were up to something, but couldn't figure out what?"

"That tracker in your bag... well, I planted it on that truck. Needed confirmation that the guys in the SUV were the ones behind it. That SUV pulling out of the alley was all the proof I needed."

"Uh, right. So, what's our play now?"

"I'm waiting for two more vehicles to show up."

"Does your crystal ball also give you the make and color?" Josh asked a little sarcastically, sounding slightly irritated at my acting all mysterious.

"You know what, pal, it does. One's an SUV—a beefed-up black Tahoe, identical to the one we saw. The other's a gray pickup. F-150. In fact, here comes the Tahoe," I said, glancing at the rear-view mirror. "Take a quick peek through the rear windscreen."

"You've got to be kidding me," he muttered, stealing a glance before turning his head forward again.

"I'm serious. And it's time for you to duck again. Even though their eyes are going to be peeled on the SUV up ahead, we can't risk one of them catching sight of you."

Josh promptly slid into the space between the seats. The SUV soon passed us.

"It wasn't that complicated, by the way," I explained to him. "Logan tipped me off about the second SUV staking out the approach to the FBI building. Both the SUVs were initially posted there, ready to pin you down if you showed up. When we made a brief stop after entering Chelsea, they split up to investigate what was going on. Then the moment that truck with the tracker on it hit the road, I knew both crews would soon converge on it before making their move."

"I get it now," Josh replied, things beginning to make sense. "But I still don't get one thing. Back at Starbucks, four men got out of the van. Why did they split up? If they had the tracker on me, why not head straight there?"

"I've been thinking about that. I figure we lucked out with all the skyscrapers around us. Those trackers run on GPS. When you're among tall buildings, the signal's a mess due to interference. You won't get a pinpoint location like you would out here in the open. So, all they knew was we were in the area, but not exactly where."

"Yeah, makes sense. And what about the gray pickup? When's that going to show up?"

"I can already see it in the distance in the rear-view mirror. Logan's behind the wheel. It's a rental we picked up at the airport last night. He's tailing the SUV. You can sit up now, by the way."

"You guys really thought this through," Josh remarked, sitting up on the seat again. "Man, I feel like such a klutz. You knew just warning me wouldn't cut it. You knew I wouldn't grasp the extent of the danger from Nick and the Russians."

"Don't blame yourself. Nobody leading a typical city life anticipates assassins appearing out of thin air on busy streets. This is a whole new game. It's what we've been trained for. When you brought up Russian money, I understood the danger was real. But we're not out of the woods yet. I wish I could say it's over. But it's far from it."

"I get it now. But I'm still struggling with the idea of someone planting a tracker in my bag. And what you were talking with Logan on the phone, about a mole in the FBI. Are you sure about that?"

"I wasn't to begin with. But the more I think about it, it sounds logical. Think about it—how would all these guys have information about your testimony, it's exact time and location? It's not like the Feds put up a public notice about the day's testimonies. A big deal like a SAC's flying over for the testimony, and your guy Nikolai finds out about it and sends his assassins. Can you come up with any other explanation?"

"None that I can think of."

"What's even more concerning is that someone intentionally kept you in the dark about the postponement. I can see only one motive behind that—to draw you out of your office so these guys could get their hands on you."

"You mean actively luring me into a trap?"

"Looks that way. That's why I'm being super cautious in keeping you hidden from sight. We'll have to work out a plan to draw out the mole. Think about it while I call Logan."

Logan's truck was getting bigger in my sideview mirror. He was about to overtake me in the next few seconds. I called him.

"I've got a visual on both SUVs up front. Where are you?" Logan asked as he answered the call.

"Notice the grey Civic that looks like it hasn't had a wash in years, the one you're closing in on."

"Got you. That's one hell of a ride you've got. And that hoodie really screams 'gangsta'."

"It's called going undercover, pal."

"Is that Josh sporting those badass shades in the back seat?" Logan asked, chuckling.

"Yup."

"What's our next play?"

"We need to root out the moles. But first, find a secure spot for him until the testimony tomorrow morning."

"You got a plan in mind?"

"Trying to wrack my brain. I know there are guys from back in the day in and around Boston, solid guys, but it's been years. I'll have to dig out the details."

"You know what, something just occurred to me. Don't you go wracking your brains. There's a Corporal from my old crew—Declan Lawson. Went by the handle Router. Comms specialist. Thrives off the grid. Solid guy. You might not be acquainted, but he sure as hell knows you... because of Ryan, you know. Everyone in Ryan's old company knows you."

Logan was talking about my brother—Captain Ryan Blaze. He was a Marine. Logan was a Staff Sergeant in his company. I had crossed paths with nearly every Marine in Ryan's company, piecing together clues about what happened to him. Logan had later informed me that word of my hunt and finally tracking down Ryan's killers had spread through the whole company. I had earned their respect for that.

When Logan vouched for someone, trust wasn't a question. Logan had tagged him as a "solid guy". That was all I needed to know. The only question was whether he would be willing to dive into what was clearly a risky mission.

"I guess I might have crossed paths with him. Might recognize him if I see his face."

"I have a feeling you will," Logan said mysteriously and left it at that.

"If you say so. You think he'll be up for this?"

"You bet. And it won't be just for me. I told you you've got a fan base in our old Marine company. He'll jump at it when I tell him you're involved. The main challenge with off-the-grid kind of guys like him is making contact. Luckily, I ran into him a few months back. I'll give him a call and circle back. You stay focused on the next moves."

"Roger that. You good with tailing the Russians?"

"Yup. I'm not gonna lose sight of these guys. Once they realize you've given them the slip, they'll likely head to wherever they're holed up. I'll keep you posted. You carry on."

"Copy that. No engagement for now."

"Roger that," Logan confirmed, before stepping on the gas and overtaking us.

I turned off Everett Avenue onto a side street. The first part of my plan had been successfully accomplished. Josh was secure, and the assassins had absolutely no inkling of his whereabouts. I aimed to keep it that way until I had gotten to the bottom of the conspiracy.

CHAPTER 9

There wasn't any immediate need for Josh to be lurking in the back. I pulled over, signaling him to join me in the front.

"All clear for now. You can come up front. But keep the hood and shades on," I directed Josh.

As he settled into the front seat, I merged back onto the street.

"Logan's riding solo on tailing the Russians?" Josh asked, his voice betraying his concern.

"Yup. Logan was a Scout Sniper in the Marines. When it comes to recon and surveillance, you can't get better than that. That guy's like a ghost."

"Got it. Your confidence in him says it all. Where are we headed now?" Josh asked.

"You've got me there, pal, I don't have a clue. I'm just cruising around, trying to clear our heads and think this through. Our main priority is finding you a safe place to lay low until tomorrow. Bunking in your office is no longer an option. Any suspicions about who might've planted that tracker in your bag?"

"Um, I don't know, it could've been anyone. I've got this open cubicle space to work in. The bag just sits there all the time. I do have a locker, but it never crossed my mind to lock the bag. I've never felt the need to do it. It's the fundamental trust you have when you're part of a team. And there was nothing important in it. Whatever was important was on the laptop and tablet."

"Right. It could've been anyone. Tough to pin down unless we set up a trap."

"Yeah, I guess. But does it matter now? Whoever it was, they've done everything they could. Security in the building is generally solid. They can't prevent an insider from doing something like this, but they don't just let anyone stroll in. Don't you think I could crash at the office for another night?"

"Not now. It was fine yesterday because these guys had plans to come after you in a way that wouldn't leave any breadcrumbs linking it to them. They didn't make a move even though they knew your location. But now, they're going to be desperate. Their aim will be to take you out by any means necessary. Discretion is no longer their priority. I've been in the witness protection game long enough to know how resourceful desperate men can become."

"Are you talking about WitSec from your Marshal days?"

"Yeah. The only way we could keep witnesses safe was by keeping them on the move and never disclosing their location outside a very tight circle. You've been a crime reporter for a long time. You must know how this works. The only way WitSec works is when the mob is left guessing about the witness's location. If they get a fix on you, security can never be foolproof. If this Russian crew gets wind of your location, you won't be safe anywhere—not in your office, not in the FBI building. They've got moles in both places and can easily get to you. Snipers in nearby buildings, poisoned snacks, hidden explosives... the possibilities are endless. That's why we need to keep this circle real tight."

"Whatever you say. You're the expert here. I won't even try to second-guess you."

"The big problem you've got is a long list of people who can't be trusted until we're sure where they stand. That includes people at your workplace and within the FBI, until we've identified the mole. How about we start with people you have full confidence in and take it from there?"

"I guess," Josh replied in a slightly defeated tone. "The only ones I can be sure about at this point are you, Kelly and Jason."

"I can see poor old Logan hasn't made the cut yet."

"Yeah, of course. By you, I meant the both of you," he replied defensively.

"I know. I was just pulling your leg. But seriously, we need to flush out the mole in the FBI and figure out who we can trust implicitly. You'll have to turn up there again tomorrow. We don't want a repeat of what's been happening today."

"I couldn't agree more. We certainly don't want that. I can see the logic in your theory of a mole in the FBI, but I can't see Special Agent Jess or Vasquez doing it. I mean, they were the ones who pulled the strings to get the SAC to fly in. It doesn't make sense that they want to stop me from testifying."

"I get what you're saying. And maybe they're in the clear. But we can't take any chances. It's your life we're talking about. One wrong step, one bad decision by trusting the wrong person and that would be it. Do you catch my drift?"

"Yes, of course."

"When I realized those guys in the SUV were closing in on us, my initial thought was that your burner might be tracked. But after discovering the tracker in your bag, I'm not entirely sure about that."

"Should I pop the battery and SIM back in? Jess might be trying to call me and wondering what's going on," Josh suggested.

"I think it's safer to err on the side of caution and steer clear of using that phone again. I'll keep an eye out for a phone shop to grab a few burners. Use a new one to call. In the meantime, we need to figure out a place for you to lay low until your testimony tomorrow. When I say lay low, I mean going completely off the grid. Typically, the best move under these circumstances would be to have the FBI place you in a safe house for the night, but that's off the table because of the leak there."

I pulled up along the curb when I spotted a phone shop. Just as I was about to step out, a question popped into my mind.

"I never got to ask, what's your living situation? The way you bunked out at your office yesterday, I'm guessing you live alone."

"Yes. Divorced. I've got an ex-wife. And a son who's twelve. We share custody, but he mostly lives with his mom. And they're on holiday in Europe. I'm not even sure which city they're in on any given day. That's why I wasn't too concerned about them."

"That's good. Gives us one less thing to worry about. I'll grab a few burners and be back in a minute. In the meantime, rack your brains to think of a place to lay low. Somewhere completely under the radar. No friends or family. No one who could be connected to you."

I bought a bunch of fresh burner phones, all wrapped up in shiny shrink packaging. As I was walking back to the car, my phone buzzed again. It was Logan.

"What's the sitrep, Marine?" I asked as I got on the call.

"I've got eyes on a bunch of steamed-up Russians having a heated discussion," Logan replied, letting out a chuckle.

"They made their move?"

"You bet. They made their move and quickly realized they've been played. The guys in the pickup have just driven away. That gave me a breather to make the call to Lawson. That's the main reason I called. He's in the loop, standing by for my next call."

"Perfect timing. Where's he based?"

"Place called Topsfield, a small rural town about 20 miles north of Boston. He's got this place on the edge of town, even sent me some photos. Looks like a cozy little place on the edge of a forest, but inside, it's like a full-blown high-tech command center. Maps and schematics plastered on the walls, a beefy computer with multiple screens. He's a straight-up tech whiz."

"Got it. You mentioned he was Comms. Was he a field operator or systems admin?"

"Systems. MOS 0671. Data systems administrator."

"Hmm... no wonder he's a tech whiz. What's his current gig?"

"He mentioned this fancy title—Off-Grid Technology Consultant. Specializes in setting up comms for businesses located out in the boonies."

"Sounds like his kind of thing. But I'm guessing he doesn't rock the nerd look."

"Hell, no. You'll see when you meet him. He was a damn fine Marine out in the field. Do you need more time with Josh, or are you ready to hand him over now?"

"I need Josh to make a couple of calls. We'll wrap it up in about fifteen. The time's 1226 hours right now. How about we reach his place by 1315 hours?"

"Copy that. He'll be ready and waiting."

When I hung up, I noticed a message from Kelly: *"This is the new number. Waiting for updates. K."*

I replied: *"About to drop our mutual friend at secure location. Call back in 30 mins."*

She responded with a thumbs-up emoji. I returned to the car, clutching a bunch of phones.

"Any luck figuring out a place to lay low?" I asked Josh as I got back inside the car.

"You know what, I've lived in this city my entire life. I could crash in twenty different places, but with your 'no friends or relatives' rule... I don't know, man, but I can't think of a single place that's completely off the grid. Maybe someone from way back, someone I haven't met in years... but I'll have to dig out their details."

"Don't worry about it. I've got it covered. Just wanted to get you thinking along the right lines. I think now you're beginning to get what I mean by going dark."

“Yeah, I guess I’m getting the hang of it. So, are you telling me you’ve got a place in mind?”

“Logan fixed it up. It’s an ex-Marine from his old crew. Bit of a loner and a tech wizard. No connection to you, me, or anyone else you might vaguely know. Once you’re there, forget about making any calls. The only contact you’ll have with the outside world will be through me. You’ll use a fresh burner with only my number fed in. That’s what I meant by going dark.”

“Sounds like an airtight plan. But my conversation with Jess kind of got cut off midway. She’ll be trying to reach me.”

“Yeah, I was getting to that. You do need to ring her up to find out exactly what happened. She must’ve looked into it by now. And you’ve got to confirm the exact plan for tomorrow. But this is the only conversation you’re going to have with her. After that call, you’re going off the radar until it’s showtime at the FBI tomorrow. So, make sure you’ve got your story straight before you dial her up,” I told him.

“Yeah, right. What do you think—shall I tell her about the mole?”

“I’d say give her a hint that you suspect someone’s leaking information somewhere. Keep it vague. Let’s see what she makes of it. Don’t flat-out mention an FBI mole. She won’t simply take your word for it. She might not say it straight up, but she’ll probably think you’re getting paranoid. That’ll make whatever else you tell her less believable. People struggle with accepting stuff like this. Imagine if I told you there’s a mole in your office without showing you the tracker. You might play along, but you wouldn't just take my word for it."

"I guess you've got a point."

"But do tell her about the men coming after you, right from the time you left your office. Say there were some men lurking around the FBI office. But keep it vague, skip the details. No need to mention the SUVs or the Russian mercs."

"Any reason for feeding her selective info?"

"Yes. Whatever you tell her, she's going to share with her crew. The main reason for you to call her is to get all the facts from her. Why were you left in the dark about the meet getting pushed? You mentioned some Agent Miller was supposed to fill you in. You ever cross paths with the guy?"

"No. Never laid eyes on him. No clue who he is."

"Find out all you can about him. Get the exact details about tomorrow's meeting. If there are any updates, tell her to shoot you an email. Drop the hint that you think your phone might be bugged. Plant the seed of doubt about a mole. Arrange a rendezvous outside the office for a face-to-face. When she shows up, I'll back up your story with solid proof. That's when she'll really see the big picture and start moving on it."

"Should I clue her in that you'll be the one meeting her instead of me?"

"That might not fly. She won't be keen on an outsider meddling in FBI matters. Even I wouldn't roll with that on official business. I'll have to earn that trust. I've got plenty of proof to back it up. But when you call her, keep it vague. Let her think she's linking up with you."

“Do I throw your name in the mix? I mean, I can bench 175 pounds on good days, but if I tell her I took out six killers solo, I don’t think she’s going to buy it,” Josh said very earnestly.

“Right, I see the problem,” I replied, struggling to keep a poker face. “Just keep it vague. An old army buddy of yours. No need to drop any names right now.”

“Got it. And the meeting spot? Where should I ask her to show up?”

“Pick a public spot, where folks are milling about. And keep it close to your office. Let the mole feed the Russians the intel that you’re hanging around your office.”

“Alright,” he replied, sounding unsure. “But what if she asks why I don’t just swing by her office?”

“She won’t, not when you tell her you saw those guys staking out the FBI building. Even if she doesn’t buy that, she can’t overlook the attacks on the T station. That’s easily verifiable stuff. Tell her to check it out. She’ll have to play along.”

“Makes sense,” he replied, sounding convinced. “What about the time?”

“Let’s see... I’ll drop you at the secure location and hit the road by 1320 hours. It’s a 30-minute drive back. Then I need at least half an hour for a perimeter check around the rendezvous point. Call it 1430 hours.”

“You got it.”

“Does Jess know about the possible murder witness—Frankie?” I asked as the thought suddenly occurred to me.

“Not really. I mean I mentioned there might be a possible witness who could verify that Grant’s death wasn't a suicide. But I didn't give any details or mention names. As it is, tracking down Frankie won't be easy. And the way things are, he'll disappear if he finds out that cops or the Feds are on his trail. I was actually planning to task Kelly with it—she's plugged into Dorchester. Likely to dig up something quicker than I can. But after your call yesterday, I figured I'd hold off till today before asking her to dig it up."

"Works for me. Once I've linked up with Jess, maybe I'll grab Kelly from your office and we could poke around for this Frankie. Got a spot in mind for the meeting with Jess?"

"I'm leaning toward Faneuil Hall. It's got a good-sized pedestrian zone and a bunch of shops and eating places. Should tick the boxes, right?" Josh asked.

"Yeah, that works. Reassemble the old burner and make the call," I instructed him, pulling over once again. "I'll hit the road once you're done. If anyone's tracing the phone, they should only pick up Chelsea. Take the phone apart again after the call. Then we'll roll out."

Josh nodded and made the call. Five minutes later, he got off the phone and looked at me, looking like something was bugging him.

"Well, the meeting's all sorted. Jess will be..." he said, before stopping mid-sentence. "Just give me a minute. I need to check something," he added, before punching in a number and putting the phone on speaker.

It was the number to access Josh's voicemail on his work landline. A message soon played out, with a male voice informing Josh that the meeting had been pushed to the same time next day because the

SAC was held up on important business and couldn't take the flight into Boston.

"Who's that? Agent Miller?"

"Nope. A technician working under him. What Miller told Jess was that he asked this technician, Stevens, to inform me about postponement of the meeting. I don't really get why, but Stevens couldn't reach my cellphone, so he left a voicemail. But on my landline? Who uses a landline these days? It just keeps lying around on the desk. I don't remember accessing that in a long time."

"Smart move."

"What do you mean?" Josh asked, as he removed the battery and SIM card from the burner.

"It leaves us guessing. We can't say for sure if he deliberately didn't inform you. The timing of the voicemail is perfect as well. It was left at 11.15 a.m. It's a safe guess you'd be out of your office by then."

"The thought occurred to me as well. They've covered their asses. You think Stevens is the mole?"

"Your guess is as good as mine. Could be him, could be Miller... Whoever it is, we'll have to dig him out."

"Any ideas how?" Josh inquired.

"Not really. I'm sure something will come up. Let's just focus on the meeting for now."

"Yeah, right. Well, that's all sorted. Agent Jess will be at this open-air café, Urban Oasis, next to Faneuil Hall. Can't say for sure if she'll be flying solo or have Vasquez riding shotgun."

"Did you specifically ask her to come alone?"

“Not really. All I said was to keep it close as I had a feeling information was getting leaked.”

“That’s fine. It doesn’t make much difference either way. I’ll handle the rest. Give me that burner. I’ll use it to establish first contact with Agent Jess.”

“There you go,” Josh replied, handing me the phone.

“Now just kick back and take it easy. The next stop is Topsfield.”

“Is that where I’m going to be holed up?”

“Yeah. Ever been there before?”

“No, dude. It’s not exactly a dream destination. It’s a quaint little town in the middle of nowhere.”

“Sounds like just the spot to keep off the grid.”

“You bet it does.”

We made our way to the north and away from Boston, soon getting onto US-1. It didn’t take us long to leave the urban streets and the mass of traffic behind us. The scenery gradually changed. The cityscape gave way to a beautiful view of sprawling farmland and lush greenery on both sides of the road.

About fifteen minutes later, we veered off the highway, taking the exit for Topsfield. Hitting a quieter road, we wound our way to the outskirts, finally rolling to a stop outside a house perched on the edge of town, nestled against the backdrop of a dense forest.

CHAPTER 10

The front door was already open. Standing inside the open doorway, leaning against the doorframe, was an athletic-looking man of about forty. About five foot ten, the man had a wiry frame, the veins crisscrossing his sinewy forearms clearly visible under the rolled-up sleeves of his well-worn overalls.

The baseball cap turned backward did little to conceal the thick, flowing curls of long straw-blond hair. However, it was the defining feature of his deeply-tanned face that immediately drew attention — a thick, bushy mustache cascading down toward his chin, framed by long sideburns, giving him a rugged and distinctive appearance.

It was the mustache and sideburns that triggered a recognition at the back of my mind. Despite the lines etched around the eyes over the intervening decade since our last encounter, the size and shape of the mustache and sideburns remained the same as I remembered from nearly a decade ago. While the face might not have been immediately familiar, those distinctive whiskers were unforgettable. Logan was correct when he said that I would recognize the guy when I saw him. The man standing in the doorway, sporting those killer whiskers, was none other than Corporal Declan Lawson.

Ten years ago, Lawson was the man who gave me the first real evidence that something was fishy about the circumstances surrounding Ryan's death. Something he had picked up on the chatter on a closed channel. That's what got me on the scent of Ryan's killers.

Lawson appeared to be absentmindedly toying with a screwdriver, effortlessly twirling it between his fingers in a smooth, continuous motion, like the tool were a natural extension of his hand. The nonchalant posture as he leaned against the frame, seemingly carefree, might have deceived a casual observer. But the precision with which his sharp eyes scanned the surroundings, evaluating the situation like a seasoned soldier, told me that this was a man not accustomed to lowering his guard.

As I pulled up into his driveway and got out, Lawson swiftly straightened up. He deftly sheathed the screwdriver into the toolbelt hanging low on his waist with a quick move, before walking forward to meet me.

"Major Axel Blaze?" Lawson inquired, extending his hand.

"That feels like a lifetime ago. Just call me Axel," I responded, shaking his hand.

"Fair enough, Axel. We met once, but I don't think you'll remember me," he said, a hint of uncertainty mixed with hopefulness in his voice.

"Not easy to forget that impressive 'stache you're still sporting. Of course I remember you, Lawson. Back in Sangin, right?"

"Yeah, man, Helmand Province. It's been a long time."

"I take it Logan has briefed you on the situation."

"Yup."

"Appreciate you doing this."

"Don't even mention it. I don't mind a little excitement. This place out here, it isn't exactly a thrill-a-minute like we had back in the day. The biggest thrill for folks out here is an agricultural fair. Not that I'm the kind that socializes, just saying. And anything that helps a brother in a good cause—I'm in."

Lawson did a double take when Josh got out of the car rocking the graffiti-covered hoodie and track pants with his sunglasses still on. Josh quickly took off his shades when he saw the expression on Lawson's face.

Once I did the introductions, Lawson led us inside. His house contained three rooms—a cozy living room, a compact bedroom, and a spacious study doubling as a computer room. That was Lawson's pride and joy. And it was exactly like Logan described, housing an impressive array of computer hardware. A large desktop computer held center space with its multitude of cables and LED indicators. Monitors, displaying an intricate web of data and communication interfaces, flanked the computer. In one corner stood a server rack, meticulously organized with blinking lights and neatly coiled wires.

"Logan wasn't kidding about your place resembling a high-tech command center."

"Well, what you see is literally the beating heart of half the IT infrastructure in town. This stuff is what keeps it alive. That's what I do these days—mostly mundane tasks. But I stick to businesses, handling everything online, no need for face-to-face interactions. Not exactly a people person."

"I hear you, brother," I replied.

"But I think I can help you more than simply provide a secure spot for Josh. Logan mentioned these guys have been tracking his phone. Is that right?"

"We're not sure, but we think so."

I gave Lawson a quick recap to bring him up to speed.

"It sounds like Agent Jess is on the level. Once you meet her and give her the all clear, I can help you get your mole," Lawson offered.

"I'm listening."

"I can fix it so Josh can make a call from this place, using the same number as in this burner you've dismantled, but the location that'll show up on any surveillance monitor will be entirely different. Are you familiar with VoIP?"

"It's about making calls over the internet. That's about all I know," I confessed.

"I once covered a story on some scammers masking their location during calls to trick victims. But I'm no expert," Josh added.

"Well, that's about right. What I'm talking about is using digital obfuscation techniques to circumvent location tracking. We employ encrypted connections and dynamic routing. The call's origination point will be concealed as it traverses a tangled network of servers spread across diverse geographic locations. Each server acts as a relay, deflecting and redirecting the call's location information in real-time. It's basically location spoofing. It confounds any attempts to trace the actual physical location of the caller."

"Can you try breaking it down in regular English?" I inquired.

"Yeah, sorry, I tend to geek out a bit, talking tech all day. I seriously need a life," Lawson explained a little apologetically. "Anyway, I can use VoIP to make the call bounce through a bunch of servers in different parts of the world. Each server will make it look like the call is coming from somewhere else. Like a digital game of hide-and-seek—they'll never pin down the location. But not only that, I can easily feed them a false location."

"And that'll keep them chasing their tails. Sounds perfect. I'll call back once I've touched base with Jess."

I soon hit the road again, making my way back to Boston. The first thing I needed to do was to call Kelly.

Another text from her had dropped on my phone five minutes ago: "*Still waiting for the call back. Hanging around in office twiddling my thumbs. No pressure. Take your time. I've got all the time in the world. K.*"

"I thought ex-army types are supposed to be punctual," Kelly complained as she took my call.

"Sorry, I was out in the boonies. Just managed to get enough connectivity to call," I lied.

"Never mind. I take it that's where you've stashed our mutual friend, somewhere safe, someplace no one can touch him."

"Yeah, that's a big load off my mind."

"I won't ask you where. If you say he's safe, that's all I need to know."

"Well, I appreciate the vote of confidence."

"What's the plan now? Josh must've told you about this guy, the witness... Um, it's cool to take names on the call, right? No one's eavesdropping?" Kelly asked a little nervously.

"Yeah, we're good. These are fresh burner phones. Only you and I have the numbers."

"Got it. So, I was talking about this dude named Frankie."

"I know. Josh briefed me. He also said you're plugged into Dorchester better than him."

"Hell, yes, that's my turf. No one knows it like I do. We call it Dot, by the way."

"Well, alright, Dot it is. From what I've heard, it's like a city of its own."

"You bet it is. Nearly a fifth of Boston's population calls Dot home."

"That's literally like finding a needle in a haystack. And the clock's ticking. I guess you've got a plan in mind."

"I've already made a few calls. But calls don't quite cut it when you're looking for someone who doesn't want to be found. You've got to hit the streets. You've been a Marshal, I'm sure you know how it works."

"You've got a point there."

"I know I do. Where are you right now? How about we meet you someplace?"

"Who's 'we'?"

"Me and Jason, of course. He insists on being my shadow. Says it's too risky for me to go solo... I need him to watch my back," she replied, giggling.

I couldn't suppress a laugh. At 110 pounds and five foot five, Jason wasn't exactly the muscle you'd expect for backup. But his unwavering loyalty to Kelly in any situation showed he had guts. That counted for something.

"Josh has set up this meeting with the Feds. I'll explain everything when we meet, but this meeting is crucial to kickstart this investigation."

"Who are you meeting? Jess? Just a heads up, she's a bit of a hard ass."

"Well, I'll keep that in mind. It's 1:30 right now, how about we rendezvous at 3:00?"

"OK. But we're not going to hang around anymore. It's time to hit the streets. Jason and I will do some digging. How about you come meet us there after you're done with the Feds. Cool?"

"Alright. Cool. But watch your back, Kelly. I know it's your hood, but we're dealing with some dangerous characters. You saw what went down at Starbucks."

"I'll be careful, cowboy. And I've got Jason with me. We'll be fine."

Leaving the open roads behind didn't take much time. Before I knew it, I was cruising through Chelsea once more. My thoughts were drifting toward Logan when he finally dialed in.

"About time. I just dropped Josh off with Lawson. He seems like a stand-up dude, just like you said," I said, taking the call.

"Great. Well, I've tracked down where these guys are holed up."

"Nice work. I know once you catch a scent, they've got no chance of getting you off their tail. Where are you?"

"Outside the Apex Pharmaceutical facility. It's a massive gated compound outside Cambridge. But there's a bit of a problem. They've got guards manning the gates. Both SUVs went in, but I got stuck outside. Can't get in without a valid reason. I've been waiting outside the gates, trying to figure out the next move. I could try bullshitting my way in, but it might raise suspicion."

"You're right. Best to hold off for now. If we do need to make a breach, we'll wait until nightfall."

"That's what I was thinking. But, hold on... they're exiting the facility. What do you want me to do? Do I continue surveillance or rendezvous with you? What's your current location?"

"I'm about to reach Faneuil Hall. Meeting the Feds there. I think you better keep on their tail. You don't know what else you might uncover."

"Roger that."

"You know what, they might lead you straight to me. I expect the Russians to have a strong presence there to take out Josh."

"Well, if that's the case, I'll be on my way... oh, wait, they're splitting up. One's heading east, the other south."

"Oh, man, that's a bummer."

"Yeah, no kidding. Tough call. I'll flip a coin and hope for the best."

"I have a hunch. If they're coming from Cambridge, the one heading east might be headed my way. Take your chances and tail the one going south."

"Roger that. Watch your six, Ranger."

"Roger that. You too, Logan. The heat's on. Head on a swivel."

By the time I got off the call, I was in the vicinity of Faneuil Hall, looking for a place to park. It was 1350 hours when I finally parked and made my way toward the hall. I had a good 40 minutes until the meet at 1430 hours. Plenty of time to find a vantage point and wait for the Feds to arrive. But before they showed their faces, I knew the Russian crew would make an appearance.

CHAPTER 11

Faneuil Hall is like Boston's beating heart, pulsating with the rebellious spirit of days gone by. This is where the Sons of Liberty took a stand against British tyranny, kickstarting the whole Revolution. The Hall has stood the test of time, holding its ground for over two and a half centuries. But it isn't just some relic collecting dust. Right smack in the heart of the city, it's the nucleus of a larger zone known as Faneuil Hall Marketplace—a buzzing hub for pedestrians, with cobblestone paths winding through both historic brick buildings and modern structures. It's where history collides with the present, and the energy is undeniable.

On that crisp fall afternoon, the place was buzzing as people ambled through the array of shops, artisan carts, restaurants, and watering holes. The chosen rendezvous point, Urban Oasis, a breezy open-air café adjacent to Faneuil Hall, offered plenty of outdoor seating under vibrant umbrellas—an ideal spot for people-watching and savoring a laid-back cup of joe.

But I wasn't there to soak in those easygoing vibes. I had taken up position on the fourth floor, the highest level inside Faneuil Hall, next to a massive glass pane, surveying the scene below. The roomy pedestrian plaza and open spaces outside Faneuil Hall do not prepare you for the busy vibe as soon as you open the wooden doors and step inside. The large hall almost begins to feel a bit cramped, filled with a bunch of busy shops lined along the perimeter. A long array of stalls in the middle adds to the whole chaotic scene.

Two sets of stairs led to the upper floors, one near the front entrance and another at the back. I had gone up the front steps and assumed my position by 1355 hours—plenty of time to scope out anyone who didn't fit in, lurking amidst the casual diners and window-shoppers.

I already had my eye on five dudes who stuck out. A pair strolled in first, walking casually before taking a table at the café. Both rocked that seasoned look, the kind you earn through military miles. They played it cool, shooting the breeze like any two Joes enjoying a laid-back afternoon. But their eyes were too damn sharp, sweeping the scene like they were on high alert, blowing the cover of their supposed chill hangout.

A few minutes later, another pair strolled into the plaza, settling on a bench about forty yards from the café. They pulled out a compact chess set, unfolding it between them, engaging in what seemed like a casual game. Simultaneously, a fifth man strategically placed himself on a bench at the opposite end of the café. Together, they covered both approaches to the café. Confirming my suspicions, the men exchanged meaningful glances, and my doubts deepened when the solo occupant lowered his head, muttering into a concealed mic. These five characters must have been the crew Logan opted not to tail.

Ten minutes before the scheduled 1430-hour meetup, a woman casually ambled toward Urban Oasis, and took a seat at an empty table. It didn't require Sherlock Holmes to figure out she was none other than Special Agent Jess. A telltale sign of her law enforcement background was in the way she carried herself. The way her eyes methodically scanned the surroundings revealed a subtle yet honed vigilance, an innate awareness of her environment.

She had already pre-selected her spot before she began weaving her way through the other tables. She zeroed in on the one where one of the chairs had its back against a wall. The strategic seat restricted potential directions of approach and offered her a clear view of her surroundings—weeks of rigorous training at Quantico having conditioned her to maintain situational awareness and prioritize security. Even though she sat conspicuously at the unoccupied table, she retained a degree of influence over potential outcomes in case of an unexpected twist of events.

Her clothes were further proof of my initial assessment. She was rocking what's like the standard FBI uniform—dark suit paired with a crisp white shirt. No tie, but she didn't need it. That suit did all the talking, loud and clear—official business. I figured it was her way of sending a clear message to Josh, reassuring him that she had the situation under control.

In case I needed any further confirmation, her appearance matched perfectly with the details Josh had given me—a fit woman in her late thirties, standing about five foot three, with short dark hair and an attractive face that usually sported a don't-mess-with-me expression. She had pounded the pavement back in her Boston PD days before making the leap to Fed. Her suit jacket had enough slack for her to stash a small piece for concealed carry, but my gut told me she was packing a backup in an ankle holster. Always prepared, these cop-turned-Fed types.

It didn't take me long to identify Special Agent Vasquez either, even though he was nowhere near Jess. The tall, almost lanky man playing the role of an overly enthusiastic tourist screamed desk jockey—a guy with zero real-world field experience. Sporting a map in hand and feigning deep interest in market souvenirs, he couldn't resist sneaking periodic glances toward the café.

His cream-colored cotton jacket seemed a size too big, probably on loan from some burlier colleague back at the office. The slight awkward angle of his left arm hinted at a shoulder holster securing a substantial firearm. It also suggested he wasn't accustomed to lugging around that particular piece. The good thing was that they were taking Josh's intel seriously. They must have confirmed the morning's subway station incidents, which must have added weight to Josh's words.

In fact, his lack of experience in field surveillance inadvertently helped me in locating the third member of the FBI crew—a well-built guy of about thirty, who looked like he knew how to handle himself. Something about him spelled ex-military to me. An ineffable blend of a certain efficiency of movement, a straight yet somehow relaxed posture, and an unmistakable awareness of his surroundings.

Unlike Vasquez, this third agent seamlessly blended into the scene, engaging in casual banter with a couple of stall owners—just a regular guy, charming two lovely women on a pleasant fall afternoon. I might have overlooked him entirely if

Vasquez hadn't kept stealing glances in his direction. Then came the telltale sign—a moment where the charming dude lowered his head and mumbled something seemingly to himself. Bingo. That was confirmation that he was covertly communicating into his mic, staying connected with the others.

The presence of the other men around the café had already confirmed my suspicion that there was a leak within the FBI. It was time to share my concerns with Special Agent Jess. The main problem I anticipated, apart from the fact that she wouldn't easily warm up to the idea of an anonymous voice on the phone accusing her agency of a leak, was that I wasn't sure if she herself could be the leak. Or if it was Vasquez, or the other dude flirting with those women at the stall like he just stepped off a ship on shore leave.

The only way of getting to the bottom of it was by diving in headfirst. I didn't have any specific script in mind. I pulled out my phone and dialed Jess's number.

"Special Agent Hayes," she answered in a crisp and business-like tone.

"This is Josh's friend. It's about your meeting with him at 1430 hours. I need you to listen carefully to what I have to say."

"Who are you?" she demanded, her tone turning curt and authoritative.

"Like I said, Josh's friend. Names don't matter right now. But what I have to say does. Josh's life depends on it."

"Are you the vet who took out those men on the T?" she asked, not yet in a mood to listen to what I had to say.

"Yes," I replied, opting to reveal some of my cards.

"If you think going all vigilante will help you score points with me, you're dead wrong."

I wasn't expecting it to be an easy ride to convince her about the Russian threat, but I didn't expect it to head south right from the get-go.

"Let's get one thing very clear—I'm not here for any brownie points," I retorted, struggling to maintain a steady voice. "My sole concern is keeping Josh out of harm's way, a task that's been made harder by the sloppy handling by your team. And if you believe saving a buddy from armed hitmen is anything but self-defense, you need a refresher on the facts. All I've done is keep him alive despite the mess created by the leak in the Bureau."

"What leak? What the hell are you talking about? Josh was caught up in the same delusion. Don't go adding fuel to his paranoia with this crap," she snapped, her voice controlled but seething with anger.

"Paranoia? Seriously? Josh was lured out of his office today so that these men could finish him off. Do you really think a case of such magnitude, with truckloads of dirty Russian money, won't have repercussions for him? You really buy that feeble excuse of 'Oops, I couldn't reach him, left him a voicemail' when killers are on the prowl? Or do you just not give a damn about what happens to him so long as you get your hands on whatever he's dug up? Are you fine with Josh as collateral damage?"

That seemed to hit a nerve. Instead of trying to bite my head off, she went silent for a few seconds. She must have realized that no matter how she tried to spin it, she couldn't deny with a straight face that not informing Josh about the meeting's postponement was a total disaster.

"Alright, let's dial it back a notch," she said, raising a white flag. "What exactly are you saying? Who were those men at State station?"

"Nick Templeton has put out a hit on Josh. That crew was the one sent to carry out the hit."

"How do you know that?"

"That's not the point. What matters is that six men with unmarked guns showed up to take down Josh, right in the heart of downtown Boston. Knowing that, how could you think for a second that Josh was just getting paranoid?"

"Do you know who those men are?" Jess asked, sidestepping my question, still trying to decide if she could trust me.

"Some lowlife crew. Your guess is as good as mine. What you need to be more concerned about right now is that there's another crew gunning for Josh after the first one failed. And we're not talking your run-of-the-mill thugs here. These are Russian mercenaries."

"Russian mercs?" she asked, sounding skeptical.

"They were stationed outside your building in Chelsea. Two crews in tactical SUVs, monitoring the approach from Everett Avenue, waiting for Josh to show up so they could take him down."

"You do understand why I would find that hard to believe?"

"Yeah, I get it. If some anonymous guy called me out of the blue claiming there's a mole in my division, I might react the same way. But coincidentally... actually, not coincidentally, but because of another leak from your end, one of those crews is out here right now, ready to take Josh out when he shows up for your meeting."

Jess went silent for a few seconds.

"You mean they're here right now? Staking out the place?"

"Exactly."

"How do you know for sure?"

"Because I've been keeping an eye out for them. They showed up here before you and your crew did."

"What crew? I'm here by myself," she replied quickly.

"Special Agent Vasquez must be here to buy souvenirs for his desk, I guess. And there's this other dude who can't stop flirting with those women... Looks ex-military, maybe also fresh out of Quantico, but I guess he might be here for some casual window shopping."

Jess didn't try to contradict me. She was genuinely at a loss for words.

"Who are you?" she asked.

"I'll tell you later. Right now, the important thing is to show you what you're dealing with. Don't look directly, but there are two men at your two o'clock, pretending to be sipping coffee on a leisurely day. You've been a cop long enough, I'm sure you can make out that they're packing heat under those loose jackets."

Jess casually glanced around as if seeking a waiter, extending her hand to signal one over. Smart move. The two men didn't get any clue that she had just scoped them out.

"I see them. What makes you think they're Russian? Couldn't they just be a local crew?"

"I observed them before they sat down. The way they carry themselves, both are ex-military. Can't say for sure if they're Russian, but it'd be one hell of a coincidence if another crew of vets showed up targeting Josh."

"You do have a point there. Are these two the only ones? Or are there others?"

"I've spotted five men. Two guys on a bench acting like they're playing chess, at your one o-clock, about thirty yards behind those two at that table, blocking the approach from the east. The fifth guy is on another bench at your ten o'clock, blocking the west. If Josh was here with you, he wouldn't have anywhere to run."

"Hmm... maybe you're on to something. But, please, humor me—how do you know Vasquez? How did you spot him?"

I could tell she was beginning to believe what I had laid out for her. But she was still testing me just to be sure she could trust me enough to make a move in coordination with me.

"Josh gave me a general description—tall, lanky guy. As for how I spotted him, well, he sucks at this. I'm guessing he doesn't have any field experience."

"Well, he's the best forensic examiner we have at division. Not everyone's a field agent," she explained a little defensively.

"I never said he isn't good at what he does. I only stated what I know he isn't good at."

"And how about the other guy—the one you said was flirting. What makes you think he's one of ours?"

"He's actually good at this. I might have missed him. But Vasquez's furtive glances led me to him. As I said..."

"I know. Vasquez sucks at this. But you clearly are good at this. Who are you?"

"I think it's better I stay in the shadows until you've caught your mole."

"We haven't yet established the existence of a mole."

"You seriously believe the person who left a voicemail for Josh, without ensuring he received the message, simply made an innocent mistake? The only reason I've been one step ahead of these guys is that they didn't know I was on to them. And that's because your mole didn't have a clue about it."

"Well, I'll hand it to you, most of what you say kind of makes sense. How about we cross that bridge later and deal with the current situation first?"

"Fair enough."

"Good. Now I'm not saying you're some random conspiracy theorist..." Jess stopped mid-sentence.

"I hear a but coming..."

"Yeah, you got that right," she said, holding back a laugh. "I mean, these guys do look like pros. All I'm saying is how can we be sure they are here for Josh."

"There's a way to confirm that."

"I'm listening."

"These guys must've already clocked you as being on a call. They've got no idea who you're talking to, but they're probably wondering if it's Josh at the other end."

"Yeah, I guess."

"When you're ready, get up from your table, and make your way inside Faneuil Hall, letting them clearly see that you're still on a call. If they're indeed after Josh, they'll assume you've changed the meeting spot to somewhere inside the hall. It's enclosed, crowded..."

"Easier to meet him there unobserved," she finished my thought.

"Exactly. They'll follow you inside."

"And if they don't?"

"Then I'm just a random nutcase, cooking up conspiracy theories. And you can go home happy there isn't a leak at your end. But if they do, then there's only one explanation of how these guys got here."

"Agreed. Tell you what, I'm getting the gut feeling you're going to be proved right about this. Are you willing to tell me where you are?"

"It's driving you nuts, isn't it? Not being able to pinpoint me."

"You bet it is. I need to know you won't escalate the situation inside the hall. We can't have bullets flying in there."

"I'm not here to escalate things. I want you to grab these guys, even though I doubt it's going to happen—you don't have enough manpower."

"I realize that. Not to take on five armed guys," Jess conceded.

"So, let's just test my theory. If you can manage it, put a tail on the guys later."

"Sounds like a plan, considering the circumstances. I'll try to grab one of them, then go after the others later."

"Play it by ear. But be super careful about these guys. They're not your typical street muscle. They're trained soldiers. At least one of them is special forces. And they'll be well-armed. It's not going to be a routine operation."

"Special forces? You mean Russian special forces? Are you sure?"

"Quite sure. Also, I spotted five, but there could be more, maybe in sniper position. Don't engage until you're absolutely certain."

"Copy that. Let's get this rolling then. I'll ask my guys to secure both entrances, and then I'll head inside. What do you think?"

That was a welcome turn of events. A basic level of trust had been established. She was asking for my tactical advice.

"Makes sense. Ask Vasquez to tone down the eye contact. You don't want those men flanking the café to spot him."

"Roger that. The other guy... you got that right, by the way, he's one of ours. Ex-Marine. Special Agent Walker. That's me laying my cards on the table."

"Appreciate the gesture. I'll share my location. See the golden grasshopper?" I asked, referring to the iconic weathervane perched atop Faneuil Hall.

"Are you inside the Hall?"

"Yup. Gives me a sweep of the area. I'll keep tabs on those mercs as you make your way inside. But I'll follow your lead. No engagement until you make a move. Sounds good?"

"Sure does. Stay connected. Give me a sitrep once I'm inside the hall."

"Roger that."

"I'll give the heads up to my guys. Then make a move."

"Copy that."

I reassembled the components of Josh's dismantled burner, reinserted the battery and SIM card, and powered on the phone. If my hunch about the burner being tracked was true, the Russians outside would soon receive the message that Josh was in the vicinity.

In the meantime, I observed Vasquez and the other agent strategically advancing to opposite ends of Faneuil Hall. Walker walked toward the entrance at the far end while Vasquez made his way to the one up front. Meanwhile, Jess got up from her table and made a beeline for the Hall, walking purposefully.

I had been immobile for too long. I squared my shoulders, stretched out, and made my way down from the fourth to the second-floor windows. As I walked down, I flexed my neck and wrists to get the circulation going, getting ready for action. Even though I had warned Jess to be careful about approaching any of the mercs, I had a gut feeling she wasn't just out for a leisurely stroll. She would try to take prisoners. If she wasn't careful, things could go south very soon. It could all explode in a moment.

CHAPTER 12

As soon as Jess exited the café, the two men from the other table got up and began following her. One of them spoke into a discreet collar mic, issuing instructions to the other three men. One of the two chess players immediately got up and moved to the back entrance, but the other two maintained position.

"The two guys from the café are on your tail. One of the chess players has moved to the rear entrance. Warn Walker to watch his back. Same for Vasquez. The two men flanking the café are holding steady," I relayed to Jess.

"Copy that," she replied. "I'll walk through the hall, taking my sweet time, giving those guys ample time to keep an eye on me. I'll head for the rear stairwell. If they follow me in there, you'll have proved your point. Means they're thinking I'm meeting Josh there."

"Copy that. Head on a swivel," I cautioned her.

I didn't see much point in lingering by the window. If any action was going to happen, it would be in the rear stairwell. I descended to the ground floor. The air down there was filled with a lively hum of activity as I swung open the stairwell door and entered the market hall. I immediately spotted Vasquez. He was inside a souvenir shop on the opposite side, holding a snow globe, ostensibly fascinated by the falling snowflakes while keeping a vigilant eye on the wooden doors of the front entrance.

Right on cue, the front doors swung open, and in walked a woman—Special Agent Jess. She shot a quick glance in Vasquez's direction but barely registered him. Then she turned her head to look in my direction, sizing me up with a quick glance. I kept my expression poker-faced, not giving her any hint that I was the guy who was live on the line with her on the phone. She turned away swiftly, strolling slowly along the shops, making her way toward the rear stairwell at the opposite end of the hall.

The shops and stalls were laid out in a way that offered two paths toward the rear. On either side were rows of shops, with a central row of stalls in between. Upon entering from the front, one could choose to veer slightly left or right, navigating the passage flanked by shops and stalls. Jess opted for the leftward passage.

I remained near the front window, waiting for the men to show up. While I no longer had the elevated advantage of the upper floors, I still had a clear view of the men seated on the benches. My attention was soon drawn to the front door as it swung open to admit the two men from the café. They swiftly assessed the surroundings before homing in on Jess. They spread out, one following Jess, maintaining the same pace as her. The other guy took the passage on the right, walking swiftly so he could make his way to the rear before Jess did.

"The guys from the café have fanned out. One's tailing you, and the other is moving to intercept you from the front," I relayed to Jess.

"Copy that. I take it you're on the same floor now."

"Yes," I confirmed, without giving her any other details.

Vasquez was soon on the move, trailing the man shadowing Jess. But I decided to hold my position so long as l I still had them all in my sights. It proved to be a good decision, as a couple of seconds later, another man entered the scene—one of the two guys flanking the café. He had taken off his jacket and had it kind of folded over his right forearm. It didn't take a genius to know he had a gun under it.

My plan had worked. The men had reached the conclusion that Josh was definitely inside the hall. Activating Josh's burner seemed to have worked in luring them inside, and Jess's movements likely confirmed it for them. But I needed to tread very carefully—these men had come to Faneuil Hall with the clear intention of taking out Josh.

The man with the gun took the passage on the left, walking purposefully to narrow the gap between him and Jess. I couldn't stay still anymore. I began following him, keeping a few steps behind him. The door to the rear stairs soon became visible. The man who had taken the right passage had opened the door and walked inside, the door swinging shut behind him. Jess wasn't one to hesitate. Without breaking step, she opened the door and headed inside.

As soon as she did that, the man tailing her followed through the door. On his tail was Vasquez, who also immediately headed inside. Meanwhile, the gunman ahead of me reached inside the pocket of his cargo pants, pulling out a suppressor. Nonchalantly, he screwed it on in plain view, but people around were too busy doing their own thing. Even if someone glanced his way, all they would perceive was a man attaching a cylindrical pipe to something—the gun remained concealed under the jacket on his forearm.

Weaving through the crowd, I swiftly closed the distance to the gunman. By the time he reached the stairwell door, the suppressor was securely screwed onto his gun. As he opened the door and stepped inside, he began raising his weapon. Though I couldn't witness the scene beyond the door, the sounds of a struggle echoed through my earpiece. I couldn't risk the gunman taking out one of the agents.

Before he could line his gun, I launched myself at him, smashing my fist into the side of his head. The man stumbled and bumped hard into the wall in front of him. He got a little disoriented, but he didn't lose his grip on the gun. He began raising it again as he caught a breath and turned around. But that crucial two second window had given me enough time to assess the unfolding situation.

I never got to see how, but by the time I entered, the petite Jess, standing at five foot three and barely weighing 130 pounds, had already subdued a six-feet tall, 200-pound man. The man was on the ground, but fully conscious and itching to have a go at her. However, Jess's drawn gun pointing straight at him made a convincing argument for him to stay still. Her gaze briefly flickered when I burst through the door, but she had witnessed me taking down the gunman about to shoot her. She quickly connected the dots and kept her firearm trained on the grounded man.

Simultaneously, the six-foot-four Vasquez was locked in a struggle with the second man. Despite managing to draw his gun, Vasquez found himself in a fierce struggle, the assailant clamping down on his gun-wielding arm, both locked in a desperate bid to gain control of his gun.

But I had my own immediate problems to deal with. As the gunman turned and began raising his gun, I launched myself at him once more, this time using the hard top of my head to strike him on the temple, while clamping my hand onto his gun-wielding arm. My head butt proved effective, sending the man crashing into the wall behind him. He was already in the process of losing consciousness from the head butt. The smash on the wall completely blew his lights out.

However, I had no time for a victory lap. Vasquez's grip on his piece was shaky at best. If that other dude got a hold of it, we would have a hail of bullets flying everywhere. I already had the silenced gun I had taken from the guy I just knocked out. I aimed low and fired a round into the man's right knee. He immediately lost all interest in the gun as he let out a howl. I cut his scream short, smashing the butt into his head, knocking him out cold.

"Cuff him. I'll cover the door," I instructed Vasquez, who was still catching his breath after the struggle.

While I covered the door, ready to take out any potential threats, Vasquez secured the guy's hands behind his back. Meanwhile, Jess was having trouble getting the other man to cooperate.

"Face the ground. Hands behind your back," she snapped at him.

"Make me," he snarled back in a thick Russian accent, glaring defiantly from his position on the ground.

Jess snapped at him again, but he refused to budge. I wasn't in the mood to deal with this bullshit. While his civil rights might have been of concern to a Federal agent, I couldn't care less for a killer.

"Cover the door," I instructed Vasquez.

I moved toward the man who was still daring Jess. The look on my face must have clearly conveyed my intentions. The man tried to sit up, extending a hand to push me away. Without hesitation, I seized his pinky, twisting it enough to make him compliant. I began hauling him to his feet, but before he could fully rise, I kicked him hard on his right shin, making his leg buckle. I simultaneously pulled him forward, sending him crashing to the floor face down.

Keeping his pinky in my grip, I twisted his arm behind his back.

"You're a dead man. I've seen your face. I don't forget," the man spat.

"You've got me quaking in my boots. One more word out of you and you'll end up with a broken hand," I warned him, giving a slight jerk to his twisted hand.

He glared at me sideways with murder in his eyes, but kept his mouth shut.

I glanced at Jess and remarked: "All yours."

She looked like she was about to chew me out for my no-nonsense tactics, but thought better of it. Instead, she opted to simply shake her head with a hint of disapproval, retrieved a pair of cuffs from her belt, and slapped them on the man. Once she was done, she looked up and said: "You and I, we need to have a chat...."

Her words were cut off as the door suddenly swung open, revealing a young couple bursting in, eager to race each other to the floor above. Their enthusiasm faded when they found themselves staring down the barrels of three drawn guns.

"FBI," Jess declared, flipping open her jacket to unveil the badge. "This is a crime scene. Use the other staircase."

Without missing a beat, the couple spun around and hightailed it out of there.

"There are two more men still out there," I reminded Jess as I took position by the door, scanning the hall.

She nodded and spoke into her radio to warn Walker. Meanwhile, I quickly field stripped the gun I had taken and discreetly tossed the parts out of sight under the stairs.

"Walker got the guy at the back entrance. I'll go get him and call for backup," Jess updated us.

"I'll check out the guy at the front. There's a chance he might still be lurking around," I replied.

Jess nodded in agreement. But before I could make a move, Vasquez chimed in.

"We can't hold them here. We'll need a room or something until backup arrives," he pointed out.

"You've got a point. I'll figure something out. You've got them covered, right?" Jess asked Vasquez.

Vasquez nodded, straightening up and looking alert, gun in hand. Jess and I exited through the door into the hall.

"Thanks for stepping in back there. You saved my life," Jess acknowledged.

"I think you had it covered."

"No, the gunman who burst in could've got me. It happened too fast. I was too focused on the other guy."

"Don't worry about it. He won't be waking up anytime soon."

"Yeah, speaking of that..."

"Are we going to have that chat now? About that guy's civil liberties?"

"Actually, let's forget it for now. Sometimes, lines blur, especially in moments like the one back there."

"That's a big weight off my mind," I said, a solemn expression on my face.

"Yeah, right, I could tell the idea of that guy's pain was eating you up inside," Jess chuckled. "Do you have a name? Or are you still the man in the shadows?"

"Where do you stand now? Still think there isn't a mole in the Bureau?"

"No, you were right. There's a leak at our end. And that guy's Russian accent was unmistakable."

"That's all I needed to hear. I'm Blaze."

"Great. Call me Jess," she said, heading toward the back entrance to meet Walker.

I swiftly made my way to the front, exiting the hall to scan the area near the café. The fifth member of the group was nowhere in sight. Realizing there was no point hanging around, I made my way back. But instead of walking through the hall, I decided to circle the exterior perimeter for additional clues.

As I re-entered through the back door, I found a sense of tension hanging in the air. Walker stood guard outside the stairwell door, his expression tight and his gun at the ready. Unfamiliar with my face, he shot me a warning glare that would make any guy back off.

“I’m the guy on the phone helping Jess,” I said as I approached him. “What’s wrong? Have the Russians made a move?”

My words seemed to ease his tension slightly.

“Vasquez is down. They stabbed him and managed to escape with one of the prisoners,” he replied in a grim tone.

CHAPTER 13

I couldn't believe what I had just heard.

"Escaped? Damn! Where did they go? Which way?" I asked.

"They headed up the stairs. Must have gotten out the front by now. I was torn between rushing upstairs and holding the fort here. But I had to secure the perimeter," Walker explained regretfully, almost like he was apologizing to me.

"You did right. How badly is Vasquez hit?"

"I think he'll pull through. The knife missed the vitals. Weird knife, though. Not like anything I've seen before. Jess is inside, holding the stairwell. Go check it out. Backup's on the way."

"What about your prisoner? Is he secure?"

"Yes. He's in there."

I nodded and dashed inside. Jess had taken her stance on the steps, gun drawn, wearing a fierce expression. Vasquez lay flat on the floor, conscious but in considerable pain. A knife was lodged in the fleshy part of his chest, just below the right shoulder. A woman from the stall outside was by his side, applying light pressure with a towel above and below the knife to staunch the bleeding.

That knife would have to stay put until Vasquez was in surgery. Contrary to popular belief and the natural instinct to pull out any external object from your body, yanking out a knife embedded in the body of a stabbing victim is a bad idea. When a knife enters the body, it causes significant damage, slicing through skin, muscle, tendons, blood vessels, and organs. But while it's in, it acts as a plug, reducing some bleeding from the severed vessels. Pulling it out not only worsens the bleeding but can cause further damage on its way out.

I kneeled beside Vasquez and examined the wound closely. One glance at the knife confirmed what Walker had told me—it was indeed a strange looking knife, with a hollow cylindrical metallic tube behind the blade, instead of a regular haft. The fact that he hadn't seen anything like it before was simply because such knives are illegal. The blade, coupled with its attached tube, constituted the projectile component of a ballistic knife.

A ballistic knife is essentially a blade attached to a hollow tube designed to fit within an outer casing containing either a coiled spring mechanism or a compressed air system. This hollow cylinder acts as the launching mechanism, enabling the blade to be forcefully ejected. A trigger on the outer casing releases the knife, propelling the blade forward like a bullet.

These specialized weapons are commonly associated with the Spetsnaz, the elite Russian special forces. Once more, Logan's suspicions were validated—at least some members of the Russian crew were Spetsnaz operatives.

"I'm not sure what happened," Vasquez spoke in a voice barely above a whisper. "I had my gun drawn and ready. This man comes down the stairs from the second floor, fiddling with this metallic tube thing. I didn't see any imminent threat. I warned him to back off, use the other stairs. Next thing I feel is this searing pain as that knife slams into me like a bullet."

"It's not on you, pal. Could've caught anyone off guard. That guy was packing a ballistic knife. Unless you've seen one before, you wouldn't know what hit you. But hey, you lucked out. It could've been way worse. I mean, it's gotta hurt like hell, but you'll pull through," I offered, aiming to reassure him.

Vasquez nodded. I rose to my feet and surveyed the scene. The two men I had knocked out were still out cold. But they were joined by a third guy, unconscious as well. I assumed he was the guy Walker had caught at the back entrance. All three had been propped up against a wall in a corner, kind of leaning into each other. Knocking them out turned out to be a good thing, or else, they would have been in the wind. I approached them, crouched down, and inspected their forearms for any distinguishing tattoos. Once done, I made my way over to Jess. She looked mad as hell, but I sensed the anger was directed more at herself.

"Don't beat yourself up about it," I comforted her. "What I said to Vasquez wasn't just to make him feel better. No one could have seen it coming. Those knives are tricky weapons—they seem harmless, nothing more than a shiny tube. If you know how to use them, they're deadlier than guns because they catch you off guard. I'm sure he must've had a gun on him as well, but it wouldn't have caught Vasquez by surprise."

"How do you know all this?" she asked.

"I used to be in the Special Forces. There was a time many years ago when we had some joint military exercises with the Russians in the Balkans. That's where I first encountered one of these. Standard gear for Spetsnaz."

"Russian special forces?"
"Yes."
"So, you were right all along."
"Guess so. I wasn't sure until I saw the knife. That and the tattoo on than guy sleeping it off in the corner."
"What tattoo?"
"It's like the batman symbol, a bat spreading its wings over a globe."
"That's Spetsnaz GRU, isn't it?" she asked.
"Yeah. Many have turned into mercenaries for hire. Will do anything for the right money," I replied, not surprised by her familiarity with the symbol of the Russian military intelligence agency.
"Vasquez was lucky, in a way. No vital organs injured, mostly muscle tissue injury. Anywhere else on the torso..."
"It would've been fatal. That knife went in about five inches deep. But I don't think it was luck."
"What do you mean? You think the attacker aimed for that spot?"
"Yes. Those guys at Spetsnaz, they're good at this stuff. Really well trained. If you're aiming to stab someone in the torso without killing them, it has to be either where Vasquez was hit, or around the left side of the lower abdomen, where the risk of hitting something vital is lower. There's no way that guy would've missed at such close range. If he wanted Vasquez dead, he'd be lying there dead."
"But why?"
"It wasn't out of the goodness of his heart, that's for sure. It was tactical. Even though they're desperate to eliminate Josh, they don't want to mess up so bad that they get top spot on the hit list

of every cop and Fed in town. Injuring Vasquez will surely get them heat, but that would be nothing compared to what would happen if they killed him. You would've been out gunning for blood. Don't you think so?"

"Yeah, you've got a point. But why do it at all? I mean, he's still going to be on top of a city-wide hunt. An APB must've gone out by now. He could've just vanished."

"He came to free these men we'd nabbed. These three being knocked out screwed up his plans. They couldn't carry them and make a run for it. All he could do was bail out with the one guy who was still conscious and able to run."

"You've got a point. So, I guess you knocking them out kind of saved the day."

"Well... I don't know about that."

"It's true, even though I can't say I approve."

"Are we about to have that chat again?"

"We will, eventually. Right now, there's too much evidence countering what I had in mind. Once these three sleeping beauties wake up, I'm hoping to get something out of them," Jess said, indicating the three unconscious men lying in a corner.

"I wouldn't hold my breath on that. These guys are hardcore. They won't talk."

At that moment, paramedics burst through the doors, immediately getting busy attending to Vasquez and the knife lodged below his shoulder.

"I'll need to hit the road if that's cool with you. Can't stick around for statements. I don't know anything more than you about went down here."

"Is Josh safe? I can arrange a safe house for him," Jess offered.

"He's safer than he'd be in a safe house until you smoke out the mole."

"Believe me, that's top of my mind. Vasquez got stabbed because of that asshole. I won't rest until he's taken down."

"That's mission accomplished for me. That's the reason I came here."

"Alright, I'll get you out of here. Any leads on the witness Josh mentioned? He didn't say much except that it could bust the cops' suicide theory about Frank Grant's penthouse plunge."

"That's on my radar. It's a long shot but needs to be done if you guys are serious about bringing down Nick Templeton. Josh will never be safe otherwise."

"Can I ask why you're doing this? I get why Josh is putting his life on the line. He's just too committed to this investigation to let it go. But what's your stake?"

"You know what went down with Josh in Wyoming?"

"Yeah, he got shot while digging into Raven's business. Barely survived."

"Yeah, right. Well, I kind of stumbled upon his location in those forests out there, when the whole world was going nuts trying to find him. And once I helped him stay alive, it'd be a real shame if something were to happen to him now."

"Were you part of the Wyoming scene too?"

"Yep."

"Working with him?"

"Nope. Like I said, just stumbled onto him unconscious. Met him awake for the first time this morning."

“Uh-huh. Can’t say I’m much wiser than before.”

“Well, he’s a buddy. How about that? And I hate seeing crooks slip through the cracks. It’s a hangover from my Marshal days.”

“You mean you were a U.S. Marshal?”

“Yeah. Until about a year ago.”

“Why’d you leave?”

“Long story. I guess I like the simple cowboy life back at my ranch in Colorado.”

“And yet here you are, hunting Russian mercs in Boston. Guess I’ll need time to figure you out. Anyway, keep me in the loop. Don’t go dark once you leave this place.”

“I can’t. Not until Josh is safe. That’s not going to happen until all these guys are accounted for. I’ll keep you posted,” I assured her.

“But don’t start going Rambo on all these guys. Remember that conversation that we haven’t had yet?”

“Got it. I’ll take it easy.”

“I don’t know why I’m finding that a little hard to believe.”

Before we could leave, one of the paramedics attending to Vasquez signaled me to come over. Vasquez had something to tell me. I knelt beside him.

“Watch your back,” Vasquez warned me. “That guy you tackled earlier, the one you helped Jess restrain...”

“What about him?”

“When the man who stabbed me took off this guy’s cuffs, he was about ready to shoot me, but that knife guy held him back. But he asked me to tell you he'll be coming for you. And he didn't look like he was bluffing."

"Thanks for the heads up. You focus on getting better soon."

I stood up as they took him away. The look on Jess's face told me she had caught Vasquez's warning. But she didn't say anything as she guided me out through the police cordon.

"You need anything at all, just say the word. What you did today won't be forgotten. These mercs would've nabbed Josh if it weren't for you. And right under our noses," Jess said, extending her hand.

"Staying off the grid helped. You guys were on their radar," I replied, shaking her hand firmly.

"I guess. But watch your six, Blaze," she cautioned as I turned to leave.

That was a piece of advice I intended to take. As I blended into the flow of pedestrians moving through the plaza, I kept my movements casual, but every sense was on high alert. Even with the mercenary slipping through our grasp, the day hadn't been a total bust. Josh was in a secure place. Jess was hot on the tail of the FBI mole. But, till then, I had been merely reactive, firefighting all along. I couldn't keep playing catch-up. It was time to flip the script and seize control. I needed to locate the witness, Frankie, before Nick's crew did.

CHAPTER 14

My next destination was Dorchester. Kelly had already texted me the location. Pub called Murphy's Alehouse. It was about a twenty-minute drive.

Leaving the historic heart of downtown behind, I hit I-93 and headed south. The scenery changed as I cruised along the Waterfront, catching glimpses of the harbor, with sailboats dotting the glistening waters. The air tasted like salt, reminding me of the sea. South Boston flew by, and Dorchester soon came into view.

Pushing further south, I rolled through Savin Hill, one of Dorchester's quieter neighborhoods. The vibe shifted to residential. Victorian houses lined the streets, with well-manicured lawns and classy fronts. Seemed like folks in the neighborhood had some cash to throw around.

After leaving Savin Hill in my rearview, the scene started shifting. It went from upscale to blue-collar real fast. It was like flipping a switch. Approaching Fields Corner, things got real gritty, real fast. The streets got tighter, the buildings lost their fancy veneer, getting more basic. Everywhere you looked, it was tightly packed triple-decker houses, all painted up in faded pastel colors. They looked beat up, with paint peeling off and makeshift fixes all over. Graffiti tags covered brick walls like tattoos. Sidewalks looked like they had seen better days.

The main street was packed with mom-and-pop joints crammed into skinny storefronts—diners, corner stores, and local dives. Signs advertised car repair shops, laundromats, and local bakeries, all worn down like the neighborhood itself.

The outside of Murphy's Alehouse looked like it had been through the wringer. The brick front was beat up, but just about sturdy enough. A wooden sign hung above the door, weathered but still holding on, screaming out the pub's name in big, bold letters. Small Irish and American flags around the sign flapped in the breeze. I decided to leave the car down the block and stroll back. It's always smart to scope out the scene before you dive in.

As I was about to step out of the car, a text from Logan popped up: "*I'm in Dorchester. Mercs have exited vehicle. Possible recon. Any updates on your meet? Call when free.*"

I immediately dialed his number.

"Any luck with the Feds? Are they buying the mole theory?" Logan inquired as soon as he picked up.

I gave him a quick recap of what went down at Faneuil Hall.

"Ballistic knife, huh? No wonder it caught everyone off guard. Where are you at now?" Logan asked.

"Guess what? I'm in Dorchester as well. Fields Corner."

"No kidding. I just passed through there minutes ago. I don't know what's going on, but these guys are searching for something. They stopped in Fields Corner, a couple of guys got out, went inside a joint, then got back to the vehicle within a few minutes and hit the road again. Made their way south to where we are right now. It's about a couple of miles from where you are."

"What's the deal with those guys? You mentioned they're on some recon," I inquired about his earlier text.

"Not entirely clear. It looked like they were hooking up with someone specific back in Fields Corner. There were five men in the vehicle but only two got out. But out here, four have exited the vehicle and fanned out. Doesn't scream coffee break. Looks like they're hunting for something—or someone."

"Someone, huh?"

"Yeah, possible. I've got eyes on the vehicle. There's one man inside. But I decided not to follow any of the guys. Best to avoid showing my face as long as possible."

"Makes sense," I agreed.

"I'm filling up at a gas station while I have the time."

"Got it. Stay sharp. I'm hot on the trail of this possible murder witness. If we luck out and find him, it might crack the case wide open. Just heading into a joint called Murphy's."

"Is that a pub? Mind trading spots, buddy? I'm parked at this beat up gas station."

"Trust me, the pub isn't looking much better."

"I'll take your word for it," Logan replied before hanging up.

As I stepped into Murphy's Alehouse, I was pleasantly surprised by the inviting atmosphere. The interior exuded warmth, with exposed brick walls adorned with vintage Guinness posters and framed photos of old Ireland. The worn but sturdy wooden tables and chairs offered ample seating, despite the sparse crowd. Not more than a handful of people inside.

A long bar counter ran along one side, with bar stools lined up in front, mostly vacant except one. Contrary to the stereotypical image I had in mind, there was no beefy Irish bloke named Murphy holding down the fort. Instead, I locked eyes with a tall, lean woman, maybe pushing forty, giving me the once-over with a look that could cut steel. Sharp eyes, sharp demeanor. Despite her slender build, she exuded a tough vibe. Her fiery red hair was pulled back in a loose ponytail, accentuating her freckled face. She was rocking a black bartender's apron over a dark shirt, sleeves rolled-up like she meant business.

"Over here," Kelly's voice beckoned from a corner table, pulling my focus away from the bar.

I nodded to the woman behind the counter before heading toward the table. Kelly and Jason were already seated, joined by a third figure occupying a chair against the wall. It didn't take a detective to recognize the telltale air of law enforcement surrounding him—either active duty or retired.

The man must have been in his early fifties, but the general weariness about him made him look older, closer to sixty. The man was well built, even though his broad shoulders slouched slightly. His stubbled jaw, streaked with gray, framed a weather-beaten face. I noticed him give me a quick once-over as I entered, a reflex honed from years on the beat. But by the time I reached the table, his weary gaze had shifted to the swirling patterns of condensation on his half-empty mug of beer.

"Meet Declan, my cousin," Kelly introduced him. "And this is Axel."

"Declan Murphy," he said, offering his hand, then quickly added, "no relation to the sign outside. That Murphy is Siobhan, the woman behind the bar."

"Pleasure. Axel Blaze."

"Welcome to Dot's grim backyard," Declan replied dryly.

"I used to catch fugitives for a living. Believe me, I've been to places that'd make this look like a walk in the park."

"Fair enough. These two have been telling me about your Marshal gig and Special Forces background. You've got quite a fan club going. That crew you took out on the T, that wasn't a random bunch of gun-toting bozos. It was a hardened crew from Philly. Takes some serious chops to handle that, but you know there's always more where they came from," he cautioned.

"I know. Thanks for the heads up. So, how long were you on the force?"

"That obvious, huh?"

"Practically stamped on your forehead."

"Declan was detective for, like, forever," Kelly jumped in.

"More like seventeen years," Declan clarified. "Retired as soon as I could cash in my pension. Tried the whole cabin by the lake and fishing routine for all of two weeks before realizing it wasn't my thing. But enough about me. Looks like you guys have far more pressing problems of your own."

"I asked Declan to do some digging on Frankie. He's the best in the business," Kelly informed me.

“Well, I don’t about the best ... but when Kelly called and filled me in, it sounded like these Globe hotshots had bitten off more than they could chew. But things are worse than I figured. That’s why I called this sit-down, to lay it out for you straight. Before I dive in, anyone need a brew?” Declan asked.

“Um, I’m good,” Jason replied. “I, uh, tend to fall asleep if I have beer in the daytime.”

“Too much information, Jason,” Kelly chimed in. “How about you?” she turned to me.

I passed on the beer, figuring Jason might feel a bit left out. Despite the kid’s tendency to be a target, I had a soft spot for him.

“I’ll stick to black coffee. Got a long day ahead, need to stay sharp,” I replied.

“Same here. Jason?” Kelly asked, looking at him.

“Yeah, sure. Um, you think they do vanilla soy lattes?”

“Seriously? Why don’t you ask Siobhan at the bar?” Kelly suggested, gesturing toward the woman with the steely gaze.

Jason quickly reconsidered after a brief glance and settled for black coffee.

“Good call. Let’s grab them. It’s self-serve right now. They switch to table service in the evening,” Kelly informed us.

We headed to the counter, where Siobhan poured from the kettle. With our coffees in hand, we returned to the table, all eyes on Declan.

“You all on the hunt for this Frankie kid, right?” Declan’s question hung in the air, more of a statement than anything else. Still, we nodded in agreement before he continued.

"I've done some digging, and what I've gathered is Frankie's just a scared kid trying to keep himself and his kid sister, Fay, above water. His older brother, Jimmy, was like the man of the house after their folks died in a wreck a few years back. Jimmy was barely out of his teens then, but he stepped up, kept the family together. He was dead set against the kids winding up in the system. Jimmy had a knack for fixing cars and worked at a repair shop. He was a good kid that way. But it's tough to steer clear of trouble in this neighborhood, especially without folks to set you straight. Jimmy got caught trying to hotwire a car and did a year behind bars."

"Did that straighten him out?" I inquired.

"It sure did. After his release, he ditched the trouble and got his act together. Landed a gig as a parking attendant at a swanky high-rise near the Waterfront. Even did odd jobs for the wealthy folks around there."

"Is that the same high rise where the Raven CEO took a dive?"

"Yeah, the same, where Frank Grant's alleged suicide happened," Declan confirmed.

"And they're still sticking with the suicide story?"

"Yeah, despite a ton of red flags. The biggest one's a fifteen-minute blackout in the security footage. Apparently, there was a power outage. Now in these high-end places, backup generators kick in like clockwork, so none of the residents would've noticed anything more than a blip. But the elevators and security cameras went dead."

"So, that's it? No further investigation."

"Not as thorough as it should've been. There wasn't any evidence of foul play inside the apartment. But that's not surprising when you've got pros arranging the killing. Word on the street is there was some heat to tie it off pronto. So, suicide it remains, unless whatever got Jimmy killed comes to light."

"What's your take on what got Jimmy killed?" I asked.

"I can only speculate. But judging by how Nick Templeton's all riled up, there's likely a connection tying him to the killing. There's talk that he's into all sorts of drugs, snorting anything that'll get him high. And when he's high, he likes to play the unpredictable badass gangster type of dude. It's not out of the realm of possibility that he was at the scene when Grant was offed. I wouldn't be surprised if Nick was the one who threw him off the balcony. But it's all just guesswork. The only one who might have the answers is Frankie."

"What if he's got nothing to spill? What if Jimmy took his secrets to the grave?" I countered.

"I considered that possibility. But if that were the case, those guys wouldn't be hot on Frankie's tail, and he wouldn't be hiding out in a panic," Declan reasoned.

"How old are these kids—Frankie and his sister?"

"Frankie's pushing sixteen. Fay's around ten. Jimmy was barely twenty."

"Any leads on who killed him?"

"None. They fished his body out of the river. Clean execution—two bullets to the back of the skull. Professional work. No piece recovered to match the slugs."

"When was the last time anyone laid eyes on Jimmy?" I asked.

"Same night Grant bit the dust. Jimmy vanished too. Cops had their eye on him at first, but he turned up dead the next day.

"Have you laid eyes on Frankie?"

"Nope. Never laid eyes on the kid. He's gone into hiding. Him and his sister too. These triple-deckers you see crowding the streets around here... they're packed tighter than sardine cans, and so are the folks living in them. In Fields Corner, there are three tight-knit communities—Irish, Black, and Vietnamese. If you're an Irish kid laying low in the Irish block, you're practically invisible. It's a community thing, looking after your own. If someone's laying low for a good reason, like avoiding a bullet, nobody's turning them in."

"No one squeals?"

"Usually not. There's this feeling of looking out for each other. But hey, humans are humans. It's been three days since the kids went into hiding and no one's singing yet. But you can't bet your life on it. Someone might spill the beans, maybe without even meaning to. If Frankie's got brains, he should be looking at skipping town soon."

"But for now, you think he's holed up nearby, not skipped town yet?" I probed.

"That's my gut feeling. They lived out here in Fields Corner, so my guess would be they aren't here. There are Irish enclaves scattered throughout Dorchester. But I've got a hunch he's still lurking. Thing is, Frankie may be scared, but around here, family loyalty runs deep. He's likely itching to square things with whoever offed his brother, even if he's clueless on how to do it. But if we can track him down, earn his trust, and offer him a shot at payback, I bet he'll spill whatever he's holding onto."

"You think there's any way we could get that message to him—that we're his only shot at bringing Jimmy's killers to justice?"

"I'll get the word out. I'm retired from the badge, but I've walked these streets long enough to spread the word. Gotta do it low-key though. You're messing with some dangerous dudes here. You've got to watch your step. Like I said earlier, even though you took down a bunch of them, seven or eight from what I heard..."

"It was eight. I've been keeping score," Jason butted in, sounding almost excited.

"Eight, huh? Well, there you have it. But like I said, there's always more where they came from," Declan cautioned.

"Couldn't agree more. We can't take any of this lightly. Just so you know, looks like the Philly crew's out of the picture for now. Some Russian mercs have taken over," I informed him.

When I walked into the pub, I wasn't sure what Kelly had in mind and what to expect. But Declan was a straight shooter, and he had gone above and beyond to dig into Frankie. And he was family for Kelly. That sealed it. I decided to take him into confidence. Figured it was best to bring him up to speed, so I briefed him on the Faneuil Hall situation.

"Ballistic knife, huh? That's a new one for me," Declan remarked.

"Yeah, it's a Spetsnaz specialty. I came across those back in my army days."

"No wonder I haven't come across them. But hitting a Fed? What kind of game are these guys playing?"

"I doubt it was part of their grand scheme. It was more of a heat-of-the-moment decision when we nabbed four of their crew. The last guy got desperate, even though he made sure not to kill Vasquez."

"You think he deliberately missed?"

"Yes. These guys are well trained. They don't miss," I answered.

"That good?"

"Yeah. But I bet he must be kicking himself now. It wasn't worth it just to get one guy out."

"The others didn't bolt?"

"They couldn't. They were out cold."

"How many?" Jason asked.

"Three."

"That brings the tally to eleven."

"Jason, pal, I'm not really keeping score. But with Russian mercenaries in play, the game just got deadlier. We'll have to tread extra carefully."

"I agree," Declan declared. "Kelly, you two need to clear out. Head back to your office, start making calls. I'll handle things here."

"Not happening, Declan," Kelly shot back, her tone resolute. "We can cover more ground if I'm out there with you. We can split up and regroup later."

Declan's suggestion to send Kelly back to the office hadn't landed well. Simply telling Kelly to return to her office wasn't going to fly, especially since I had already made her do that once. I knew by then that she had a fiercely independent streak that wouldn't let her see the sense in what Declan was saying—there was too much risk for her and Jason to be out gathering intel on those streets. Instead of letting Declan make another futile attempt to convince her, I intervened to handle the situation differently.

"We also need someone to check out the apartments where all this chaos went down, where Jimmy and Grant ended up dead. We might just uncover the clues to what got Jimmy killed," I pointed out.

"How do you figure?" Kelly asked.

"What went down the night Grant took that leap from his penthouse? There's bound to be someone there who saw or heard something off. Doesn't sound like the cops put much effort into digging deep. And people might be more inclined to talk to reporters than to cops. Time's not on our side here. And finding Frankie's a long shot. We'll only find him if he wants to be found. All we can do is for Declan and you to spread the word, then sit back and wait for him to make a move."

"Well, that's true," she conceded.

"That's what I thought. Jason, if Kelly's sticking around here, you'll have to be the one to do it. We're short on people we can trust implicitly. How are you at knocking doors and sweet-talking people into revealing secrets?"

"Um, I'm not sure. I guess I can give it a try," Jason responded, glancing uncertainly between Kelly and me.

"Not exactly filling us with confidence, Jason. You'll have a bunch of doors to knock, security guys to schmooze, and who knows what else around the building with security cams... It's a big task, but it could be our ticket. I need to hear you're going to nail it."

I deliberately leaned on Jason, hoping Kelly would come to his aid. It worked.

"Yeah, sure," Jason replied, trying to sound resolute.

"Maybe I should go with Jason. What do you think?" she proposed, stepping in.

Declan shot me a knowing glance, almost like giving me a mental high-five.

"Sounds like a plan to me. How about it, Declan?" I asked him.

"Yeah, time's not on our side. You two can cover more ground together. I'll hold down the fort here," Declan agreed, remaining pokerfaced.

"Alright, that's settled then," I concluded.

Kelly's car was still parked at North Station. She and Jason were alternating between taxis and the T to move around. While they were sorting out a taxi for the Waterfront, Declan and I had a minute to ourselves.

"That was nicely handled," Declan commented.

"I don't know what you're talking about," I replied, keeping my poker face intact, but couldn't help cracking a smile. "Two hours ago, I kind of ordered them to head back to their office. They couldn't argue at that time—I had just taken out two killers inside Starbucks. The threat was fresh on their minds. But there's no way they would've done it a second time. She wouldn't have budged unless there was some logic to it."

"The way you put it, checking out the place makes perfect sense."

"Yeah, now that I think about it, it adds up. I was shooting from the hip, trying to sound halfway reasonable. But once the words were out there, it started to make sense. Those apartments might hold the key."

We quickly left the pub and went our separate ways. Kelly and Jason headed to the apartments, while Declan stayed put in the pub, hoping to gather info on Frankie. I made my way back to the car. Just as I settled in, my phone started ringing. It was Agent Jess.

CHAPTER 15

"How's Vasquez?" I asked Jess as I answered the call.

"He's still in surgery, but he's stable. They've removed the knife and are stitching him up now."

"Any leads on the two who got away?"

"Not yet. We've issued an APB with their descriptions and some photos from the security footage. We'll get them, but watch your back. Vasquez wanted me to remind you again."

"I will. Send me the photos and descriptions. You never know when I might bump into them again."

"Will do," she confirmed.

"Any progress on the mole?"

"Yes, that's the reason I called. You know Stevens, the tech who left the voicemail for Josh?"

"Yeah."

"He's gone AWOL," Jess informed me.

"Gone AWOL? What happened?"

"We can't find him. He got a call, got up from his desk, and left the building without a word to anyone. Nobody knows where he is."

"What do you make of that?"

"They think Stevens was the mole."

"I'm getting the feeling you don't buy that," I remarked.

"I'm not sure. What do you think?"

"Well, from the way things look, Stevens fits the bill as the mole. But it feels a bit too neat—mole identified, case closed, let's move on. There could be more players involved, with Stevens taking the fall to shield the others."

"That's exactly what I was thinking, even though I find it hard to believe that the Bureau is crawling with moles. We're all dedicated agents here, you know."

"I don't doubt that. But there's some serious power at play here. Who knows what kind of pressure they could've applied?"

"That's true. But I gotta ask, did you ever consider the possibility that I might've been the mole?"

"Honestly, yeah. I didn't take anything for granted, even though I had a gut feeling you were clean. Catching those Russians in the stairwell cleared you and Vasquez. If you were in on it, they wouldn't have been caught off guard."

"I see your point. Well, I'm glad we got that cleared up."

"But if there's still a mole lurking, we can't let him slip through the cracks. Those mercs outside your building were ready to take out Josh. It was pure luck that I caught wind of them. The mole's an accessory to attempted murder."

"I agree. But I'm stumped on how to root him out."

"I might have a plan. Give me some time, I'll circle back with details."

"Sounds good. But right now, I'm stuck not knowing who to trust on my own team."

"Agent Walker seemed solid to me. He nabbed one of them. Wouldn't have done that otherwise."

"I agree. I'm partnering with him now that Vasquez is out of action. We've kept your involvement under wraps for now. The story is that

Josh was supposed to show up but got spooked when he saw the Russians attacking us. That gives you the flexibility to operate without the Bureau breathing down your neck. It also keeps you off the radar if Stevens wasn't the mole after all," Jess explained.

"Which, by the sounds of it, is a likely possibility."

"I don't know what to think. I'm keeping the circle small. Just ensure Josh stays safe. It's a good thing I'm in the dark about his location. I can honestly say I have no idea where he is."

"Did they press you for his whereabouts?" I inquired.

"Yeah, they did. I just stuck to the story—Josh lost faith in us after Faneuil Hall and disappeared. But he's expected to show up for the hearing tomorrow."

"Is the hearing still on?"

"Yes. The SAC's flying in tomorrow."

"What about Vasquez? You mentioned he's your best forensic examiner. With him out of action, does that affect the investigation?"

"No, we're covered. Vasquez did all the legwork to build the case, but everything's documented now. Combined with Josh's testimony, we'll have an airtight case. Keep me posted on anything else you uncover. I'm guessing you aren't just sitting around chilling."

"I'm exploring another angle."

"The witness? Any leads yet?"

"I'm still digging. Will fill you in once I have solid information," I replied.

I knew that Josh had intentionally withheld Frankie's identity from Jess, not because he distrusted her, but because he knew that heavy-handed interference from the Feds and local cops would only drive Frankie further underground. It wouldn't help with our plans of gaining his trust.

"The clock's ticking. Remember, you need anything from my end, just say the word."

"Copy that," I confirmed.

After ending the call, I figured it was time to rendezvous with Logan to get an update on the Russian crew he had been tailing. During our last conversation, he had mentioned that they appeared to be on the hunt for someone. I started to wonder if that someone could be Frankie. I called Logan to get a fix on his location.

"Hang on a sec, Axel," Logan spoke cautiously into the phone as he took my call.

I paused, trying to make out the sounds in the background, but couldn't hear much apart from muffled voices.

"Sorry, didn't expect this op to turn into babysitting duty," Logan remarked as he returned to the line.

"Babysitting? What's the deal, Logan?"

"Remember I mentioned these guys fanning out, looking for someone? Turns out they were after a kid. They were about to snatch her. Had to intervene, no other choice."

"Are you still at the gas station? What's the location? I'll head over immediately."

"We're inside a diner. It's across the street from the gas station. Less than two miles south of Fields Corner. Take Morrissey Boulevard. First gas station on your left, got a 7-Eleven inside. I'm in the diner across the street."

“Got it. I’m on my way. Be there in a few minutes. Who’s the kid?”

“No idea. Just a scared little girl. Looks about ten. Won’t say much, except that some guys were after her, and someone called Mary Anne told her to bolt and hide. When I mentioned calling the cops, she freaked out. Begged me not to, because she's convinced those men will come after her if they find out. With these Russians, who knows? They could be tapping into radio chatter. So, no cops for now. Just focusing on getting her out of here.”

“Where’s she now?”

“I’ve got her tucked away in a corner booth while I keep watch by the front door, scanning the road for any trouble. I told her we’ll slip out the back if I spot any trouble. She trusts me enough to go along with it.”

“Back up a bit. How did this all start?” I asked, stepping on the gas down Morrissey Boulevard.

“At the gas station. That’s where I called you from earlier. I filled up, popped inside to grab a coffee, and there she was, hiding between the aisles. Figured she was the owner’s kid, playing games or something. I played it cool, got my coffee and a hotdog. But I could feel her eyes on me the whole time. Then one of those Russkies strolled in. Big guy, looked like trouble.”

“He came face to face with you?”

“Yeah, but he didn’t know who I was. I played it cool, just another customer grabbing some stuff for the road, shooting the breeze with the owner. Then I slipped up—asked about the kid. That’s when the Russkie’s radar went off. Started grilling me—what kid, where she at... I could tell from the owner’s face that something was off. Claimed he hadn't seen any kid. I knew he was lying. But I improvised, said I must've seen her when I came around half an hour ago. The Russian wasn't totally convinced. Scoped out the shop and the back, but the kid was long gone."

"Did she slip out the back?"

"I guess so. The guy was eyeballing me, getting all confrontational, trying to poke holes in my story. Took all I had not to clock him, but I had to keep cool to keep my cover. Just stuck to my guns. When he split, I grilled the owner again about the kid, but he clammed up tight. Said she and those guys were trouble, didn't want any part of it. Figured I'd better get back to my truck and scope things out. But as I was heading there, I caught sight of the girl darting out and ducking into a corner store."

As Logan recounted the encounter with the girl, a nagging feeling tugged at the edges of my thoughts. A scared girl of about ten dodging Russians? Could very well be Frankie's little sis, Fay. But I needed to be sure before jumping to conclusions. I made a mental note to get a pic from Declan, just to be certain.

"Was she dodging those guys specifically? Or just spooked by everyone around?" I inquired.

"I wasn't sure at the time, but now it's crystal clear she was steering clear of those Russians. Couldn't figure why, but it felt like she was petrified of them. They weren't just hanging out either; they were hunting for her."

"What happened next?"

"One man tailed her into the store, signaling his buddy to cover the alley out back. He moved into position, blocking her exit. She bolted out the back, but hit a dead end. Froze like a deer in headlights when she saw him. Then, real slow, she turned around. Poor kid was terrified. But before she could do anything, the second guy sneaked up behind and clamped his hand over her mouth. She bit back, and he retaliated with a smack. That's when I lost it. You know how it is, seeing a punk lay hands on a kid, it's like your instincts take over.

"Yeah, I get it, pal."

"Well, I'd already hopped out of the truck, dashed across the street, and slipped into the alley. Lucky for me, the SUV driver was parked a bit away, there's this slight bend in the road after the gas station, so he didn't catch sight of the alley. I wasted no time giving those two punks a taste of their own medicine. Knocked them out and tossed them behind a dumpster. Was ready to dial 911 when the girl begged me not to. I couldn't take her back to my ride; it's across the street. If we step out, the SUV guy will spot her. Plus, I can't see the other hostiles. So, here we are, holed up in the diner."

"We got three more hostiles out there, right?" I asked.

"Yep."

"I see the gas station up ahead. What's the play—we engage or slip out?"

"I thing retreat's the smarter play. These guys are strapped tight. The two I dropped were packing SIG P320s with suppressors. Bet there's heavier artillery in that SUV. Don't want to kick off a shootout on Main Street."

"Roger that. Be ready to move in ten seconds."

“Copy that. The diner’s across from the gas station, but around the bend.”

As I passed the SUV, I realized why the driver inside didn’t have a visual on the diner. There was a slight curve on the road. The diner lay beyond it.

As I pulled up outside the diner, I reached over and cracked open the rear door without leaving my seat. At the same time, the diner’s door swung open, and Logan emerged, guiding a frightened ten-year-old girl. Her cheeks were flushed with panic, strands of disheveled hair framed her face, her eyes darting nervously as she scanned her surroundings. Yet, the way she clung to Logan's T-shirt, seeking solace in his protective presence, revealed the trust she placed in him.

With a protective arm around her, making her as inconspicuous as possible, Logan ushered her into the car and slipped in next to her, before quickly slamming the door shut. I had already begun to roll by then.

CHAPTER 16

Within five seconds of stopping outside the diner, I shot out of there, stepping hard on the gas.

"Perfect timing," Logan remarked, scanning the surroundings.

Before I could reply, the girl suddenly piped up.

"Where are we going?" she asked, leaning forward.

"Away from here, kiddo, somewhere safe where you can tell us why those men were chasing you. Is that alright?" I asked.

"No, please, I can't go. Frankie's still back there. Those men will do him in," she pleaded, looking about ready to burst into tears.

It was a good thing I already suspected that the girl Logan had saved was Fay. Otherwise, the shock of her sudden revelation about Frankie might have caused me to momentarily lose control of the vehicle.

"Who's Frankie?" Logan asked.

I realized Logan was completely in the dark about Frankie. I had told him about a murder witness I was trying to locate, but Frankie's name had never come up. And as for Fay, even I didn't know about her existence until less than half an hour ago, when Declan revealed it to me. Spotting a parking lot ahead, I slowed down and pulled in.

"Don't worry, kiddo. We won't leave Frankie behind," I assured her. Then, turning around to face her, I asked: "Are you Fay?"

I couldn't tell who looked more surprised—the girl or Logan. She didn't respond right away, but her expression confirmed my guess.

"What's the deal, Ranger? You got some kind of secret crystal ball?" Logan asked, his disbelief ringing clear in his voice.

"Sorry, pal, I only found out myself about half an hour ago, about ten-year old Fay and her sixteen-year old brother, Frankie. That's what I'd been doing in Fields Corner. Isn't that where you're from, Fay?"

Fay nodded silently, her guarded demeanor revealing her reluctance to trust a stranger. It was evident she felt more at ease with Logan, which was understandable given that he had rescued her from the menacing men she was fleeing.

"I'm Axel. This is Logan," I began again, offering my hand.

"I'm Fay," she replied, hesitantly clasping my hand with her small one.

Logan picked up on my cue.

"We're here to help you and Frankie. Can you tell us why those men were after you? And why you're worried about Frankie?" he gently prodded.

Logan's approach seemed to work better than mine. Fay opened up more readily, quickly launching into her story.

"You saw how those goons came for me, didn't you? It was wicked scary, you know? Me and Frankie were just chilling at home when Mary Anne got a call. She became super serious all of a sudden, looking real worried, and told us to run 'cause some bad guys were coming for us. We didn't waste no time. Frankie grabbed my hand, and we bolted out the back door. But one of those tough-looking fellas saw us and came after us. Frankie said we had to split up. He told me to hide behind this big old van while he took off running. I peeked out, and I saw him running like crazy, leading the man away. But the man was shooting at him."

"He was shooting at Frankie? You heard that?" I asked.

"Yes, for real. The guns didn't sound loud, not like the bang in the movies. They made these weird noises, like popping sounds. I don't know what happened to Frankie after that. Please find him, mister. He's my big brother, and he always takes care of me."

"We will. Promise," Logan assured her, before addressing me, "Suppressors on the guns tally with what I saw."

"It sure does. We'll have to engage to save Frankie. Fay, can you take us back to Mary Anne's place? Who is she?" I asked Fay.

"She's really nice and kind. I haven't known her long. Frankie and I have been staying with her for three days now, ever since Jimmy disappeared. Frankie keeps saying he's hiding somewhere and will be back, but I don't think they're telling me everything," Fay replied.

It was evident that Frankie and the others were trying to shield Fay from the grim truth surrounding Jimmy's disappearance. Mary Anne appeared to be a kind-hearted woman, willing to offer refuge to the children despite the dangers involved. People like her deserved the utmost respect in my eyes.

"Don't worry about Jimmy. Let's focus on getting Frankie to safety. Where's Mary Anne's place? Who else lives there?"

"It's close to the gas station, on the street behind it. There's her, her brother, Mikey, and her old dad, he's like really old with snowy hair... he's in a wheelchair."

"Do you know the house number? Once we get on the street, you'll have to stay hidden."

"It's kind of separate from the other houses. Mary Anne lives in the back and is fixing up the front for a little coffee place. It's the only one on the street that ain't a triple-decker," Fay explained.

"Alright, that's good enough. I'm sure we can spot it easily. Which direction did Frankie go?"

"Back by the railroad tracks. Frankie told me to hide, then took off that way," she pointed.

"Got it. I see them now," I confirmed, checking my phone's map app and honing in on the area behind the gas station, where the tracks lay.

"How did you end up at the gas station?" I asked Fay, as I showed the map to Logan, who had joined me in the front by then.

"When Frankie left me, I was, like, wicked scared, my heart thumping like crazy in my chest. I waited a whole minute and then bolted. Frankie said not to go back to Mary Anne's, so I dashed into 7-Eleven. That's where I spotted Logan. And then this other guy showed up, so I hid in the back, and snuck out of there through a window. Then I sprinted across the street to that other shop. But then I got nabbed. And then Logan came and whupped those guys, saving me."

"You've been a very brave girl, Fay. We'll make a quick plan and then get Frankie out of there. Alright?"

"Alright," she replied, nodding her head a few times.

Logan and I stepped out for a brief pow wow before we made our move.

"Those two guys you laid out, are they going to be waking up anytime soon?" I asked Logan.

"Unlikely. And when they do, they're not going to be active threats," Logan answered, adding an explanation as an afterthought, "Broken limbs."

I already knew the answer before I posed the question. When Logan's riled up, like when he sees someone lay a hand on a kid, he isn't one to handle folks with kid gloves. Still, I had to double-check, just in case the years had softened him up a bit since we last crossed paths.

"We've got two hostiles on the loose. I figure one's likely posted up at the house, making sure the kids don't circle back. The other's probably out hunting Frankie along the tracks, if he hasn't got him already."

"You think Frankie might still be alive—a kid against an armed merc?" Logan asked.

"Chances are slim, I'll give you that. But the kid's probably got some street smarts, growing up by himself while his brother was in the joint. He's a survivor. And I'm holding out for a stroke of luck."

"Yeah, let's hope luck's on our side. So, how are we playing it?"

"It's best we split up. I'll handle the house while you scout around the tracks for any signs of Frankie," I suggested.

"Roger that. Getting entry to the house won't be easy. The hostile inside will be armed and ready, likely with hostages."

"I know it's a shot in the dark, but we're out of options. Every tick of the clock lowers Frankie's odds of making it out alive. We need him, not just for Fay's sake, but to put an end to this Russian mess once and for all."

"Copy that. What about the guy in the SUV?"

"We'll have to hold off on that call until we've nailed down his position. They're bound to have caught wind that something's up. They're probably on high alert by now, likely in radio contact."

"You're right. I shut down both radios when I searched them."

"What about the kid? We can't leave her anywhere near that place. And we don't have time to drop her off at Fields Corner. She'll have to stay hidden behind the seats."

"I guess that's our best shot," Logan agreed.

We got back inside the car again.

"Alright, kiddo, let's go look for Frankie. Sit tight back there and, if we tell you to, hide behind the back seat. If we leave you inside the car for a minute, we'll cover you up so no one peeping in can spot you. Got it?" Logan talked to her, pointing to the seat covers stashed behind the driver's seat.

"Got it. I know you'll bring him back," Fay replied, hope lacing her voice.

I looked at Logan without saying a word. The odds of Frankie still being alive were slim. But either way, it was time to take the fight to the enemy.

The diner, where we had just bolted from minutes ago, was less than a mile away. Fay's desperate pleas to rescue Frankie had me screeching into the parking lot mere moments after we had hit the road.

But as we neared the diner, we spotted the SUV crawling in our direction at a snail's pace. The guy inside must have realized something was wrong—two of his crew had gone silent for almost ten minutes. He was on the lookout, scanning every alley, house, and storefront, hunting for clues. Our car still looked like it had just come out of a major sandstorm. The man behind the wheel didn't take much notice of the eyesore of a car chugging along the boulevard. By then, Logan had already instructed Fay to hunker down behind my seat.

As we cruised past the diner and rounded the gentle curve in the road, the SUV vanished from my rearview mirror.

"Better grab your truck now that no one's got eyes on it," I suggested to Logan as I pulled into the gas station, stopping parallel to the pickup.

"Yup, good idea. I might need to go off-road near the tracks. It won't work out so well in the car."

We swiftly moved Fay from the backseat of the car to the pickup's cabin. We were good to go.

"Watch your six, Axel," Logan cautioned as he jumped behind the wheel to head for the tracks.

"Roger that, Logan. Head on a swivel," I replied, as I got behind mine to make my way toward Mary Anne's house.

CHAPTER 17

I veered off the main street and into an alley leading to the back street. Ideally, I would have posed as a delivery guy to gain entry to the house, but there was no time to grab a packet. Given my car's dusty condition, I settled on a different approach. I opted to play the role of a workman discussing building material delivery. Fay had mentioned renovations were underway, so it sounded plausible.

The house wasn't hard to spot. Though modest, it stood alone, the sole single-story structure set slightly apart from a row of triple-deckers. I pulled up outside.

I had my Glock 48 snug in a holster at the back of my jeans, but I wasn't planning on using it until I had a clear picture of what awaited inside. Besides, flashing a gun at the door wouldn't exactly help me pull off a discreet entry. My top priority was ensuring Mary Anne and her family's safety.

Instead, I opted for my boot knife—a double-edged carbon steel blade—holding it in a reverse grip with the blade flat against my wrist. With my graffiti-covered hoodie still on, the blade remained hidden up its sleeve. I grabbed some papers from the glove compartment, using them to conceal the knife's haft as well.

I was ready. I pulled the bill of my cap low, and got out of the car, slamming the door hard, not making the slightest attempt to be stealthy.

Striding up to the front door, I rapped firmly on the frame and pressed the doorbell multiple times.

"Hey, Mary Anne, where should I drop off these tiles?" I called out, projecting my voice.

I was met with complete silence from inside. I waited a few seconds, then pressed the doorbell again, determined to convey the impression of an impatient delivery worker with urgent business. I could sense movement within, someone cautiously approaching the window to investigate. After a brief pause, I rang the bell once more, keeping up my act of a persistent deliveryman.

"Mary Anne," I hollered once again.

"Hold on," a gruff voice came from inside the door.

Someone unbolted the door from inside. I fought the urge to slam against the door, sending the man behind it crashing. But I couldn't be sure how many adversaries stood behind it. I couldn't risk bullets flying around while there were other people inside. Instead, I remained composed as the door opened slightly, revealing a big guy who stood glaring at me.

"What do you want?" he demanded in a thick Russian accent.

"Looking for Mary Anne. Pretty sure that's not you," I retorted, matching his unfriendly tone.

"She's not here. What do you want?"

"I've got a truck waiting up the road. With the tiles she ordered."

"You can leave them outside."

"That's fine with me. Will you be making the payment?"

"What payment?" he growled.

"$2,150 for the tiles," I came up with a random number.

"I don't know about that."

"Exactly. That's why I wanted to talk to Mary Anne. She doesn't take time in paying. I've been dealing with her for years. Who are you? I haven't seen you before," I pressed, trying to gauge his reaction.

"A friend. Family friend."

"Well, why don't you get her on the phone and sort out the payment?"

"Come back after an hour. She will be here then."

"Not happening, pal. I've got an entire route to cover. She booked a delivery time. This is the time I deliver. Just get her on the phone, will you? Or ask the old man. He's surely inside. He was around when I came over yesterday for the order."

The look on the man's face conveyed that he had realized I wouldn't go away without talking to Mary Anne. I expected him to ask me to wait while he went back in and got Mary Anne to talk to me with a gun pressing into her back. But to my surprise, he opened the door wider and asked me to come in.

"Come inside. I'll give you the payment."

It wasn't difficult to figure out why he invited me inside. He couldn't have me causing a scene at the door, drawing unwanted attention. His plan was to lure me inside before shutting me up properly. The door was barely open enough for me to squeeze through. His right hand was concealed behind the door. I didn't have to be Sherlock to guess that he held a gun in that hand. As I stepped inside, I felt the cold metal of the gun pressed against my abdomen. With a forceful shove, he pushed me into the room and swiftly locked the door behind us.

It was a big room. Fay had mentioned that Mary Anne planned to convert that front part of the house into a café. Planks of wood and some paint cans were stacked at one end. But there was no sign of any hostages. It was possible the gunman had tied them up in a backroom and threatened them not to make a sound. Or there could be a second gunman keeping them quiet. Either way, my immediate concern was the gun pressed against my back. I needed to neutralize the guy quickly and quietly.

"Woah, easy now, pal. No need to take it to heart. You don't wanna pay? That's cool with me," I said, turning halfway to face him.

"Hands in the air," he snapped. "I told you to fuck off. You should've listened."

The urgency of taking him out was weighing on me. If a second gunman emerged from inside, I needed to be in control of this guy.

"It's my partner in the car, man. He's the one pushing me," I bluffed.

It had the intended result. His gaze shifted toward the window, diverting his attention. It was only for a second, but that was all I needed. I was already following his order to raise my arms. I grabbed the wrist of his gun wielding hand with my left, deflecting it downward to take myself out of the line of fire. In the same move, I used the knife in my right hand to slash him deep on the inner side of his elbow, just below the bicep.

The sharp blade sliced through flesh, ligaments and nerves, paralyzing his arm, rendering it useless. There was no immediate pain—when a sharp blade cuts deep, it tends to numb before the agony sets in. Initially, there was no blood either. Instead, his fingers involuntarily loosened their grip on the gun, which I swiftly snatched before it hit the ground. It had a suppressor screwed on.

I immediately moved behind him, sheathing my knife as I pressed his own gun into his back and pushed him toward the backrooms. He moved without protest, the surprise on his face at losing control of his fingers had been replaced by the shock of seeing blood oozing out of the deep cut. I had been careful not to sever any major arteries. A couple of inches above and his brachial artery would have been cut. There would be no coming back from that. This way, he had a chance of survival—unless he did something really stupid and got in the way of a bullet.

He clamped his left hand around his right, trying to stem the blood, while I prodded him forward with his own gun, using him as a shield as I checked each room. The first bedroom was empty, as was the next. But as I began pushing him toward the kitchen at the back, I sensed his reluctance, a shift in his body language that hinted at something ominous.

Upon reaching the kitchen doorway, I understood why. It was clear why he wielded a gun with a suppressor. Seated around the table were three figures—a young woman and a man, along with an elderly man in a wheelchair. Three kind souls who had offered refuge to desperate kids. But their compassion had cost them dearly. They sat lifeless, victims of their benevolence. If they hadn't warned Fay in time, she would have met the same fate.

A surge of raw, seething rage hit me like a freight train, twisting my guts into knots. My veins pulsed with the heat of my boiling blood, a hurricane of fury tearing through me.

Memories, dark and haunting, clawed their way back from the depths of my consciousness. I saw it all again—a godforsaken village on the edge of Kandahar, the haunting gaze of Omar Haq, our loyal Afghan interpreter putting it all on the line for the promise of a better future for his family. And then, the gut-wrenching horror—Omar, his wife, their innocent kids, all butchered in cold blood in their own home, branded as traitors by heartless savages.

The injustice of it all clawed at my soul, igniting a firestorm of vengeance deep within me. It took us relentless pursuit spanning two agonizing days to track down those responsible. We were dropped from the sky under the cover of darkness, with the only sound being that of the rotor blades of the MH-60 Black Hawk slicing through the night air. We served up the justice those killers had coming. While it couldn't bring Omar back, there was a grim satisfaction in knowing we didn't let evil slip through the cracks unpunished.

"Why?" I asked, my voice emotionless, cold as ice, posing the question before passing judgment on the perpetrator of such senseless violence.

I struggled with the urge to end the man right then and there. I felt the same boiling fury. Thirst for payback consumed me once more, just like it did back then—the whirring sound of the chopper's blades invading my consciousness once again.

Folks who spill blood just for a payday don't warrant second chances. There aren't any golden-hearted contract killers. Hollywood's got that all wrong—there isn't any redeeming quality in men who kill for money. Such guys are pure darkness, no light to be found inside them. There's a blackness in their souls that can't be scrubbed clean. You can't rehab the devil.

The guy stayed quiet, thinking he could pull a fast one while I was lost in my own head. He was trying to snatch a backup piece from his ankle holster while I was distracted. But even in the midst of my rage and flashbacks from Afghanistan, I was tuned in, hyper-aware of every twitch. His left arm, previously clenching his right, trying to stem the blood, had slid down to his side. His left leg was bent at the knee and off the ground, bringing the gun strapped to his ankle closer to his grip.

I caught it all in my peripheral vision, even though my eyes were locked onto the scene in front of me. I let him grab the gun, waiting for him to line up the shot from the hip, before I put a bullet in his wrist at close range, shattering it, making the man cry out in pain. I deliberately gave him that glimmer of hope before I crushed it.

"Why?" I repeated, my voice cold and firm, the suppressed barrel now digging into his right shoulder.

I stripped away any illusions of escape. He could sense it, see it in my eyes—I would keep drawing blood until I had answers.

"I didn't do it," he muttered, almost in a whisper.

"Lies won't save you," I countered, my pressure unyielding. "Give me the truth, and you might meet your end without suffering. You took the lives of innocent folk. There's no coming back from that."

His face told me he was convinced I wasn't bluffing. Beads of sweat broke out on his brow.

"I'm not lying. Viktor, my commander, came in and shot them all. Caught me off guard. I didn't know he was about to do that. He just shot them. Said leave no witnesses. I'm a soldier. I don't kill women and children. Viktor laughed at me when I said it. That's why he left me here while he's out there hunting them," he rasped, grimacing as fresh pain shot through his shattered wrist, both arms hanging limp at his side.

"Prove it and maybe I'll let you live."

"You can match up the bullets that killed them with my gun," he gasped, nodding toward the gun in my hand. "They didn't come from this gun."

"Nice try. You think I'll wait for a ballistics report? You're not going to last that long."

"What can I do to make you believe me?"

"Call your boss. If he owns up to it, maybe you'll see tomorrow," I said, calling his bluff.

"I'll do it. You'll believe me then?"

"We'll see. Who are those other men hunting?"

"The boy and girl who lived here. I didn't know until we came to this house that we were looking for them. When we came in, they escaped from the back. I was the closest to them. Viktor asked me to shoot them, but I took too much time putting the suppressor on the gun. And then shot wide. I don't kill women and kids."

"Yeah, you said that. But I'll need more than just your word for it. Is the boy still breathing?"

"I'm not sure, but I think he is. One other guy went after him. He radioed back saying the boy had definitely taken a bullet but escaped. They're tracking him now."

"How many men on his tail?"

"I think two. Two others have gone silent on the radio."

"Are the two together?" I asked, testing him. I knew there was one guy driving the SUV. So, the two couldn't be together, unless he was bluffing.

"No, Viktor is in a vehicle, driving around. Dmitri went after the boy on foot."

What the man said tallied with what I knew. The two guys who had gone silent were the ones Logan had taken out.

"But they've called for more backup. More men are on the way," the man added.

"Why are you telling me this?"

"I don't want the kids to die. If they catch them, they'll kill them. I didn't realize that until Viktor killed these people," he said, looking at the three bodies around the kitchen table. "I'm not afraid to die. But I don't want to die labelled as a child and woman killer," he added, looking me straight in the eye.

Something in his eyes told me he wasn't trying to play me. Still, I needed to be sure that he wasn't the killer. If he had blood on his hands, he would catch a bullet himself, no questions asked.

"Call Viktor. Prove you're not the killer. Make him say he did it," I told him.

"You'll have to operate the radio. My hands don't work anymore," he said in a matter-of-fact voice.

I grabbed the radio hanging from his belt. Simultaneously, I also took out my phone and pressed the record button to record the conversation.

"Ready?" I asked.

He nodded. I pressed the push-to-talk button and held it out before him.

"Alexei to Commander. Over," he transmitted.

There was a brief pause before a response crackled through.

"Commander to Alexei. What's the status?" queried a gruff voice with a heavy Russian accent.

"I've seen the girl moving around the back of the house. What should I do?"

"Shoot her, you fool. No mercy. We're not taking prisoners."

"I cannot shoot a little girl," Alexei looked pointedly at me as he refused to obey his boss's command.

"Like you couldn't shoot the woman? You need me to do it for you, you pussy. But remember, if I come, I'll put a bullet in you too. We don't have any room for weaklings."

Alexei's boss had just incriminated himself, though it wasn't explicit if the woman he mentioned was Mary Anne.

"They weren't a threat. You didn't need to gun down the woman and the old man in the kitchen. We could've just left," Alexei retorted.

"We don't leave any witnesses. What's so difficult to understand about that. Shoot the girl if you see her. That's a direct order. And if you miss this time, you'll be the one getting shot. I'm on my way," he declared ominously.

That removed any doubt that the woman being discussed was Mary Anne, and all three people lying dead around the kitchen table were shot by Alexei's boss, Viktor. That didn't completely exonerate Alexei—despite having some scruples, the man was still part of the crew. But he had absolved himself to some extent by getting Viktor to implicate himself.

"Are you convinced now? I'm not saying I'm a good man. I have killed men, but there are some things I won't do."

"You were speaking the truth," I conceded. "I'll let the law decide what to do with you. You're going to prison."

"I know. I've seen the inside of Russian gulags. American prisons don't scare me. But I know I won't last long when the others find out what I've done."

"They won't. Viktor is the only one who knows. He's not getting out of here alive."

"He deserves what's coming to him," was all Alexei had to say in reply.

I grabbed a piece of cloth, ripped it into two, and quickly tied each strip around his wounds on both arms. They would stem the bleeding until the cops arrived and got him looked at. Alexei expressionlessly watched me do it. Once I was done, I ushered him toward the bathroom tucked in the corner.

"I need you out of the way. Get in there and stay put until I give the green light," I directed him, locking him inside.

Alexei complied without protest.

Aware that Viktor could roll up any second in his SUV, I unlocked the front door. Before taking position, I sent a text to Logan: "*Frankie's been shot, but likely alive. One merc looking for him near the tracks. House is secure.*"

Logan texted back: "*Copy that. You on your way to the tracks?*"

I replied: "*Waiting for SUV guy to show up any sec. Stand by for my all clear.*"

Logan's reply came back within seconds: "*Copy that.*"

I had deliberately opted to send Logan a text instead of ringing him up. I would have had to disclose the grim scene inside the house to Logan. I didn't want to do that until I had dealt with Viktor. Nor did I want to give Logan a hint of what I planned to do to the man who was about to walk in through that door. While Logan might have taken similar measures, I didn't want to drag him into this. If I talked with him, he might have sensed something more was up than I was letting on.

This was my own brand of justice, a burden I preferred to bear alone. Viktor had spilled innocent blood. There was only one way he could make up for it. He would have to pay his dues. Period.

CHAPTER 18

I didn't have any specific plan for dealing with Viktor. I already had his confession on tape. I wanted to make him look at his victims before taking him out. I shut the blinds on every window, making the interior as dark as possible, so that anyone coming in from the brightness outside would be disoriented. The haunting images of the three lifeless bodies around the kitchen table lingered in my mind as I stood in the center of the room, holding Alexei's suppressed gun in my right hand, my boot knife in the left, waiting...

Moments later, I heard the sound I was waiting for. A vehicle pulled up outside. I was able to make out from the slits in the blinds that it was the same SUV that had prowled the main street. I heard footsteps before the door was pushed open and a big guy appeared in the doorway. He took a couple of steps inside, before realizing he wasn't alone in the room. I saw him looking in my direction. All he could see was a dark shape, but he could make out that the shape didn't look familiar. But by then, it was too late.

"You twitch a muscle, and you're a dead man," I snarled as his hand inched toward the gun at his hip.

The man froze. He was a seasoned pro. He had seen enough shit in his life to realize from my stance and the sound of my voice that I wasn't bluffing.

"Who are you? What do you want?" he asked, his voice confirming it was the same man Alexei had talked with on the radio.

"I ask the questions. Why did you kill them?" I questioned, gesturing toward the kitchen with a subtle nod.

"What are you talking..."

His words got cut off midway as I shot him, the bullet grazing his left arm below his shoulder. But when you're shot, even it's just a graze, the bullet takes off flesh and skin, inflicting sudden, intense pain. It had the desired effect. It got his immediate attention as his hand instinctively clutched the wounded arm.

"Why did you kill them?" I asked again, my voice icy.

"You think you're very tough with that gun in your hand?"

I shot him again. Another bullet, another graze, this time on his other arm. He winced, switching hands to nurse the fresh wound.

"Why did you kill them?" I demanded, unrelenting.

"Wait, listen to me, you've got the wrong man..." he cried out, sounding less cocky by the second.

This time, I aimed for the top of his left ear. He let out a yelp, the close call with the bullet rattling his nerves.

"Why did you kill them?" I asked a fourth time.

"Those were my orders. Leave no witnesses. I'm a soldier, I follow orders."

"You're just a cheap gun for hire. You would've been safer back in the gulag."

"You wouldn't be so tough if you didn't have that gun..."

His words trailed off as I hurled the gun to the corner, locking eyes with him, waiting, daring him to act. As I expected, the man was a spineless coward. With an evil smirk, his hand crept toward the gun at his side.

"Stupid man. This was your last mista..."

Viktor's words got cut off midway as I whipped up my left hand and released the knife I had been holding with a powerful flick of my wrist. The blade sliced through the air with deadly precision, sinking deep into his neck with pinpoint accuracy, severing his trachea and spinal cord.

Viktor wouldn't be killing any more innocents. Ever.

But the threat wasn't over yet. Just moments later, another SUV, identical to Viktor's, screeched to a halt outside. Three men emerged from it. Two advanced toward the house, while the third remained behind, retrieving something from the back of the vehicle.

My demons had been laid to rest with Viktor's death. I was done with bloodshed. But I knew the three guys wouldn't just turn around and head back, simply because I wasn't in the mood to kill. Not that I was planning to let them walk away. I aimed to make sure as few of them as possible would be left standing when I escorted Josh to the FBI hearing the next morning.

I recalled spotting a baseball bat in one of the bedrooms. Without hesitation, I dashed inside, snatched the bat, and positioned myself behind the partially opened door, concealed from view. I bided my time, waiting for them to get inside. The two men, chatting casually in Russian, entered one after the other, unaware of the impending danger, too lax in the belief that their buddies had secured the house. The guy at the back never even got a whiff of danger. With a swift swing, I struck him on the back of his head. He went down without a sound.

The second man was quick to react. He tried to swing around immediately while drawing his gun. But he didn't really have a chance—I was already moving on him by the time he began to turn. I struck him hard on the kneecap, shattering it. The incapacitating pain made him forget about drawing his gun. Before he could even open his mouth to let out a scream, I had swung the bat upward, hitting him hard on the bottom of the chin, breaking his jaw. The force of the strike lifted him off his feet before he crashed beside his fallen partner.

The action inside the house had unfolded in near silence. The guy outside didn't have a clue about what was up. When the unsuspecting man stepped into the house, I was ready and waiting. Took him out just like the last guy—a swift strike to the knee followed by a knockout blow to the jaw.

The immediate threats had been neutralized. I needed to leave the scene fast.

I retrieved my knife from Viktor's neck before frisking him. He wasn't carrying any ID, but I found his phone. It was one with facial recognition. I pointed it at him and, once I unlocked it, disabled the Auto-Lock. I scrolled through the messages. All of them were in Russian.

That was a bummer. Finding someone trustworthy enough who could also read Russian was going to be a hassle. Jess was the quickest bet— there must be some agents who could read Russian. But it would mean a delay—sending her the messages and then waiting for her to find a translator. I didn't want to overload her—she had enough on her plate dealing with the mess I was leaving behind.

Feeling a little disappointed, I was about to stash the phone when it hit me—most smartphones have a translate feature. It just hadn't occurred to me in the heat of the moment. I used the translate feature and converted the text to English with a few taps.

The message at the top was from some guy called Maxim. Scrolling down, I checked out the exchange between Viktor and Maxim over the last few hours. There was a quick back-and-forth a couple of hours ago.

Maxim: "*There was a trap at Faneuil Hall.*"

Viktor: "*Fuck. How bad?*"

Maxim: "*Managed to get Igor out, but the others got nabbed.*"

Viktor: "*You think they'll spill?*"

Maxim: "*No. Nikolai is taking care of it. They won't talk.*"

Viktor: "*Good. Send me the address.*"

Maxim: "*Beantown Pawn & Loan, Adams Street, Fields Corner.*"

Viktor: "*Who's the contact?*"

Maxim: "*Liam.*"

The messages were turning out to be a goldmine. It was evident that Maxim was the one who took out Vasquez with the ballistic knife. He seemed to be the Spetsnaz guy, perhaps the leader of the group. The man he helped break out, the one who held a special grudge against me, was named Igor. I couldn't quite figure out the significance of the pawn shop address.

There was a 30-minute gap before the next messages.

Viktor: "*Got the address. Heading there now.*"

Maxim: "*Good. Let me know when it's done.*"

Viktor: "*Roger that.*"

I couldn't figure out what address Viktor was talking about. It could be a delayed response to the pawn shop address Maxim had sent earlier, but I couldn't be sure.

There was a 25-minute gap before the next messages.

Maxim: "*Is it done?*"

Viktor: "*At the location. Targets escaped but our men are after them. Three witnesses at the house. We leave no witnesses, right?*"

Maxim: "*No witnesses.*"

After Maxim's chilling response, there was a five-minute pause.

Viktor: "*Witnesses down. Alexei isn't reliable.*"

Maxim: "*Take care of him when the job is done. Make it look like he did it and then killed himself.*"

Viktor: "*Good idea. Will do.*"

The last message had landed two minutes ago.

Maxim: "*Are the boy and girl dead? Nikolai is waiting for confirmation. Let me know when it's done.*"

Viktor was unable to reply to the message. He was dead by the time it landed on his phone.

CHAPTER 19

Before I left the house, I needed to make an urgent call to Jess. Her involvement in this mess was vital. Without her help, I would be tangled up with the cops for hours, and time wasn't on my side. It was also time to tell her about Frankie.

Jess answered on the second ring.

"Can you hold on a sec?" she murmured.

After a brief pause, Jess returned.

"Playing it safe, can't risk anyone overhearing. What's up?" she asked.

"I need your help. And I need it fast. I'm running out of time."

"Sure. Go on," she replied promptly, picking up on my urgency.

"Remember that witness Josh mentioned to you, the one who could bust the suicide theory?"

"Yes."

"His name's Frankie. Sixteen-year-old kid scared out of his wits. His brother worked in the building where Grant was killed. The brother saw something and got killed for it. Frankie and his kid sister have been hiding for three days with a family at a place near Fields Corner. The Russians found out about it somehow and landed there to take him out. I happened to get there before they could take out the two kids."

"You landed at the right time? How?"

"I'll explain later. Can you trust me and just focus on what's to be done?"

"Yes. Go on," she replied with conviction.

"It's a gruesome scene at the house. The mercs executed all three members of the family that sheltered the kids."

"Oh my God. Any clues about the perps? Could it be the same two who escaped?"

"No, it wasn't those two. Others from the same crew. All the perps are here in the house."

"Inside the house?"

"Yes, I took them out. You need to come and grab them. As it's your active investigation, and there are Russian mercs involved, you can take over jurisdiction from the local cops, right?"

"Yes. It's going to ruffle some feathers, but not a problem. I'll handle it. Are the cops there yet?"

"No. You're the first person I'm calling. I dealt with the perps seconds before I called you."

"How many perps are there?"

"Seven."

"Seven?" she exclaimed.

"Yes, take down the details," I replied, trying to keep the conversation focused. "It's 25 Melville Street. The street behind the gas station on Morrissey Boulevard, about 1.5 miles south of Fields Corner. Only single-story place on the street, followed by some empty lots and then a row of triple-deckers."

"Got it," she replied, taking notes.

"Two men are lying knocked out inside an alley beside Liam's Diner on the main street. Five men inside the house. One of them is dead. Before you ask, it was self-defense. He was about to draw. I'll give you guys a detailed statement tomorrow when I bring in Josh. But right now, I need to leave the scene. These guys are out for blood. If there's any evidence, I need to secure it before they do."

"Let me get this straight. Seven men. Six are alive. Right?"

"Correct. And I'm not fleeing the scene. I'm leaving to find the kid who took a bullet and is hiding somewhere close by. Once I find him, I'll call you again. If he needs treatment, it'll have to be on the low. If those guys find out, they'll come for him. And they're a determined lot. They'll find him unless he stays hidden and under protection."

"Alright. It's not going to be easy... but I'll manage. Get out of there. Once I make the call, cops will swarm the place within minutes."

"Copy that. I'll get moving," I replied, ending the call.

Before leaving the house, I unlocked the bathroom door to have a final word with Alexei. His eyes lingered on the dead Viktor before scanning the other men sprawled around the room. But he didn't say a word.

"Whatever it is you guys thought you were doing, your operation is more or less over," I told him, eyeing the broken men on the floor. "I'm leaving, but the cops will be here soon. I could've left you locked in, but I'm giving you a choice since you spoke the truth earlier."

"What choice?"

"You can try to escape, but you've got nowhere to go. And trust me, you don't want to become a hunted fugitive and a target for Marshals. But if you're willing to testify exactly what went down here and everything you guys have been up to, I can see to it that things go easier on you. Think about it. I'll talk to you later."

Alexei didn't need time to think—he had already made up his mind.

"There's nothing to think about. I'm not going anywhere. I'll do what you say."

"Good," I said, turning to leave.

But a thought suddenly struck me. I wanted to test his sincerity and strip away any loyalty he might have felt to the rest of the crew. I retrieved Viktor's phone from my pocket, changed the messages back to Russian, and showed them to Alexei.

"This is Viktor's phone. I need you to translate these messages for me," I said, holding Viktor's phone in front of him.

He read them aloud, his otherwise stoic expression showing a flicker of emotion as he reached the part where Maxim instructed Viktor to eliminate Alexei.

"Well, well, looks like your pals were planning to kill you," I remarked.

"They're not my pals," he almost snapped.

His expression told me that he was ready to talk. Time was ticking, but I couldn't pass up this opportunity to gather as much intel as possible.

"I can believe that. Are these Maxim and Igor?" I asked him, showing him the photos Jess had sent me earlier from the security camera footage.

"Yes," Alexei confirmed.

"Is Maxim the leader of your crew?"

"Yes. Very dangerous man. He was in Spetsnaz GRU. Everyone fears him and Igor."

"Igor's Spetsnaz too?"

"Yes. Not a good man. Watch your back around them."

"Got it. Who's Nikolai? Maxim sounds like he works for that guy."

"That's right. Nikolai is a rich American guy. Russian by birth but American. He doesn't like being called Nikolai."

That remark triggered a memory. Earlier that day, when I was driving Josh to Chelsea, he had uttered those exact words about Nick Templeton.

"What name does Nikolai prefer?"

"Nick. Nick Templeton."

Bingo. The shadowy Nick was beginning to emerge from behind the curtains.

"What's Nick's role in all this?"

"I don't know. I've seen him but he never talked to me—I'm not important enough. All I know is Nick has a lot of money. That's all that mattered to Maxim. We were promised a hefty payday tomorrow. Until then, we followed Maxim's orders and went wherever he sent us."

"Until you were asked to take out the kids?"

"Yes. That's when I decided I was in the middle of something I wanted no part of."

This time, I believed him.

"Where are you guys holed up?" I asked.

"There's a warehouse on the premises of a pharmaceutical company."

That matched with what Logan had told me earlier.

"Did Nick come to the warehouse, or did you go to his place?"

"He came to the warehouse. I have no idea where he lives."

"Alright. Think about what I said earlier. If you're looking for a fresh start, I can help you do it."

Alexei's willingness to cooperate, coupled with the message I read about Maxim's intention to kill him, convinced me he wanted to get out of the mess and go straight.

"As I said, there's nothing to think about. I'll do what you say. I'll stay here for the cops. What should I tell them about you?"

"For now, don't say anything. I'll contact you once this is all over. You trust me on this?"

"Yes."

"Good. When the cops arrive, lie flat on the floor. You don't want a nervous officer mistaking you for a threat."

I exited the house, hopped into my car, and drove off. Once I reached the next street, I pulled over and dialed Logan.

"What's the situation? All threats neutralized?" Logan asked as he answered the call.

"Yes," I replied, without explaining further. "Any trace of the hostile?"

"He's been neutralized. We're headed toward some abandoned freight train cars near the tracks. Frankie might be hiding there."

"Sounds promising. I'll make my way to you. Send me the exact coordinates on my phone."

"Roger that."

"And Logan, the house is off limits now. Is Fay listening in on this?"

"Negative."

"The mercs wiped out everyone in the house—Mary Anne and her family."

"Jesus!" Logan exclaimed in shock, before quickly composing himself. "Copy that. Any retaliation planned?" he asked in a matter-of-fact voice.

"It's been done. The perps are all down."

"Breathing?"

"All except the triggerman."

"Copy that. You did well, brother."

"He got what was coming to him."

Logan shared his real-time location, and I reached them in no time. Logan and Fay had disembarked from the pickup truck. Logan carried Fay in his arms as they peered inside the abandoned train cars along the tracks. Covered in foliage and surrounded by neglected tracks, the cars seemed forgotten. Most of the doors were left ajar, revealing dimly lit interiors illuminated by thin beams of sunlight filtering through the cracks.

Fay called out Frankie's name at each car they approached. By the time I caught up with them, they had combed through a dozen cars. Finally, their perseverance paid off. Fay's call was met with a weak response from inside one of the cars.

As we peered into the dim space, all we could make out were rows of corroded shelves along the walls. Then, our eyes settled on a figure—a sixteen-year-old boy slumped in a corner, his clothes stained with grime and blood. Beads of sweat dotted his forehead. His cheeks were drained of color as he fought to remain conscious.

"Frankie!" Fay's voice rang out.

Logan gently placed her inside the car, and she dashed toward her brother, with Logan and me close behind. Frankie had been shot in the back of his right shoulder. The bullet had passed through, fracturing a rib, but fortunately, it missed any vital organs. Just a few inches to the left or lower, and it could have been fatal. Despite his injuries, he managed to acknowledge Fay's presence.

"Hang in there, Frankie. You and Fay are safe now," I reassured him, kneeling down beside him.

I turned to Logan. "He needs surgery. Carry him to the truck. I'll arrange for medical assistance off the grid."

Frankie was just a boy, barely weighing a hundred pounds. Logan effortlessly lifted him and carried him toward the truck, with Fay trailing behind. Frankie urgently needed medical attention. I decided to call Declan.

"I've got a few leads," Declan answered as he took my call.

"We've located the kids," I informed him.

"What? How?" he exclaimed.

"No time to explain. Frankie's been shot. He needs urgent ER attention. I'm not calling 911. The Russians could be monitoring police frequencies. It needs to be off the record. No names in the police report. Can you make that happen?"

"Yes," he replied without hesitation. "Where are you?"

"About a couple of miles south from you. Near the gas station on Morrissey Boulevard."

"I know the place. It's got a 7-Eleven, right?"

"You got it."

"The closest to you will be Carney Hospital. Go south on Morrissey for about a mile and a half until you hit Dorchester Avenue. Take a left and you'll see the place. I'll meet you at the entrance to the ER. Five minutes tops. I'm running toward my car as we speak."

Once Frankie was settled on the pickup's back seat, we wasted no time. Leaving my car behind, I hopped into the driver's seat of Logan's truck. We could already hear the sirens of approaching cop cars as we headed toward Morrissey Boulevard.

Cutting across Melville Street, we spotted the strobe lights of a couple of cop cars parked in front of Mary Anne's house. Fay was too preoccupied with worrying about Frankie to inquire about her. Frankie himself was teetering on the edge of consciousness, barely coherent. We would have to wait until after his surgery to have a chance to speak with him.

CHAPTER 20

I had a lingering suspicion gnawing at me—how did the mercenaries find their way to Mary Anne's place? Someone had betrayed us. That someone wouldn't escape unscathed if I had any say in it. I wondered if the mercenaries encountered the informant at the pawn shop mentioned in the messages. Otherwise, there didn't seem to be much reason for them to make that stop. Glancing at Logan, I found him engrossed in something on his phone.

"Logan, you mentioned the mercs made a stop in Fields Corner and two men exited the vehicle. What did they do?"

"Are you considering the possibility of a snitch?" Logan asked.

"Yeah."

"It's like you're reading my mind. That's exactly what I've been checking on my phone," Logan responded, flipping his phone screen toward me, revealing the map app. "I didn't get a good look at the time—I was keeping an eye on the guys in the SUV from a distance. But I just zoomed into the street view. I'm pretty sure it's this pawn shop."

"Beantown Pawn & Loan?"

"Now you're getting into my head."

"I spotted the name in the messages on the phone of a merc I took down back there."

"Right. That pretty much confirms it."

Pulling up to the ER entrance five minutes later, I saw Declan had everything handled. A team of medical staff stood ready, efficiently transferring Frankie from the vehicle to a stretcher before whisking him inside.

We trailed behind as they wheeled Frankie through the hospital corridors, the atmosphere filled with the beeping of machines and the soft shuffle of footsteps. Fluorescent lights flickered overhead, casting a sterile glow on the bustling scene. Finally, they reached the operating room doors, where Frankie was taken inside.

Declan managed to arrange for Frankie to be admitted under a false name—Mike Dalton. I tasked Logan with ensuring Fay wouldn't accidentally reveal Frankie's real name. We were keeping our circle tight, trusting only those in the know. To simplify things for Fay, we referred to Frankie as Mikey and Fay as Mary Anne.

While Logan explained things to Fay, I pulled Declan aside to update him on how Logan bumped into Fay by chance. Then I delivered the grim news about the mercs' massacre of the kids' host family.

"The kids got away, but the mercs shot everyone inside—Mary Anne, her brother, and their elderly father."

"Jesus! Shot, as in killed them all?" Declan asked incredulously.

"Yes."

"Any leads on the bastards who did it?"

"The guy who pulled the trigger is inside that house. Dead."

"Oh. What about..."

"The rest of the crew are inside the house as well," I said, cutting him off, pre-empting his question. "Broken, but breathing. The cops must've taken them all into custody by now."

"But how did they land at that house?"

"Someone snitched. I think I've got a lead on who it might be."

"Care to share? I've been feeling pretty useless. I was supposed to be the one doing the digging."

"Your tip about ten-year-old Fay helped me connect the dots. And it was pure luck that Logan happened to be tailing that crew and intervened in an alley when they targeted Fay. Otherwise, they'd have taken her out too."

"He did that, huh?" Declan asked, glancing at Logan with newfound interest. "So, how did you figure out who the snitch might be?"

"It's just a hunch for now. I found the address of a pawn shop on one of the mercs' phones. Wasn't sure what it meant until Logan's intel confirmed it. He's been tracking these guys for a while. Before they hit the house, they stopped in Fields Corner. Just minutes before we met up at the pub. Logan spotted two of them heading into a pawn shop called Beantown Pawn & Loan. Ring any bells?"

"I think so. It's a rundown joint on Adams Street," Declan confirmed.

"That's the one. I don't see any reason for Russian mercs to stroll into a pawn shop unless..." I trailed off.

"...they were there gathering intel. I know the place. A real sleazeball runs that joint. If he was the snitch, he's got blood on his hands. The law might not nail him for snitching, but he won't escape justice. I'll spread the word. He'll get what's coming to him. We won't need to lift a finger," Declan declared through clenched teeth.

"Let's scope out the place. We might need to lift more than a finger to get him to talk, but after that, it's open season for justice."

"Sounds good to me."

"What about Frankie? You think he'll be safe here?" I asked Declan.

"No one knows his real name. Now that he's admitted and in surgery, no one's going to dig deeper. Even if they do, I've got some buddies at the local precinct. The paperwork's sorted. That kid on the operating table is Mike Dalton. No one's the wiser. A cop's posted here until I say otherwise," Declan assured me.

"Sounds good. I'm thinking of asking Logan to stick around until Frankie's up, just to be safe."

"If you say so. What's his deal… though I can guess just by looking at him."

"Ex-Marine. Anyone thinking of causing trouble here better think twice. He's not someone you want to mess with."

"I'll take your word for it."

"Logan's also hit it off with Fay. Right now, she trusts him the most. Once Frankie's up, we'll need her to help convince him we're on his side and he doesn't need to be scared anymore. Fay's got a part to play in all this."

"Makes sense," Declan agreed.

I pulled Logan aside to fill him in on the plan.

"What? You want me playing babysitter again while you go kick ass out there," he grumbled, feigning indignation.

"Come on, Logan, pal. If the kid followed me around like a puppy like she does with you, I'd gladly switch roles."

"I was just messing around. Yeah, it makes sense. These Russians are sneaky. One cop on watch duty won't be enough if they decide to storm this place. I'll stick around."

"Good. And make sure Fay's prepped to grill Frankie the moment he wakes up. She's key to getting him to spill the beans."

"Copy that. Keep me updated. And if things heat up too much, give me the word."

"Roger that. We're taking Declan's ride. You hang onto the truck," I said, tossing him the keys, then gesturing to Declan.

The drive from the hospital to Fields Corner took less than ten minutes. Once we hit Adams Street, I would have had trouble spotting the pawn shop without Declan. Wedged between a convenience store and a boarded-up storefront, its weathered facade displayed a fading sign that read "Beantown Pawn & Loan". Metal bars and grime covered the front windows, offering a glimpse of dusty merchandise—old electronics, second-hand tools, all stacked haphazardly on worn-out shelves.

As Declan pulled the car into a parking spot, I stepped out and headed toward the shop. Its door appeared weather-beaten and aged, with paint peeling and fading. Inside the door hung a double-sided board, one of those flappable signs saying "Open" and "Closed" on opposite sides. Oddly enough, it showed "Closed", despite the time being 1600 hours. No reason for the shop to be closed. Not that a simple door sign was about to turn me away.

I tried the door and found it unlocked. With a ding, the bell above announced my entrance as I pushed it open. As I stepped inside, I flipped the board to "Open". The air was thick with the scent of old upholstery and aged wood. Dim fluorescent lights cast a faint glow across the cluttered space, revealing rows of dusty display cases along the walls. Among the assortment of items were tarnished jewelry and vintage vinyl records, each adorned with faded price tags.

There wasn't anyone manning the worn wooden counter, its surface showing signs of wear and tear. Behind it, a door led to a back office.

"Hello, anyone around?" I called out from the counter.

The doorbell dinged behind me as Declan entered.

"No one's around. I'll check out the back office," I told him, lifting a wooden flap on the counter and slipping behind it.

I walked into the back office, my senses on high alert, half expecting a cranky guy to be sitting there with a shotgun by his side. But I needn't have worried. The scruffy-looking guy sitting on a chair behind the large desk wouldn't be a threat to anyone. Ever. Somone had blown his brains out. Shot him in the back of the head at close range.

The cluttered desk before him was strewn with papers, receipts, and assorted trinkets. Leaning back in his chair, head cocked to one side, his sunken eyes peered out from under heavy brows. Even in death, his face bore a scowl, an aura of unwelcomeness lingering about him.

Declan entered the room behind me. "Looks like he got what was coming to him," he remarked.

"Yeah, those guys aren't in the habit of leaving loose ends."

There was little we could do at the scene besides alerting the cops. We set our story straight before a patrol car arrived. Declan was following up on a case and wanted to check up on a stolen watch that might have made its way to the pawn shop. The rest of the story was exactly as it happened.

While Declan talked with the cops, I was alerted to a message landing on my phone. When I checked my phone, I found nothing new. Then I realized the message had landed on Viktor's phone. In my rush to get out of the house and save Frankie, I had forgotten I still had his phone with me.

CHAPTER 21

The message was from Maxim: "*Have you got them? Nikolai is waiting.*"

It was obvious Maxim was clueless about what went down at Mary Anne's place. But if I didn't hit him back with something, he would call. That would end the game. I needed to make him feel comfortable and keep him in the dark about Fields Corner for as long as possible. Meanwhile, I could task Jess with tracing that number.

I texted back: "*We've got the girl. Using her to track the boy. Won't be long.*"

I ran it through the translate function to switch it into Russian before hitting the "Send" button.

Maxim's response came back immediately: "*Do it quick. Keep me posted.*"

I replied: "*Roger that. Updates coming soon.*"

Once I had sent the text, I called Jess without losing a second.

"I'm en route to the scene. But we've got one agent already on the ground. ETA five minutes. We're all over it," Jess briefed me the moment she picked up the call.

"Good. I'll forward you the number of the merc who coordinated that escape at Faneuil Hall—the one who stabbed Vasquez."

"What? How did you manage that?"

"Long story. That guy with the ballistic knife is called Maxim. The one who escaped is Igor. Both are Spetsnaz GRU special forces, just as we figured. I've got Maxim's number."

"How did you...? Well, never mind, I know it's a long story."

"Yeah. Can you trace it? Maxim's clueless about what went down at the house. Thinks his guys have it under control. But he'll catch on soon. And then this trail will go cold."

"Got it. Send me the number. I'll get on it. Where are you right now?" Jess asked.

"Doing the same grind as you guys. Trying to track down the mercs. But so far, all I've got is another dead body."

"What the hell's going on? Where's this body? I can't keep covering up, Blaze."

"Relax. The cops are on it. It's a pawn shop over in Fields Corner. The owner was the one who snitched to the mercs about the kids' location. Didn't work out well for him. Those guys don't leave loose ends."

"I can't believe these guys are being so brazen about it."

"They're getting desperate. Makes them more dangerous. But also prone to slip-ups."

"True. Shoot me that number before the trail goes cold."

"On it. And one more thing..."

"Yeah?"

"There's a merc back at the house. Name's Alexei. Cops must have got him by now. Keep him isolated if possible. That guy won't talk to anyone but me."

"Why's that?" Jess asked.

"Hard to explain. We've got this weird trust thing going."

"How was that? You mean you didn't break him up like the others?"

"It's not that. I had to slash him to disarm him, and then had to shoot him in the hand when he tried to pull again."

"Ah, got you. No wonder he's warmed up to you. Who wouldn't?"

"It does sound bizarre," I replied, chuckling. "I told you it's hard to explain. Can you trust me on this? Keep him protected. Those guys might make a move if they find out he's in cuffs. We're still not sure if we got the real mole at your end."

"I know. I'll have him kept in protective custody. Send me the number."

"Roger that."

After I hung up, I mulled over the next steps. All I could do was wait—for Frankie to wake up after surgery and for Jess to pinpoint Maxim's phone. Logan had already notified me that Frankie was out of the operating room, but he wouldn't be conscious for a while. A call from Kelly made up my mind for me.

"Hey, how's the sleuthing going on?" I asked her as I got on the call.

"You know what? It's a good thing we're on the ground here. We managed to get our hands on the security footage from that day. It wasn't easy, took some serious convincing, a mix of charm and subtle threats, but the guards finally caved. And let me tell you, there's definitely something off about what went down here."

"Go on. What did you find?"

"One of the guards was up to something in the basement just before the big power outage. He keeps darting in and out of the footage. There's nothing outright incriminating, but the basement houses the power system. He had no business being there. And five minutes after he left, boom, power's out."

"Any signs of foul play?"

"Well, that's the thing—right before the lights went out, there's a flicker on the camera, then the screen goes black. Hard to say exactly what it was, could've been a deliberate short-circuit. Jason's got this geeky buddy who's all about this stuff. He says there are plenty of ways to rig a system to fail. But it could've also been an odd power surge... Still, doesn't quite add up in a place like this."

"What do you mean?" I asked.

"These aren't your run-of-the-mill apartments tucked away in some dodgy corner. It's top-notch, high-end luxury. Private power lines, security on call 24/7, staff at your beck and call for everything from gourmet grub to concierge services, rooftop pool, private gym... the works. You catch my drift?"

"I'm getting the picture."

"Oh, and one more thing—there are two service elevators, each with its own backup power source. They're supposed to keep running even if the main power's out and the regular ones are down. That's to keep essential services running, you know, in case of an emergency when the main system's down."

"And the cameras inside? Still rolling?"

"You bet. Not just that, but there's a hidden one outside the elevators, trained on the elevator doors. But here's the catch, they've all been wiped clean."

"Are you sure about that? Can you tell if they've been wiped clean? Do they still record the footage on discs? Don't they store everything in the cloud these days?"

“Spot on, Marshal. It all goes straight to the cloud. But someone scrubbed it clean from the account. Jason’s got a knack for this stuff. He found the digital fingerprints, then had his tech-savvy buddy verify. There was definitely footage. Someone intentionally wiped it.”

“So, someone’s been trying to cover their tracks?”

“Yep. And here’s the kicker—before it was deleted, there was a download. Whoever tried to cover up wasn’t quick enough. Somebody got there first.”

“No kidding.”

“I’m dead serious. And get this, there’s a solid chance Frankie’s brother Jimmy was the one who downloaded that file. How’s that for some undercover sleuthing?” she asked, clearly thrilled by the revelation.

I was a bit taken aback by all the dirt she had managed to unearth. Sending her and Jason to the apartments was supposed to keep them out of harm’s way, away from the chaos in Fields Corner. But her uncovering solid evidence of wrongdoing—that’s something I didn’t see coming.

“Nice work. I’m impressed,” I commended her.

"Well, you better be. What’s been cooking on your end?”

“Not much, really. Declan’s with me. We’ll head your way soon.”

“Any luck with finding the kids?”

“Well, yeah, we found them.”

“Found them already? Declan helped?”

“Yeah, he sure did.”

“So, what’s the word from Frankie? Anything about the stuff Jimmy downloaded?”

"I haven't been able to speak to him. He got shot, had to undergo surgery."

"Shot? Oh my God!"

"He'll be fine, but it'll be a while before he wakes up."

"Got it. Well, you make your way here. I've got a few more leads to chase in the meantime."

"Right. But stay sharp. Those guys have eyes and ears everywhere. I won't be surprised if someone tips them off."

"Will do," she assured me before ending the call.

I was beginning to get a little worried about Kelly. What she had uncovered wasn't your typical scoop—it could be concrete proof of a conspiracy surrounding Frank Grant's demise. If Nick Templeton had managed to have an inside source within the FBI, it wouldn't shock me if someone from the apartment staff tipped him off about nosy reporters snooping around.

Kelly and Jason needed to get out of that place soon. But I knew that once Kelly got a whiff of something, she would be locked in until she finished whatever she had left to unearth. I banked on the idea that even if there was a leak, it would take some time before the message reached its recipient.

By then, Declan had wrapped things up with the cops and joined me by the car.

"We gotta move," I informed him.

Sensing the urgency in my tone, Declan slid into the driver's seat without hesitation.

"Where to?" he inquired.

"The apartments at the Waterfront. Kelly's got some intel, and I'm worried the mercs might catch wind of it. How long till we get there?"

"Twenty minutes tops," he replied, stepping on the gas. "Place is called Marina Heights."

I briefed Declan on everything Kelly had told me.

"The plan didn't pan out like I hoped. I might've thrown them into a risky spot," I admitted.

"I get it. But who could've seen this coming? Seemed like a smart move to get her out of there. Problem is, it's just a gut feeling that she might be in hot water. We can't dial 911 and ask for a patrol car to stand by, just in case," Declan reasoned, navigating through traffic.

I decided to send a text to Maxim to keep him kind of busy. Any distraction might buy us time, diverting his attention from potential messages from a mole at Marina Heights.

I wrote: "*We've got the boy. Both kids are dead.*"

My plan kind of backfired as Maxim rang me up seconds after I hit send. He must have been amped up about the news, but there was no way I could take his call.

I texted back: "*Can't chat now. Neighbors are getting suspicious. We're leaving this place.*"

A minute later, the reply came back: "*Good work. Head to HQ. Await further orders.*"

I was keeping my fingers crossed for Jess to lock down Maxim's location soon. In the meantime, I pinged Kelly: "*All good? Keep me posted.*"

She replied: "*Sure. Heading to the basement for a look-see. Will call back soon.*"

We had left Morrissey Boulevard by then and hit I-93, picking up speed. The Waterfront was just a couple of miles away.

CHAPTER 22

As we approached the Waterfront, the imposing silhouette of Marina Heights loomed against the skyline. Kelly had been right. This wasn't just any apartment complex. Marina Heights was the epitome of luxury, a gleaming high-rise exuding opulence and sophistication. Its towering structure boasted floor-to-ceiling windows, offering breathtaking views of the harbor and cityscape. The shimmering glass panels reflected the serene blue waters below.

Even from a distance, the building's grandeur was evident. A lavish entrance adorned with meticulously manicured landscaping and designer lighting greeted visitors, leading to a spacious driveway where luxury vehicles awaited their affluent owners.

We were still about a minute away when Viktor's phone buzzed with another call. It was Maxim. I declined the call, preparing to respond with an excuse, but before I could, a text from Maxim flashed on the screen.

His message was ominous: "*I know who you are. You can't save them.*"

I knew the game was up. I dialed back immediately, uncertain who he meant, though my instincts screamed Kelly and Jason. The call went unanswered, straight to voicemail. Maxim had likely powered down his phone, maybe even destroyed it. If Jess hadn't pinpointed his location yet, we had lost him. But there was no time to dwell on it as Kelly's call came through.

"Hey. Everything OK?" I asked.

"I'm not sure..." was all she said, before the call abruptly got cut off.

I tried calling her again, but only received an automated message stating her phone was out of range. By then, we had entered the building compound. A guard gestured for Declan to veer off to the side, guiding us toward the underground parking level.

My phone had lost connectivity by then. We were in a dead zone, and a sinking feeling told me it wasn't a coincidence. The mercs were likely employing signal jammers, closing in on Kelly and Jason. They weren't looking to take any prisoners. I would have to handle them accordingly.

My suspicions were confirmed when I spotted a dark SUV amidst the parked luxury cars—resembling the reinforced vehicles the mercenaries favored. They had control of the front entrance. It was a trap waiting to snap shut. Plus, Kelly's last text hinted she was heading to the basement—that's exactly where I wanted to reach. But Declan seemed poised to ignore the guard's directions and proceed to the front entrance.

"Forget the main entrance. Head to the underground parking," I directed him.

"You sure? What's up?"

"The mercs might be inside the building. Someone likely tipped them off about Kelly snooping around. Her call dropped, then I lost signal. Check yours?" I prompted.

"You're right. Nothing," Declan confirmed, glancing at his phone. "You think they're using jammers?"

"I'm sure about it," I affirmed, unbuckling my seatbelt and sliding to the backseat. "The jammers kicked in less than a minute ago. They might be taking control of the reception and the basement. We can't risk driving to the front and walking in. If we run into armed guards inside the parking and we're stuck in the car, we'll be sitting ducks. We need to play it stealthy. They won't have guards at the back so quickly, but they'll be monitoring through cameras. I'll stay low behind the seats. Once we're inside, I'll pop open the back door and slip out whenever you find a blind spot."

"Copy that. How do you want to handle this?"

"I'll enter through the basement. Kelly was heading there moments ago. Once you're in the underground parking, scout around. Look for any signs of a utility area—generators, service elevators, stuff like that. That's where she was last before she lost contact."

"Copy that," Declan acknowledged, his hand instinctively checking the gun in the shoulder holster under his jacket.

"After you drop me off, make your way out and call the cops. You can't do it until you're clear of the building and out of range of the jammers," I instructed.

"Are you sure you don't want backup?"

"Ideally, I'd prefer you with me, but we can't enter together. We'll get picked up by the cameras. The only way this works is if you drop me at a blind spot."

"You've got a point," Declan conceded.

"If you end up stuck and they won't let you leave, you'll need a cover story. These guys play rough. You can't say you're looking for Kelly or investigating the suicide," I warned.

"Don't worry about that. Making up stories is part of the PI job description."

Declan pulled up to the barrier at the underground parking entrance. There was no attendant. It was all remotely controlled via security cameras. I slipped into the space behind the front seats and kept low. After about twenty seconds, the barrier lifted.

Declan navigated the parking lot slowly, his gaze scanning the area for any signs of surveillance. Bright fluorescent lights overhead cast a harsh glow over the neatly marked parking spaces, making it challenging to find a discreet exit. I remained low, relying on Declan's expertise to pinpoint the right moment to leave the vehicle.

"Security cameras everywhere. I'll be on the lookout for a blind spot. Elevator access is still a way off," Declan provided a steady stream of updates, his eyes scanning the surroundings. "But the good news is, the signs are clear. Up ahead, I see a door marked 'Authorized Personnel Only' with a sign beside it for 'Utility Access'. That's our target. I'll slow down once I notice a blind spot between the cameras."

"Copy that. Watch your six. Don't engage. Just keep them distracted as long as you can."

"Will do. Best of luck. Get out now," Declan replied, easing off the accelerator and reducing the speed to a crawl.

I trusted Declan's judgment implicitly. If it were anyone other than a seasoned cop behind the wheel, I would have been more cautious about potential cameras. But without hesitation, I cracked open the door, rolled out of the car, and crouched close to the wall, keeping low. I watched as Declan maneuvered the car toward the exit. All I could do was hope he made it out safely. Once he was out of sight, there was no way for me to confirm his fate.

I drew my focus back to the task in hand, drawing a boot knife, holding it in a reverse grip, keeping the blade flat against my wrist. I still had the hoodie on, which helped me conceal the blade under the long sleeve. I pulled the hood well over my head. I knew I would move out of the camera's blind spot once I walked to the door.

As I approached the door, I saw large block letters painted on the door shouting: AUTHORIZED PERSONNEL ONLY. No wonder Declan could read that from a mile away. The door itself wasn't as formidable as the sign. It was an ordinary door, and it was unlocked. I simply pushed it open and entered.

Inside, I found the reason for the door's simplicity. It led only to a vestibule, beyond which lay the actual door. This one was formidable as hell—a sturdy thing made of solid iron, with a wall-mounted card reader next to it. There wasn't any way I could ram my way through it without a proper access card.

Feeling a little frustrated, I yanked at the door handle more out of irritation than any real expectation. But to my surprise, it swung open. I was suddenly confronted with a suppressed Uzi aimed directly at my chest. Holding the gun was a guy in combat gear, with a Heckler & Koch HK416 assault rifle slung across his back.

I didn't need any confirmation that this man was one of the Russian mercenaries. Security guards in apartment buildings don't typically carry suppressed Uzis and assault rifles. Moreover, the way he opened the door with his gun pointed at me, it was clear he had received intel about my presence in the vestibule from someone monitoring the security feed. He began speaking as he opened the door, the Uzi poised menacingly.

But he wasn't able to go beyond "Who the fuck are..."

By the time he uttered the second word, I recognized his accent. And by the time he spoke the fourth word, I had changed my grip on the knife, flipping it from a reverse "ice pick" grip to a forward one, and drove the blade deep into his throat in one fluid motion. At the same time, I swept the Uzi's barrel aside with the other hand.

It all unfolded in a split second, more reflex than calculated action. The man was taken completely off guard. A man pointing an Uzi at someone at close range doesn't anticipate resistance. That's why he isn't ready and primed to pull the trigger. The usual tendency of the target in such a situation is to flinch, cower in fear, and raise his hands. But in that rare instance where the target retaliates, it takes a second for the gunman's mind to process and react.

That second cost the man his life. When you have spent hours and hours honing knife skills, they get ingrained in your muscle memory. You don't think about it. Your body knows exactly what to do. I flipped the grip midway while driving my hand toward his throat. The 5.4-inch double-edged carbon steel blade sliced through everything in its path, severing the jugular vein and carotid artery.

A gurgling sound escaped the man's lips as blood gushed forth. His finger reflexively squeezed the trigger, sending a burst of 9 mm bullets into the wall behind me at a rate of 600 rounds per minute. The muffled staccato filled the room for the brief two seconds it took to empty the 20-round magazine. Thankfully, the suppressor dampened the noise. Otherwise, it would have been deafening in the enclosed space.

As the magazine emptied, the man slumped to the floor, lifeless. I wasted no time, swiftly unshouldering the HK416 rifle from his back. I stripped him of his bulletproof vest, black cap, and crossbody bag containing extra magazines, and put them on. I also found a magnetic card on his belt—the kind that opens doors. I grabbed the card, not knowing exactly which doors it would open for me.

The timing of the door opening and our encounter wasn't a mere coincidence. The man, gun poised, had actively sought out an intruder, likely tipped off by someone monitoring the camera feeds. He was sent specifically to investigate. I had a small window of opportunity, but if I lingered too long, his comrades would grow suspicious. I was hoping that with the vest on and rifle slung across my back, I wouldn't stick out too much to anyone catching a quick glance of me from a distance.

While wiping the blood off the blade, my gaze fixed on a map mounted on a wall. It detailed the layout of the basement floor, marking service elevators, emergency exits, storerooms, a generator room, and HVAC systems. I mentally noted the layout before proceeding inside.

I inserted a fresh magazine into the Uzi, set the gun to semi-automatic mode, and shot out the light. When I opened the door to step inside, I didn't want to become an easy target by getting framed by the light inside the vestibule. Once the space around me became dark, I opened the door and stood within the doorway as I surveyed the hall.

The spacious hall stretched before me, with corridors intersecting at right angles. Fluorescent lights bathed the concrete floors in a sterile glow, supported by sturdy columns and beams. Large ventilation ducts and pipes lined the ceiling, circulating air and water throughout the building.

In the middle of the hall stood a row of sleek generators, behind which were electrical rooms and maintenance closets. Additional rooms housing HVAC equipment and utilities were located to my left, while disabled service elevators and some storage rooms were situated to the right. Despite the orderly layout, the vast space offered countless places for concealment.

Kelly and Jason could remain hidden for a while, but the gunmen had the upper hand. With the jammers in place, no calls for help could be made, and the gunmen likely controlled all building services, including security cameras and the main entrance.

There was no option but to hunt the hunters. I stepped out from the doorway and closed the door behind me. As soon as I did that, a door at the opposite corner swung open and two men emerged, carrying the same artillery and clad in identical gear to the one I had just dispatched.

I immediately moved to a cramped space behind a nearby electrical service panel, reasonably concealed. I realized I was not alone in that cramped space. Lying face down on the floor was a security guard, his back riddled with bullets. Must have gotten caught trying to rush out the back exit. The mercs weren't taking any prisoners. They were there to eliminate everyone they encountered.

My thoughts were interrupted by a burst of gunfire. One of the mercenaries, having discarded his suppressor, unleashed a barrage of bullets upon the solid metal door, each impact echoing ominously throughout the large hall.

"Come out now with your hands raised, and we'll let you walk out alive," a voice pierced the chaos. "If you don't, we will find you, and when we do, this is what you'll get," the man issued a chilling ultimatum as another barrage of gunfire erupted.

It was evident that the gunfire was merely a tactic to coerce Kelly and Jason into surrendering. I realized that they had no intention of letting them leave unscathed. With their brazen approach and indiscriminate bullet spray, stealth was clearly not their objective, unlike their covert operation to eliminate Frank Grant, which they had tried to pass off as a suicide.

Any potential witnesses, including the security personnel, were likely already eliminated. With the elevators likely disabled and cell service disrupted, residents would remain trapped on higher floors, providing the mercenaries ample time to flush out their targets.

Meanwhile, the two men entered the next room, using a keycard. I was about to move out when I saw another pair doing the same thing at the other corner. A door opened, the men exited, and soon entered the next room. They were systematically entering each room, trying to flush out Kelly and Jason from wherever they were hidden.

I realized that locating Kelly and Jason would prove as challenging for me as it was for them. It wasn't like I could call out to them. And with the phones not working, all I could do was try to make a logical guess. Two guys were scouring the HVAC rooms, while the other two lingered near the service elevators and their adjacent utility rooms. Going by my last conversation with Kelly, she was likely near the service elevators. The electrical rooms behind the generators presented a secondary possibility, while the HVAC area seemed less probable based on my assessment.

I decided to ignore the HVAC area and swiftly made my way toward the two men near the elevators. I stayed close to the walls to avoid detection. I had seen the men using access cards to enter each room and was banking on the card I had swiped from the dead guy. If it didn't work, I would be caught out in the open. But that was a chance I had to take.

I tried the card on the room next to the one they had entered. It worked. However, as I prepared to enter, the door of the neighboring room swung open, with voices emanating from within. It was too late for me to enter and close the door behind me. Those men would hear the door closing. I would be trapped inside. I had no choice but to take out both men immediately.

I already had the suppressed Uzi drawn and ready to fire. I advanced toward the room. I was a few feet away when a man stepped out. Without hesitation, I shot him in the head. A double tap.

As the first man crumpled to the ground, I swiftly lunged forward, twisting my body sideways and flicking the gun's setting to automatic mode. Landing atop the fallen assailant just outside the threshold, I remained poised, my gun aimed and ready to fire. The second gunman, having stepped back cautiously, had his weapon drawn but it was aimed too high. Before he could lower his gun, I unleashed a brief burst of gunfire, squeezing the trigger no longer than a second. Ten rounds tore into him, piercing his abdomen and moving up toward his heart. The man fell back inside the room. He was dead before he hit the floor.

Without delay, I sprang to my feet, intending to drag the other man's body into the room for concealment. However, as I moved to do so, I glimpsed two figures approaching from the opposite direction through the exit door. Once again, time was against me. I couldn't hide the bodies and shut the door before those men entered.

I abandoned the man where he lay and dashed toward the generators, keeping low to avoid detection. I took cover behind the massive generators, their towering forms encased in sturdy metal casings. But they stood silent, meant to come to life only in the rare event of a power cut. That day, the mercs weren't there on a stealth mission.

A power cut didn't figure in their scheme of things. They had simply taken over control of the building's systems, disabling all elevators.

I decided to discard the Uzi in favor of the assault rifle. It was time for a full-fledged firefight, and the HK416 offered superior accuracy and stopping power over the Uzi's 9 mm rounds. When I pointed at a target and fired, I needed to hit bull's eyes each time, and I needed the target to go down. Stashing the Uzi in my crossbody bag and retrieving spare magazines from my pockets, I unslung the rifle—a compact version with an eleven-inch barrel—ready for action.

By that time, the two men had entered the hall and discovered their fallen comrades. I pressed myself against the generators, concealed from view. Their attention fixed on the room ahead, they hurried toward it, unaware of my presence. But suddenly, a voice called out to me in a whisper, sending a jolt of surprise through me. It was Kelly.

"Axel," her voice murmured softly, seemingly coming from nowhere.

CHAPTER 23

For a few seconds, I couldn't figure out what was going on. Hemmed in by the massive generator behind me and a solid wall ahead, I was at a loss until I felt movement beside me. To my surprise, a panel between the generators shifted, revealing Kelly's face. She extended her hand, and I grasped it firmly, a silent exchange of reassurance in the midst of chaos.

Kelly had been cleverly concealed behind one of the large metal panels interspersed among the rows of generators. These panels, serving as protective barriers, spanned a few feet in width. Though cramped, the hiding spot proved to be a lifesaver.

Equipped with sliding mechanisms, the panels were designed to be opened and closed manually, providing access for maintenance and inspection of the generators. Small perforations allowed for ventilation and heat dissipation, which enabled Kelly to observe her surroundings while remaining hidden in the darkness behind the panel.

"Are you both alright?" I asked in a whisper, feeling a wave of relief wash over me.

"Jason and I are fine. But we've got one of the guards with us—Dewayne. He took a bullet," she whispered back, trying hard to keep her voice from quivering.

"How bad is it?" I asked, keeping a watchful eye around me.

"It hit his thigh. It's hard to see clearly, but he says the bullet went through. Jason's applying pressure to stop the bleeding. Dewayne says he's got no plans to die."

"That's the spirit. You guys will be fine. Don't worry about it," I reassured her, giving her hand a squeeze.

"I can't understand why these guys are such psychos. They just came inside the building and started shooting," Kelly replied, a shiver running down her spine.

"They're getting desperate. You've uncovered their secrets, and now they're scrambling. They won't last long," I replied in a firm voice.

"We never saw this coming," Kelly whispered back, sounding kind of mad at herself.

"No one did. I'm the one who sent you here, remember?" I reminded her.

"Yeah, that's right. It's all your fault," she replied, a smile breaking through her strained features.

"I know. But I'll get you out of here. This hiding spot is genius, by the way. Good thinking," I whispered back, trying to bolster her confidence.

"It was Dewayne's idea. He knows this place inside out."

"Good for him. He might've saved all of your lives."

"I'm sure he did. We were counting on you to figure it out eventually. We just weren't sure if you'd make it in time," Kelly admitted.

"After that last call got cut off, I could guess what was up."

"I told you he'd come through in the end," Jason chimed in with a whisper.

"Jason, pal, you two are making a habit of landing in tough spots. But don't worry, we'll make it out."

"I know we will," he replied, sounding determined.

"What do we do now? Shall we come out?" Kelly asked.

"No, too risky. Too many hostiles out here. Heavily armed. Stay put. I'll draw them away."

"How many are there?"

"I'm not sure. I've taken out a few, but there might be about six more. Don't worry, I can handle it."

"Six more? Maybe we should all hide in here and wait for them to leave. It's tight, but we can make it work," she suggested, concerned about the number of men I was facing.

"No. These guys aren't going anywhere until they find you. I'll stay out here and change their minds. Is Dewayne armed?"

"He's got a handgun."

"Have you or Jason ever fired one?"

"Not Jason, but I let loose once... way back," Kelly replied.

"That'll have to do. Grab this. It won't come to it, but better safe than sorry," I said, handing her my Glock.

I couldn't trust a rookie with an Uzi. In that cramped space, she could end up shooting herself or one of the others.

"This is the safety. Turn it off, aim and fire," I directed, jabbing a finger at the safety without taking my eyes off the perimeter.

"Uh, got it," she mumbled, not exactly sounding super confident.

All this while, the guys out there were raising hell in Russian. I couldn't understand a damn word, but it wasn't difficult to guess what they were mad about. The men searching the HVAC rooms had walked over to join the other pair where I had left the two dead men. I knew I had to move away from the generators—I didn't want those boneheads thinking they needed to carefully check that area.

"Ask Dewayne if all those HVAC rooms are connected from the inside?"

"Yes, they're all linked up," Kelly confirmed. "The HVAC and electrical rooms have connecting doors. You'll need a key card to open them. Hang on a second, he's getting it out of his belt."

"That's fine. I've got the card. Ask him two more things—where's the security camera control room and where are the controls for the elevators located?"

"Both on the ground floor. All central controls and monitoring system are tucked behind the front desk," Kelly relayed after checking with Dewayne.

"That's all I need. I've got to get moving now. Close the panel tight. Keep sharp. I'll be back before you know it."

"Be careful."

"Always am. Oh, and Kelly?"

"Yes?"

"Maybe have a serious think about a lighter gig after this. Remember the puppy parades I mentioned?"

"Smartass!" she shot back, punching me in the arm.

I chuckled and moved away. I slipped into the electricals room using the card, staying out of sight of the mercs. Through a series of interconnected rooms, I made my way to the ventilation chamber, the same room whose door those men had sprayed with bullets earlier.

With my rifle snug against my shoulder and pointed straight out, I cracked the door open to locate the targets. They were spread out, sweeping each room methodically. One guy was edging toward the electrical area near the generators. That was a no-go. I couldn't let him catch sight of those panels and figure out the hiding place.

Rifle set to automatic, I stepped out, took aim, and took the shot. Bullseye. The others were caught off-guard as their partner went down.

"Drop your weapons. Now," I commanded.

But these guys weren't rookies. Trained soldiers, ready for trouble, they reacted fast. All three dropped low, guns aimed my way. But before they could line up their shots, I took out the one closest to the generators.

As they returned fire, I ducked back into the room, slamming the door shut behind me. Bullets pounded against it, some embedding in the metal, others ricocheting off nearby walls. Solid as it was, that door held fast, shrugging off the barrage.

I used the key card to open two doors at both ends at the back of the room, one leading to the electricals rooms and the other to a heating room. I positioned myself strategically inside the heating room, anticipating their room-clearing protocol. Typically, one guy would open the door while the other provided cover, then enter to clear the immediate threats. But their plan hit a snag with the room's layout–it had three exits. As the first man opened the door, the second guy's view of my hidden exit remained obstructed until the door swung fully open, buying me crucial seconds. Those few seconds could spell disaster for them.

Moments later, I heard the telltale beep of the key card swiping. I was primed, lying flat on the floor, rifle steady against the wall, aimed at the door. A hand opened the door and pushed the heavy frame inward. The second thing that became visible after the hand was the barrel of the other man's rifle. With precision timing, I unleashed a barrage from my 30-round magazine, the bullets shattering the forearm of the door opener and slamming into the one behind, targeting his midsection and chest with unforgiving force.

The guy was geared up with a bulletproof vest, just like the one I swiped from his buddy. But his gear lacked something crucial—armor plating. His oversight proved costly. When bullets rip out of an automatic rifle with a muzzle velocity around three times the speed of sound, even with the vest on, the blunt force trauma is immense. It cracks ribs. It causes massive soft tissue bruising. The vest might leave you breathing, but you're still going to feel like you got hit by a freight train.

I sprang to my feet, swiftly moving to the door of the neighboring room, inserting a fresh magazine in the gun as I walked. Stepping out, I unleashed a storm of bullets at the midsection of the man whose forearm I had already shattered. The man had pulled a gun with his left hand. He tried lining it on me before my shots took him down. As he dropped, I switched my rifle to semi-automatic mode, targeting his left elbow and knee, then repeating the process with the other incapacitated man. The time to show any mercy to these ruthless killers had long passed.

I moved swiftly toward the fire exit, firing at each security camera along the way, systematically disabling them all. With the mercenaries likely monitoring the feeds, I aimed to keep them in the dark about my next move. As I continued to disable cameras, I weighed my options for ascending the stairs from three different directions—front, back, or near the service elevators. Once I committed to an exit, they would catch on, but until then, I would keep them on their toes, disrupting more cameras and buying myself valuable time while thwarting any chance of an ambush.

"Kelly, stay hidden until I give the all-clear. The basement is clear, but there's more action upstairs. I'll be back before you know it," I shouted as I passed by the generator, not breaking my stride.

"Got it," she replied.

I reached the side exit, swiftly disabling the camera, but instead of heading upstairs, I doubled back and made a dash for the front exit. As I burst through the door and bounded up the stairs, the distant wail of approaching sirens filled the air. Declan must have made a clean getaway from the parking lot, and help was on its way.

Stepping onto the ground floor, I surveyed the area cautiously before stepping into the lobby, rifle poised for action. Moving swiftly, I made my way toward the control room behind the reception desk. Inside, I only found a lifeless security guard slumped in a corner.

I heard the rumble of an engine revving to life and rushed outside. Racing toward the exit, I spotted the SUV pulling up, its engine roaring. In the passenger seat sat Igor, the same guy I had cuffed at Faneuil Hall before he managed to slip away, now armed with an HK416 rifle fitted with a hefty 100-round drum magazine.

When it comes to tactical ops, those big drum mags offer zilch advantage over box magazines. They are a pain to load and flaky as hell, prone to jamming. But if you're into rage-fueled spray-and-pray mode, they fit the bill perfectly. Igor must have had a tantrum in mind, hauling out that monster mag before making a run for it instead of sticking around to slug it out with me.

But I wasn't in the mood for heroics. Outgunning him out in the open wasn't an option. All I could see was Igor's head, safely tucked behind the reinforced door of the SUV. I didn't have the luxury of time for a precision shot. I hit the deck as Igor went full auto, bullets ripping like there was no tomorrow.

Bullets zipped above me, a symphony of sharp cracks and whistles tearing through the air. Debris sprayed from the walls as the bullets chipped away at the surface with sharp clinks. The rhythmic thud of rounds hitting nearby objects echoed through the space.

Suddenly, the firing ceased. I had been keeping count—it had only lasted about four seconds. It was too soon for the magazine to be empty. The HK416 spits out rounds at a rate of 800 per minute, meaning a 100-round mag should last around 7.5 seconds. There were two possibilities: either the magazine jammed, which was unlikely, given that Igor wasn't a novice, or he was hoping I would pop up, assuming he was out of ammo.

A tense silence settled over the scene, starkly contrasting the utter chaos of moments before.

"Too much of a pussy to show your face, huh? Remember what I said back at Faneuil Hall? You're a dead man. You and that Josh and the bitch you saved today—none of you will see me coming. I'll end you all," Igor taunted, trying to provoke a response from me.

The sirens of approaching cop cars grew louder. I didn't want him to escape, but there wasn't much I could do—I was on foot while he had that beast of a vehicle at his disposal. I kept him talking, hoping the cops would arrive soon.

"I took out seven of your guys down there. You're only alive because you were too chicken to come face me yourself. You won't be so lucky next time."

But my ploy didn't work. The man knew he needed to bolt. Without warning, he unleashed the remaining bullets in the magazine. The hailstorm of bullets zipping all around resumed, lasting for about three seconds. And then the SUV peeled out. There was no point chasing after it or firing shots. It was a reinforced, tactical vehicle with protected, bulletproof tires. I didn't want to give Igor the satisfaction.

As the SUV sped off through the gate, the first cop car rolled in. I headed back down to the basement. Approaching the panel behind which Kelly and her crew were hiding, I rapped on it.

"All clear. Time to come out," I called out.

CHAPTER 24

While Kelly and Jason emerged unscathed, Dewayne had been less lucky. Still, considering the body count of security guards upstairs and in the basement, he wasn't the unluckiest one.

Kelly and Jason quickly briefed me on what went down. They were waiting by the service elevators on the ground floor with Dewayne, planning to check out the electrical room to confirm their hunch of sabotage. That's when they noticed the armed men filing in through the main entrance. The men were in tactical gear, even though their guns were stashed inside hefty bags. That's when Kelly called to tell me that something wasn't right. But the jammer kicked in right then, cutting off the call.

The gunmen caught them off guard, drawing their weapons and firing at the guards with suppressed gunfire. Kelly's team only realized what was happening when bullets started flying past, one of them hitting Dewayne. They got lucky that the elevator doors opened on time, letting them escape to the basement floor. They initially hid in an electrical room, but when they saw the gunmen conducting searches, Dewayne took them behind the panels. I arrived at the scene about five minutes later.

It had been a lucky escape for them. But I knew the threat wasn't over until Igor and Maxim were still out there. They were the kind of guys who nursed grudges like it's their full-time job, dangerous to the core. From here on out, every move I made would be aimed at ensuring those two didn't live to see tomorrow.

Once the SUV sped away, cellphone connectivity returned around the building. The jammers must have been placed inside the SUV. I noticed missed calls and messages from Jess and Logan.

Logan's message was straightforward: "*Call back when you can.*"

Jess's text had a sense of urgency: "*Call me. It's urgent!!*" Those exclamation marks made me dial her number first.

"Where the heck have you been? I've been going crazy trying to reach you. Some seriously wild stuff's gone down here," Jess blurted out as soon as she answered, sounding about ready to explode with the urgency of her news.

"A whole lot of crazy's been unfolding at my end too. I'll fill you in, but you go first. What's going on?"

"I hate to break it to you, but your guy Alexei turned out to be a suicide bomber."

"What?" I nearly shouted in disbelief. "What do you mean? Suicide bomber?"

"He blew himself up, taking most of Mary Anne's house with him."

"No way. That's not possible. I don't buy that for a second."

"I'm just telling you what I heard. I'm as puzzled as you are."

"Give me the details. What exactly happened?"

"Agent Miller was the first responder, coordinating with the cops. He secured the area, marking it as a Federal crime scene. Alexei was held inside, in one of the bedrooms. Miller said he somehow slipped out of the cuffs. When Miller approached him, he was messing around with what looked like C-4 plastic explosive and a detonator. He threatened to blow everyone up when Miller confronted him. Miller backed off, evacuated himself, and instructed the cops to do the same. Moments later, there was an explosion. Either he blew himself up intentionally, or it was an accident."

"I don't get this. He miraculously got his hands on some C-4, which just happened to be conveniently stashed under the bed? Why was he inside a bedroom anyway? Surely, that's not protocol. He should've been in the living room under guard, or inside a guarded vehicle on his way to a lockup."

"I agree. It's all very fishy. Miller claims the local cops weren't too thrilled about the Feds swooping in. He felt outnumbered, so he kept the suspect isolated until backup arrived, which happened to be me and the others," Jess explained, her tone betraying her skepticism.

"And how did Miller end up being the first responder?" I inquired.

"He was out in the field at the time. Apparently, he was heading to meet a contact in Roxbury for another investigation the Bureau's conducting on interstate robberies," Jess replied, sounding like she was trying to convince herself.

But the thing with some stories is, no matter how you spin them, they still sound like complete bullshit. I was sure Jess herself wasn't buying it either. However, I understood her predicament. She couldn't outright accuse a fellow agent of lying.

"Miller just happened to be roaming around Dorchester. Isn't that a little too convenient?"

"I don't know what to make of it."

"How long has Stevens been working at the FBI?" I suddenly posed the somewhat unrelated question.

Ever since I first heard the story that Stevens, the tech guy, was the one responsible for luring Josh into a trap by leaving a voicemail on his phone, something didn't sit right. His sudden disappearance only deepened the mystery. It just didn't add up. The reason for leaving a voicemail could have been explained. It wasn't that big of a smoking gun that would make him blow his cover and vanish.

"Stevens?" Jess asked, sounding a little thrown off when I mentioned him out of the blue.

"Yeah, the techie who vanished. He's not an agent, is he? He sounded more like a freelancer."

"Well, yes, he's a freelancer. How did you know?"

"Just a hunch. It'd be too tricky for Miller to pass off an agent as the mole. He wouldn't have had time to set that up properly."

"You mean..." she trailed off.

"Miller's the mole. He's working for Nick Templeton. And now he's not just a mole, but their hired gun too. I'd bet my life on it."

"How can you be so sure?"

"Because I can prove that Miller's lying through his teeth. He would've even gotten away with it, but there are details from the incident at Mary Anne's house that only I know, because I was there."

"Go on."

"Two things. The first will prove that Miller's lying. There's no way Alexei could've escaped his cuffs, let alone set up explosives. What I didn't mention earlier is that I disabled both his arms when I disarmed him. He couldn't even hold a radio to communicate with his boss—I had to do it for him. So when Miller claims he was handling explosives half an hour later, well, do the math."

"Oh boy, I'm trying to process this. What do you mean by 'disabled his arms'?"

"A deep slash under his right bicep. Unless you're familiar with knife work, you wouldn't know, but it effectively paralyzes the arm. As for his left hand, I shot him in the wrist. You can imagine what that does to your grip."

"Well, I can take a guess. That sounds brutal, but I suppose it got the job done," Jess remarked.

"Yeah, it was brutal, but it had to be. You don't disarm a gunman holding innocent people hostage by being gentle."

"I understand. I wasn't judging, just observing. What was the other thing you mentioned? You said there were two."

"Right, the other thing. Maxim, the mercs' leader, ordered his lieutenant Viktor to eliminate Alexei. They didn't trust him because he refused to shoot Mary Anne and the kids when they ordered him to. I found evidence of that on Viktor's phone. Contrary to the picture Miller has been trying to paint, Alexei wasn't the kind of blind fanatic willing to blow himself up. And there was also a text saying that Nick would ensure no one in the house talked. I didn't get it then, but now it makes sense. Miller was Nick's assassin. Miller was tasked with making sure Alexei stayed silent. He acted like he was securing Alexei and the crime scene, but he ended up eliminating both."

Jess paused for a moment.

"You still there?" I asked.

"Yeah," came her reply, followed by a long sigh. "You've left me speechless, and that doesn't happen often. I'm trying to process it all. Trying to think where did the C-4 come from? I doubt Miller was just carrying it around town."

"It must've been in the SUV outside. These guys are rolling with heavy artillery; they could easily have had C-4 on hand. I saw cop cars show up before I left. Miller couldn't have arrived much earlier. If you check the body-cam footage of the first responders, you might catch him rummaging through the vehicle."

"You've got an explanation for everything. And I'm not saying that like it's a bad thing. I'm just thinking out loud."

"Yeah, I know."

"I'm struggling to come up with a coherent plan here. I mean, things are chaotic. An explosion in a residential area, and now our own agent might be involved."

"I know. This is way beyond a regular crime investigation. These guys are causing havoc all over the city. You better be ready to step up if you want to get a grip on it. Guess where I am right now? Ever heard of Marina Heights?"

"The Waterfront? Is that where you are?"

"Yep. I'll fill you in on everything that just went down here before you hear it through official channels."

I proceeded to tell her about everything that had happened at Marina Heights, from the jammer to the security guards' deaths and what unfolded in the basement.

"That Igor dude's got some serious luck, slipping away twice in a day. But they're running out of options. We'll nab him and Maxim soon. Even though... we lost track of Maxim's phone," Jess confessed apologetically.

"I know. He caught on to our tracking. He sent me a message telling me, before saying I wouldn't be able to save Kelly and Jason."

"But you did. That'll be a shock to him. I'm sure we'll soon track him down."

"I wouldn't count on it. They're probably planning to skip town by morning. They'll wait until then to grab Josh, but they're low on manpower. If we don't act fast, they'll vanish, along with Nick Templeton. They won't stick around for you to build your case and arrest them."

"I know. We need to act. Do you have a plan to stop them? You've been ahead of us all day."

"We need to set a trap. Use Josh as bait to draw them out. That includes not just Nick and the mercs, but even upstanding Agent Miller."

"I'm listening."

"I need to make some arrangements. Call you back in an hour."

When I got off the call, I didn't have a clear plan in mind. All I knew was that unless something happened that brought Igor and Maxim out of the shadows, my plan would largely involve dangling Josh as the bait to lure them to a place of my choosing.

Igor's last words still echoed in my ears: "None of you will see me coming. I'll end you all." I knew he meant it. Guys like him thrive on their own venom. I've dealt with enough men like him to know they won't hesitate to strike when they see an opportunity. I've stopped many such guys, but you can't end them all. But now it wasn't just about me. I couldn't risk Josh or Kelly becoming targets any time in the future.

It was time to call in Logan. We had taken out many such threats in the past. It was time to go on the hunt once again.

CHAPTER 25

When I called Logan, he informed me that Frankie was awake after the surgery. As expected, Fay had helped Logan earn Frankie's trust.

"He's just a scared kid trying to protect himself and his sister," Logan explained.

"I'm not surprised, the way these mercs are offing people everywhere they go. Did he mention anything about what got Jimmy killed?"

"Yes. Jimmy had a recording of footage from a security camera, which he downloaded onto a flash drive. It's still inside the apartment building. Place called Marina Heights."

"No kidding. That's where I am right now," I said, quickly filling him in on what transpired there.

"You made it just in time, bro. But I've missed all the action. All I've been doing is watching Fay play video games on my phone until Frankie finally woke up."

"And yet, you're the one who got Frankie talking and tracked down the flash drive. Where exactly is it in the building? We need to grab it before anyone else does."

"It's stashed in the security room where they have all the monitors. Jimmy figured he'd get patted down by the guards on his way out, so he hid it behind the false ceiling, tucked away in a corner."

"Inside the false ceiling? Stay on the line. I'm putting you on hold while I check it out."

Sure enough, the security room had a false ceiling. And it was one where you could easily hide something by lifting a flap. A metal grid covered the upper space, with intersecting strips creating a grid pattern, leaving hollow spaces. Insulated flaps had been fitted within these hollows, completing the ceiling structure. However, each insulated flap could be lifted with slight pressure, providing access to the concealed space.

Accessing it was simple, but the room was swarming with cops. I couldn't just waltz in, grab a stool, pop open a flap, and stroll out. Anything taken from there would be seized as evidence.

I wasn't about to allow anyone else getting his hands on the flash drive. Lives were at stake. I had to ensure I left without tipping anyone off that I had gotten my hands on the evidence that Nick and his mercs were ready to tear apart the city to get their hands on. That flash drive would help me make sure those guys didn't make a run for it before they got what was coming to them.

"It's not going to be easy. Place is swarming with cops. But I'll figure something out. Which corner did he stash it in?" I asked.

"Far corner from the entrance. Sound good?"

"Got it. Let me work out a plan to snatch it without the cops finding out. I'll update you once it's done. And I'll arrange for someone to take over your post. I need you here, pal. We're wrapping this up tonight."

"Now we're talking."

I studied the layout of the adjacent rooms. A plan took shape in my mind. The space above the false ceiling could be accessed via the storage room beside it. Though it was locked, I still had the key card granting access. I approached Kelly, who was keeping an eye on Dewayne being tended to by the EMTs. He was a young kid, barely over twenty. He waved at me when he saw me.

"Thanks for taking out those guys. I'm Dewayne," he greeted, extending his hand.

"I'm Axel. You did really well today. That was some quick thinking, especially after taking a hit. Not many guys manage to keep their head straight when they're shot. That saved all three of you. Well done, pal. Take it easy now."

His face lit up at my praise before he lay back on the gurney as it was rolled away.

"How are you holding up?" I asked Kelly.

"You know I hate playing the role of damsel in distress," she replied, her eyes shining. "But thanks for rescuing me yet again," she added, giving me a quick hug and a peck on the cheek.

"This madness ends tonight. You won't have to worry about those lunatics anymore. I promise."

"I believe you. When I saw you this morning... well, aside from wanting to give you a good kick for arriving out of the blue, I just knew everything would be alright. But don't you dare disappear from Boston as suddenly as you showed up. I'll hunt you down, even if I have to chase you all the way to Colorado."

"Hold on to that thought. Wild horses couldn't drive me away," I replied with a playful grin.

Our banter was cut short when Jason strolled over to join us.

"Jason, pal. I need your help," I addressed him.

"Seriously?" he exclaimed, sounding real kicked about it. "Count me in. Let's kick some ass."

"Easy there, tiger. How do you feel about climbing and squeezing through tight spots?"

"Huh? I'm not sure. What do you need me to do?" he asked, his enthusiasm waning slightly.

"You know the evidence you guys dug up today, about the security feed that Jimmy downloaded?" I asked, addressing them both. "That was some impressive investigative work, by the way."

"Yeah, it was pretty cool, wasn't it?" Kelly responded, without a hint of modesty. "But what about it?"

"Jimmy saved it on a flash drive. And then he hid it behind the false ceiling in that security room."

"No kidding! How do you know that?"

"It's a long story. But the thing is, we can't just stroll in there with cops swarming all over the place. That flash drive is the crucial evidence that'll bring down Nick Templeton. That, along with Josh's testimony, spells the end for him. We're not handing it over to anyone until we're certain they can be trusted. Nick had moles in the FBI. I wouldn't be surprised if one of these cops is in cahoots with him too."

"Yeah, that's a valid concern. So, where does Jason come in?"

"See that room over there?" I gestured toward the storage room next to the security room. "While you keep watch, Jason and I will go inside. That false ceiling won't support my weight, but it should hold Jason's."

"Um, I'm not as lightweight as I look," Jason chimed in.

"I know, big guy. But we'll have to give it a shot. I don't see any other way."

"I was just messing around. Let's go do it. If I crash through the ceiling and land on top of the cops in there, just make sure they don't slap the cuffs on me."

"Oh, come on, Jason. A night in the slammer won't kill you," Kelly teased him.

"Thanks for the pep talk, K. Just what I needed," he replied with playful sarcasm, before adding enthusiastically, "Let's get this show rolling."

"Kelly, you're on lookout duty," I instructed as we approached the room.

I used the key card to unlock the door, before Jason and I slipped inside. I didn't need to lift Jason physically—there were convenient racks with shelves already set up in the room. Jason quickly stepped up and lifted a flap near the corner that I pointed out, revealing a narrow crawl space.

"Keep your feet on the metal strips. You step on a flap and you'll crash to the floor. Got it?" I reminded him.

"Yeah, don't worry."

He took out his phone and turned on its flashlight to look around.

"I see it," he reported, placing his phone beside him to keep the area lit.

Then he disappeared into the darkness for about half a minute.

"Got it," he whispered triumphantly as his face emerged from the cavity again.

With a bit of assistance, Jason was soon back on solid ground. He handed me the flash drive, which I promptly slipped in my pocket. We exited without any trouble and headed to the apartment's main lobby. What had once been an opulent space, with marble floors, plush furniture, cascading chandeliers, and exquisite artwork, now resembled a war zone after Igor unleashed a barrage from the 100-round drum magazine. The sleek glass entrance doors lay shattered.

"Do you guys have a laptop?" I asked Kelly and Jason.

"Yeah, it's in the car?" Kelly confirmed.

"Grab it. Let's see what's on the flash drive."

We made our way to the rental Kelly was using after she had to abandon her own vehicle at North Station. It was a good thing Jimmy wasn't a techie or else it would have been password-protected, almost impossible to open. Kelly plugged the drive into the laptop and accessed its contents. All the flash drive had was a video recording.

As soon as Kelly played it, it became evident why Nick and his mercenaries were causing chaos throughout the city to obtain it. Clearly visible in the recording were four men—Nick, Igor, Maxim, and a man dressed as a security guard. The quartet entered the elevator, with the guard using his key card to activate it, and the doors sliding open moments later.

The video bore a distinct time stamp, serving as undeniable evidence that these men ascended in the elevator five minutes before Frank Grant plummeted from his balcony. Any prosecutor would charge them with premeditated murder. Coupled with Josh's testimony regarding Nick's financial dealings, this evidence guaranteed that Nick would spend the rest of his days behind bars.

"Upload the recording to your cloud and mail it to your, Josh's and Jason's email addresses so there are multiple copies," I instructed Kelly. "But keep this under wraps until I've got my hands on Nick. If he catches wind of the recordings, he'll disappear."

"Got it. I've transferred it to my laptop. Give me five minutes to send the emails."

"Sure, while you do that, I'll catch up with Declan," I said, as I spotted him pulling up.

"You're making a habit of saving the day. I heard you took down the whole crew," Declan called out as he walked over.

"One got away. I'm working on a plan to grab him. Good thing you managed to get the cavalry here in time."

I briefed Declan on what happened. He quickly understood the gravity of the threat posed by Igor and Maxim.

"I think the safest bet for Kelly is the Globe office. It's secure and well-guarded. What do you think?" I inquired.

"Sounds good to me. Keeping her confined anywhere else would be challenging, unless we knock her out and tie her up," Declan replied, with a chuckle.

"All settled then. What about the kids—Frankie and Fay? I haven't sorted it out yet, but I'll set up a trap for Nick tonight. I'll need Logan by my side."

"The kids will be safe. I'll take care of it. Do you need me for your plan tonight?"

"No, we'll manage. I'll have to involve the FBI. We'll catch their mole and use him to lure Nick out. Let's give our statements to the cops and leave."

"Sure thing."

We soon got out of there, dropping Kelly and Jason off at the Globe office. Both had been through a harrowing ordeal, witnessing death and being hunted by gunmen. They were handling it reasonably well. But it had given them enough reality bites not to need much convincing about staying put inside the building until they heard from me, even if it meant crashing there for the night.

With that worry off my mind, I headed with Declan to Fields Corner. It was time to extract Logan and get him set up to do what he excelled at—acting as a scout sniper. It was time to make war.

CHAPTER 26

Nestled among windswept dunes and tall grasses near the Cape Cod beach, the secluded two-story house exuded a quaint charm. Its steeply pitched roof, symmetrical facade, and cozy dormer windows peeking from under the eaves added to its allure. Painted in a classic white hue, dark shutters framed the windows while a brass knocker adorned the front door.

Surrounded by dense foliage and veiled by the night's darkness, the house emitted an eerie sense of isolation. Bathed in the ethereal glow of the moon, shadows danced across its weathered shingles, enhancing its mysterious aura. The steady rhythm of crashing waves, accompanied by the occasional cry of a seabird, filled the air. The salty tang of the ocean permeated the air, mingling with the earthy scent of pine needles, creating a sense of tranquility that belied the impending chaos.

Inside the house, the only light came from dimly lit lamps and the soft glow of moonlight filtering through the windows. Anyone peering in couldn't say for certainty if the house had any occupants inside. But it wasn't empty. I sat on a couch, positioned away from the line of sight of any window, enveloped in partial darkness. I had swapped my usual attire of jeans, T-shirt and cowboy boots with all-black tactical gear and boots.

The upper floor of the house was shrouded in complete darkness. Nestled beside a dormer window, Logan's silhouette lurked, clad entirely in black attire from head to toe. Thick streaks of black camo paint obscured much of his face, rendering him nearly invisible amidst the night. Gripped firmly in his hands was a 6.5 mm Creedmoor rifle fitted with a night scope and a flash suppressor.

Logan and I were doing something we had done on countless missions—waiting. Staying still until it was time to strike.

The tranquil scene was disturbed by the headlights of an approaching car slicing through the inky night, casting stark beams of light onto the facade of the house. A sleek black sedan soon emerged from the shadows, gliding to a halt before the main entrance. Its engine hummed softly as it idled.

Within the vehicle sat three occupants—Special Agents Jess, Walker, and Miller. Jess and Walker were privy to the trap I had laid for Miller that night. He was the FBI mole working for Nick Templeton, responsible for orchestrating multiple killings through Nick's Russian mercenaries. Miller's involvement in the killing of Alexei and the three knocked-out mercenaries at Mary Anne's house was undeniable.

Even though Jess and I didn't have any doubts about Miller's treachery, proving it wasn't going to be simple. That's why we set up an elaborate trap to ensure that before the night was over, Miller, Nick and the remaining mercenaries would be in custody. Except Igor and Maxim. I had separate plans for them, plans about which Jess had no idea.

Nick owned numerous properties throughout Boston, but his primary residence was on Cape Cod. It was also the location of the hangar for his private jet. If things didn't go his way during the night, he would fly away, without a doubt. Once he left U.S. shores, bringing him to justice would be impossible. None of us was willing to let that happen. We worked out a plan that would lure Nick out of hiding.

The house we chose belonged to Josh's aunt. It was crucial to tie the location directly to Josh. And for Miller to buy into the idea that Jess and I weren't buddy-buddy like he thought. Jess had to put on a show, acting like she was furious with me for keeping her in the dark about her star witness's whereabouts for the upcoming testimony. Agent Walker, a former Marine who had proven his loyalty by helping us take down those mercs at Faneuil Hall, was in the loop too.

Before I dialed Jess earlier that evening, we had rehearsed the script. She rounded up Miller and Walker for a meeting and gave me the signal when she was ready. Just moments before my call, she was laying into me, swearing up a storm about my doubts over her insistence that the FBI had caught the mole. When I joined in, she put me on speaker, and the trio swore up and down that their house was clean. I played along, acting like I was buying it, but insisted I would only talk to those three and no one else.

I laid it out straight: Josh was on my watch, and I was sick and tired of playing bodyguard, putting my neck on the line. It was time to hand him over to the Feds for safekeeping. But that wasn't all. I also wanted to hand over Frankie who had the video proof pinning Nick Templeton to Frank Grant's murder.

I gave them a deadline. They had until 2100 hours to collect them and take them to some secure location. I told them I would send them the location half an hour before that—at 2030 hours. That gave me enough time to set the stage without having to worry about the mercs trying a surprise attack before the agents arrived. At 2030 hours, I asked them to hit the road for Cape Cod. I finally sent them the exact address at 2045 hours.

The trap had been set. Miller was itching to confirm Josh and Frankie's location, eager to spill the beans to Nick. But I had a few cards left up my sleeve to keep him guessing.

"Radio check. Charlie 1, am I loud and clear?" I murmured into the mic tucked under my shirt.

"Charlie 1 to Alpha. Affirmative. Crystal clear on this end," Logan's voice crackled through the earpiece.

"Alpha to Charlie 2. You locked and loaded?"

"Charlie 2 to Alpha. Locked, loaded, and ready to roll," Lawson's voice chimed in.

Another surprise I had up my sleeve was that Josh and Lawson were no longer holed up in Lawson's place in Topsfield. They had rolled in using Lawson's pickup and were parked on top of a little hill, about a third of a mile away from the house, positioned a little toward its back. They had a clear view of the only approach road to the house. Part of my plan was to have Miller see Josh on a video call I would make to him.

Everything was in place. I rose from the couch, ambled to the front door, and planted myself in the doorway, waiting for the three agents to exit the vehicle and approach me.

"Well, we are here. Just the three of us like you wanted. Where are Josh and Frankie?" Jess asked, her tone far from friendly.

"They're close by. I couldn't risk having them with me until I was sure you weren't followed by a convoy of other Feds," I replied.

"Look, buddy, you're going to be in trouble if you're just screwing around with Feds. I hope you aren't pulling some stunt," she warned me.

"I don't play games. You guys had a leak, and my neck's on the line too. I've got to be sure. You sure you three are clean and not mixed up with Nick Templeton?"

"Oh, for crying out loud. This is getting ridiculous. You can't seriously think the whole Bureau's compromised?"

"I don't know, Special Agent Jessica. The thing is, I stepped up for Josh, but I don't want to be looking over my shoulder for the rest of my life. I'm only in if you guarantee those Russian mercs stay off my tail."

"Of course, we guarantee it," Miller chimed in. "But we need all the witnesses and evidence to build the case. You're simply delaying things."

"We could throw your ass in prison simply for withholding evidence from the FBI," Walker cut in, stepping in close, really getting in my face.

"Whoa, you guys gotta make up your minds how we're doing this. Scaring me into handing them over won't work. Those Russian mercs with nothing to lose scare me more than GI Joe here," I retorted, looking at Jess.

"Cool it, Walker," Jess snapped.

Walker glared at me, but backed off.

"Well, what do you want?" Jess asked me, sounding fed up.

"Your personal guarantee those mercs are going to be behind bars by tomorrow."

"We've got a statewide APB out. Their faces are plastered everywhere. There's nowhere for them to run. We'll nab them. Just a matter of time. Once we do, it's terrorism charges. Blowing up a house with C-4? They're lifers. Satisfied?"

"Well, I guess it'll have to do," I conceded.

"Good. Now quit stalling and start talking. Let's get down to business. The sooner we've got our hands on all the evidence, the better. Where's Josh?" Miller pressed.

"He's on his way to this place. Should be here in half an hour. I'll call him now so you can see for yourself."

I called Josh. He knew he needed to be sitting inside Lawson's pickup for the video call. This way, Miller wouldn't have any doubts about my story.

"Almost there, about twenty minutes out," Josh confirmed as his face appeared on my screen.

"Great. Say hello to Special Agent Jessica," I replied, turning the screen toward the agents.

"Hey, Josh. We're waiting to pick you up. Hang tight," Jess spoke up.

"Sounds good. Catch you soon," Josh replied and hung up.

"Happy?" I asked Jess.

"Yeah, delirious with delight. How about Frankie? Are you sure he's got the goods on Templeton?"

"Frankie's got the scoop, and it's not pretty. He's got video evidence proving Grant didn't jump.

Nick and his cronies were in the building when it went down. They had one of their guys on the security team orchestrate a power outage, knocking out the main elevators and cameras. But in these high-rises, service elevators have a separate power source. They rode those up to the penthouse, but not before disabling the security cam inside, so there wouldn't be any evidence of their little field trip."

"So, where's the evidence? All I'm hearing is this theory about service elevators, but no real proof," Jess snapped, looking ready to bite my head off.

"Frankie's holding the proof. Those killers didn't realize that the security camera facing the entrance to the service elevator runs on the same generator as the elevators. It captured them stepping into the elevator just five minutes before Grant's fall. Their mole inside the building's security figured it out later and deleted the footage. But he was too late. Before him, Frankie's brother Jimmy had downloaded a copy on a flash drive. That's why they killed Jimmy. But they must've realized later killing him was a mistake because they didn't find the flash drive on him. Hence, the manhunt for Frankie."

While I kept my eyes mostly on Jess while I spoke, I was keeping tabs on Miller's reaction to my bombshell revelation. Despite his trained composure, it was evident from his demeanor that my revelation unsettled him.

"And where's Frankie? Is he too on his way here?"

"Nope. Those guys shot him. He barely survived. You'll need to head to the hospital to see him. You and GI Joe can go meet him. Agent Miller and I can wait here for Josh."

"Works for me. Just make sure we're not chasing shadows," Jess replied.

"Hey, I'm the good guy here, trying to do the right thing."

"Yeah, I guess so. Give me the address. We'll get moving."

I stuck close to Miller as Jess and Walker headed out to their car. The plan was for them to reach the hospital and stay there until I had Miller's guilt on tape. The only thing Jess made me promise was not to leave any marks on Miller. She insisted his confession shouldn't be coerced physically. Despite my desire to rough him up a bit, I agreed. I knew she was really going out on a limb based on my hunch.

Once Jess and Walker left, Miller attempted to move away for privacy.

"Gotta make an official call," he claimed, reaching for his phone.

"Nope, you're not," I replied, drawing my gun, pressing it into his gut, and grabbing his phone.

"Are you out of your mind, pointing a gun at a Federal agent?" he protested as I frisked him.

"Get inside and listen carefully. What I'm about to propose might save your life," I instructed, confiscating his primary weapon and the second one in his ankle holster, as well as a second phone.

"What the hell are you talking about?" he demanded, reluctantly stepping inside.

"You don't have a lot of time, Miller. If Jess and Walker get their hands on that flash drive, it's game over for all of you. But before we go any further, let's drop the act and face the facts. The most crucial fact being you're the mole."

"Are you high on something? What the hell..."

"Save it, Miller. I've seen the bodycam footage form the first responders at the scene. It shows you taking the C-4 from the SUV and planting it inside the house. Your suicide bomber theory is as bogus as Grant's supposed suicide."

"Don't try to play me. I was searching the SUV for evidence and might have picked up something. There's no way the bodycam footage shows me handling C-4," he retorted.

Bingo. My shot in the dark about the bodycam footage seemed to hit the mark. I wasn't even sure if such footage existed, but his defensive reaction rather than trying to punch me for calling him a traitor spoke volumes. It was time to tighten the screws.

"We could argue all night, but convincing me won't save you. What you need to understand is that time is running out. Once those two have the flash drive, it's curtains for Nick Templeton. And when he falls, he'll drag you down with him. You can try to explain later how you could've stopped it but wasted time trying to prove me wrong."

My words seemed to sink in.

"Even if we forget everything else for now, Jess and Walker will get that drive when they reach the hospital. It's less than a 15-minute drive away."

"What if I told you they won't get their hands on the drive when they arrive?"

"I don't follow. What are you getting at?"

"Frankie is heavily sedated. He woke up briefly and gave me the flash drive's location. I have it here. I can hand it over to Jess and Walker if that's what you want."

"What's your angle? What are you after?"

"Get your man Nick to wire me $100 million, and he's off the hook."

"$100 million!" Miller laughed out scornfully. "Where did you even come up with that number?"

"From the fact that Nick's made billions laundering dirty Russian money. I don't have any love for Nick and his Russian mercs. If I'm doing this, it's going to cost a ridiculous amount of money. Otherwise, I'll do the patriotic thing and make sure all of you end up in prison."

"Show me the video."

"Over here," I gestured, leading him to a laptop on a side table and playing the video.

Miller was silent for a few seconds.

"Frankie did have the video. We didn't think he had it," he spoke almost to himself, shocked at seeing it.

"And yet you lot murdered the family sheltering him. You should all rot in prison. Maybe I don't want the money after all."

"It wasn't me who killed them."

"You did blow up the others."

"They were all Russian mercs. Who cares about them."

"Tell it to the judge when they're trying you on terrorism charges."

That made up his mind.

"I'll make the call. Give me my phone," he said.

"You're doing it right here in my presence," I stated, handing him his phone.

"He won't talk to me if he knows you're listening in."

"I'll stay silent. Pretend you're doing it in private. That's all you're getting."

Miller acknowledged with a nod. While he made the call, Lawson gave me an update on the radio.

"Charlie 2 to all teams. Vehicle stopped four hundred yards from the house. Lights switched off. Looks suspicious, but no one's stepped out yet," his voice came through on my earphones.

"Charlie 1 to Charlie 2. Copy that," Logan responded, confirming receipt of the message.

I wasn't surprised. I had no doubt that as soon as I confirmed the address of the cottage to Jess, Miller must have passed it on to Nick and the mercs. They would soon be getting into position, ready to take out everyone in the house at Nick's command.

I had been listening in to Miller's conversation all this while. It was pretty straightforward. Miller informed Nick about the video's existence, and after a brief silence, Nick recovered and resumed the conversation. Surprisingly, Nick readily agreed to the $100 million demand. Well, not so surprising, considering he never intended to follow through. He was confident he could eliminate everyone, including me and Josh. As if on cue, Miller paused the call and relayed a question from Nick.

"He's asking what's going to happen to Josh's testimony?"

"That's between you guys and him. I get my money, I walk. Josh will be here in fifteen minutes. Make whatever deal you want to make with him."

Miller passed on the message and ended the call soon after.

"It's a go. He's agreed. He'll set things up and be here in ten. Once he verifies the evidence and you hand over Josh, he'll wire the money to your account. Get the details ready," Miller informed me.

"Sounds like a plan."

It was clear that Nick's plan was to take me out soon, so that his guys would be ready and waiting for Josh inside the house. It made sense strategically—eliminating me first would get him the flash drive before targeting Josh. After that, the only small detail left for him would be to take out Frankie. And he would be home free. But I had other plans for him.

CHAPTER 27

As if on cue, Lawson's voice came through the earpiece: "Six hostiles have exited the vehicle. Headed toward the house."

"Copy that," Logan acknowledged.

"Can I use the restroom?" Miller asked, likely aware of the impending danger and wanting to get out of the way before the men took me out.

"Yeah, go ahead," I replied.

As he turned, I swiftly slipped behind him, locking him in a chokehold. My right arm snaked around his neck, locking onto my left bicep, while my left hand pressed his head forward, cutting off blood flow to his brain. After a brief struggle, Miller went limp. I swiftly restrained him with flexicuffs, securing his hands behind his back to a pillar by the fireplace. He wouldn't be going anywhere, even if he regained consciousness.

Pocketing Miller's phone, I silently opened a window and slipped into the darkness outside. I moved around the back of the house to cover the west. We anticipated such a stealthy approach by the hostiles and had planned for it. Logan was covering the east and back of the house.

As I moved, I applied camo paint to my face from a small container. Checking my weapons, I ensured my HK416 assault rifle was slung securely across my back, with a suppressed Glock holstered on my leg, ready to fire. Both boot knives were easily accessible in my boots. Flexing my neck and wrists to get the blood flowing, I prepared myself for action.

I watched the six men as they approached, their movements methodical and strategic as they began to spread out. Four of them veered toward the eastern edge of the house, establishing a wide perimeter and staying clear of the house. Two of the four men positioned themselves in the east, while the other two circled around to the back.

Meanwhile, the remaining two men continued their advance toward my position, where I was stationed to cover the western approach.

"This is Charlie 1. I've got eyes on two tangos to the east and another pair at the rear," Logan's hushed voice crackled through my earpiece.

"This is Alpha. Focus on the hostiles on the east. Stand by for my signal," I whispered into my mic.

"Copy that," Logan replied.

"This is Charlie 2. Subject secured in vehicle. Permission to advance and engage?" Lawson's voice broke the silence.

"Negative. Stick to the plan," I murmured quietly.

I empathized with Lawson's situation. Being assigned to reconnaissance duty while Logan and I engaged with the enemy had to be frustrating. Any soldier who's ever had to sit tight, itching to engage the enemy, but stuck waiting for orders, knows exactly how he felt. But Josh's safety was paramount, and he couldn't be left unguarded.

As the two men drew nearer to my position, I remained crouched low, concealed by the foliage behind a sturdy tree. They positioned themselves about ten yards apart, with one of them stopping nearly within touching distance of me. I could even discern the faint chatter from his earpiece. He gestured to his companion, who swiftly moved forward.

In a split second, I surged upward, swiftly stepping behind him, my arm snaking around his neck. With a decisive motion, I tilted his head, driving my knife into his exposed neck. The blade sliced through his carotid and jugular. His body went slack and he slumped to the ground without emitting a sound. Releasing my grip, leaving the knife lodged in his neck, I swiftly drew my Glock.

"Engage. Now," I breathed to Logan, simultaneously shooting at the man before me.

The first clue the man had that something was wrong was when he heard my indistinct whisper. By the time he began to turn, I had fired three rapid shots into his head and neck. While the man went down, I heard the suppressed pops of Logan's rifle. Two shots, two kills.

"Two targets neutralized," Logan confirmed.

The two men at the rear must have detected the shots, even though Logan's rifle, equipped with a flash suppressor, obscured the muzzle flash, leaving them clueless about the source. But they were pros. While others might have hesitated, they swiftly reacted, hitting the ground before rising in a cautious crouch and spreading out amidst the underbrush and tall grass, armed and prepared to retaliate against any threat.

"I'll draw their fire. Take out targets on sight," I instructed Logan.

"Copy that."

I stood up and unleashed a sustained burst of fire toward the position of one of the men, then swiftly dropped to the ground, executing a rolling maneuver. At least one of my shots must have found their mark, as the retaliatory gunfire came from his partner and not him. It was the cue Logan was waiting for. With precision, his next shot eliminated the assailant.

"Target down," Logan confirmed.

"Copy that. One hostile still in play, possibly injured," I reported.

"I don't have a visual on the target."

The man had moved too far. Logan's position wasn't elevated enough to give him a clear shot unless the man stood up.

"I'll advance and engage," I replied.

Maintaining a low profile, I swiftly moved forward, toward the last known location of the target I engaged earlier. Despite my approach, I encountered no hostile fire. The remaining man was either incapacitated or maintaining tactical discretion, aware of the sniper's presence and the risk of exposure.

I didn't want this to turn into a waiting game. Time was running out. If Nick arrived, heard the gunfire, and was unable to contact Miller, he would bail.

"Alpha to Charlie 2. Do you have a visual?" I asked Lawson, hoping his vantage point gave him better visibility.

"Negative, Alpha," Lawson's apologetic voice came through.

With no other choice, I had to advance toward the remaining threat, risking return fire. I slung my rifle, drew my sidearm, and moved forward cautiously, hoping to catch a glimpse. Finally spotting him, I saw the man lying motionless on his back. Approaching carefully, gun ready, I stopped a few feet away.

"No movement. Might be down," I spoke clearly into the mic before half turning away.

At the same instant the man raised his hand, holding a gun, ready to fire. But I was anticipating that. I still had my weapon drawn. Before he could aim, I fired multiple shots. This time there was no doubt. The target was down. It was Igor.

I walked over to check the other hostile Logan had taken down. It was Maxim. Neither of the two would be able to cast his shadow on Josh or Kelly again.

"Alpha to all teams. All targets neutralized. Returning to base. The big man will make an appearance any minute. Charlie 2, keep watch for any incoming vehicles."

When I re-entered the house through the back window, Miller was awake, trying to get himself loose. He looked at me in terror as I moved toward him, my gun still drawn and in my hand.

"All your Russian buddies are toast," I informed him.

Miller struggled to respond, but the fear had left him speechless.

"Charlie 2 to Alpha. Vehicle approaching," Lawson's voice crackled over the comms.

"Copy that," I replied.

Glancing at Miller with a smirk, I asked in a mocking voice, "What about my $100 million, pal? Is that happening or not?"

His eyes lit up with a flicker of hope, missing the sarcasm in my tone. "Yeah, sure. I'll talk to Nick," he replied.

Just then, his phone buzzed. I knew it was Nick even before I pulled it out.

"Tell him to come here. No games this time. If you have to, tell him I'm dead if that's what it takes to bring him here. Once he's here, we'll sort out the deal. Then you're free to go," I instructed, thrusting the phone toward him.

With no other options left, Miller complied. Whether he believed my money demand or not, desperation pushed him to play along. He relayed the fabricated news to Nick, sealing his own fate.

As soon as the call ended, I slipped back outside, positioning myself discreetly and awaiting Nick's arrival.

"Alpha to all teams. Hold your positions," I spoke into the mic.

Before long, a striking sports car roared around the corner and screeched to a stop in front of the house. It was a 1965 Shelby Cobra 427, painted in vintage Guardsman blue with bold white racing stripes. This was the same model that old man Templeton had been driving when he went for a spin and ended up at the bottom of a cliff near Penobscot Bay. Given what I knew about Nick, that was likely no accident. But that one would be hard to pin down. Not that it mattered. He was going down for multiple homicides on top of his financial crimes.

As the car door opened, a confident young man emerged, his demeanor suggesting he was accustomed to attention, his gaze scanning the surroundings with anticipation. He was about thirty, of medium height, an unmistakable air of entitlement about him. But his expression shifted from excitement to annoyance when he realized there wasn't a welcoming committee on the door. He retrieved his phone and swiftly dialed a number, his agitation evident in his swift movements.

Miller's phone buzzed silently in my hand as Nick tapped his foot impatiently, waiting for a response. I allowed him to simmer a bit longer before finally answering the call. I brought the phone to my ear without uttering a word.

"Where are you? It's all sorted out, right?" Nick's voice came through the line.

"It is, but not in the way you expected, Nikolai," I replied, stepping out of the shadows.

The realization that his game was over smacked him square in the face. He tried to slither back into his car, but I cut him off, slamming him to the ground and locking his hands behind him. He squirmed and cursed. I didn't have the patience for his antics—or maybe I was just itching to have a go at him—so I clocked him in the neck, knocking him out cold.

All threats had been neutralized. It was time for the law to step in. I reached into my back pocket for flexicuffs.

As I cuffed Nick, I spoke into my radio: "Alpha to all units. Target secured. Stand down and take a breather, Marines."

"Copy that, Ranger," echoed the pair's synchronized response.

Headlights popped up on top of a low hill to the east. Lawson and Josh would soon be on their way down.

I shot Jess a text, giving her the all clear. She had Miller's confession on tape. All that was left was for her to slap cuffs on him and the sleeping beauty lying knocked out at my feet—the mastermind behind all the murder and mayhem in the city. Maxim and Igor were already history. Josh and Kelly would be safe. My job was done.

A shadow slid out from the house, joining me—Logan's stealth game still sharp. A cool breeze swept over the Cape Cod beach house, easing the night's tension. Under the moon's soft glow, we stood side by side, watching the endless sea, a silent witness to the chaos we had just cleaned up.

It was time to head back—for Logan to Wyoming and me to Colorado. Yet, lingering in my thoughts was a gentle warning from a captivating woman who had taken hold of my senses: "Don't you dare disappear from Boston as suddenly as you showed up. I'll hunt you down, even if I have to chase you all the way to Colorado."

My response to her echoed in my mind with newfound resonance: "Hold on to that thought. Wild horses couldn't keep me away."

– THE END –

BOOKS IN THE AXEL BLAZE SERIES

BLAZE RETURNS (Book One)

US Marshal Carter has gone missing in Little Butte, Nevada. The Dawsons own the town. A Mexican cartel is moving in. A gang war is coming to town. Blaze returns for one last assignment to find Carter before all hell breaks loose.

LETHAL FORCE (Book Two)

When Blaze takes out a Mexican cartel's operations in Nevada, the cartel sends hitmen after him and everyone he cares about. Bad move. What the cartel doesn't realize is, it has messed with a Lethal Force.

HARD TARGET (Book Three)

When Blaze stops at an isolated gas station, he Prevents an execution about to go down. Blaze's intervention gets a pack of mercenaries after him.

MEAN STREETS (Book Four)

Midnight in New York City. A car stops at an intersection. A girl in the back gives Blaze a distress signal. The chase that begins in Manhattan takes Blaze on a treacherous chase through the city that never sleeps.

UNCHAINED FURY (Book Five)

There is a contract out on Blaze and his old team. Floated by the Cady brothers—ruthless arms dealers who will stop at nothing to get revenge. In this no holds barred game, there's nothing to hold back Blaze's fury.

NO ESCAPE (Book Six)

Chaos erupts in Bison Creek, Wyoming. Two slain officers. Blood-soaked ex-Marine Logan on the scene. A sinister link between a cult and a pharma company. One man will move heaven and earth to get the truth—Blaze.

FEAR CITY (Book Seven)

Blaze heads to Boston after a shadowy group of investors—rich, powerful, and ready to bulldoze anything in their way. Blaze is up against these ruthless players who would sooner bury the truth than face it. They play dirty. But so does Blaze.

DEAD CALM (Book Eight)

The book goes into Blaze's past as a US Army Ranger. Blaze promises to rescue a dying friend's kids from the Taliban. The hunt takes him from Afghanistan to a trafficking network run by the Bulgarian mafia.

NO MERCY (Book Nine)

CIA agents in the Middle East are turning up dead. Blaze must save trapped agents and stop a rogue analyst from blowing their covers. With the Italian mafia and terror outfits in the picture, Blaze has only one rule: No Mercy.

WARPATH (Book Ten)

Blaze and his Delta team head to Mexico to dismantle a powerful drug cartel. But when the cartel brings the fight to US soil and targets Americans, Blaze makes it personal and goes on the warpath.

CROSSFIRE (Book Eleven)

Americans are caught in the inferno As Yemen goes up in flames. Blaze and his team are sent to extract an Al-Qaeda informant, who is the key to saving lives. Facing betrayals and deadly odds, Blaze won't just hold the line—he'll obliterate the enemy.

NEMESIS (Book Twelve – Nov '25)

They killed his brother. They buried the truth. They thought it was over. But Axel Blaze, is coming for them. No rules. No mercy. Just a promise written in blood. The hunt is on. And it won't end until they do. The nemesis is coming.

Made in the USA
Middletown, DE
29 November 2025

23549077R00170